Henry Duff Traill

Lord Cromer

A Biography

Henry Duff Traill

Lord Cromer
A Biography

ISBN/EAN: 9783743347588

Manufactured in Europe, USA, Canada, Australia, Japa

Cover: Foto ©Raphael Reischuk / pixelio.de

Manufactured and distributed by brebook publishing software (www.brebook.com)

Henry Duff Traill

Lord Cromer

LORD CROMER

A Biography

BY

H. D. TRAILL

ILLUSTRATED

NEW YORK
EDWARD ARNOLD
70, FIFTH AVENUE
1897

CONTENTS

LIST OF ILLUSTRATIONS

LORD CROMER

CHAPTER I.

Early Years

THE family of Baring, originally of German extraction, but for now two centuries domiciled and naturalized citizens of this country, has for more than half that long period been conspicuous in the world of British commerce, finance, and politics. Its founder, John, son of Franz Baring, a Lutheran minister of Bremen, came to England in the year 1697, and established himself as a merchant and cloth manufacturer at Larkbeer, in Devonshire. His son Francis, born at that place in 1740, was sent to London to study commerce under a leading firm of city merchants. Though deaf from his youth, his indomitable energy enabled him to overcome all obstacles, and to establish his business on the surest foundations. He prospered exceedingly, and had risen to wealth and importance by the time he had reached middle age. Towards the end of the century, when Pitt had determined to strengthen the titled orders with an infusion of new blood from the middle classes, Francis Baring was a personage of sufficient prominence in the commercial world to have become a natural object of the Minister's selection. The elevation of another financial magnate, his contemporary, was celebrated by a political rhymer of the day in the irreverent distich :

> "Billy Pitt made me a peer,
> And took the pen from behind my ear."

Francis Baring was at least as wealthy as the founder of the noble house of Carrington, and had other and higher claims than any that Mr. Robert Smith is known to have possessed. He was an authority on questions of currency and finance, and a contributor of weighty additions to the literature of the subject. He had made himself specially conversant with the principles and details of Indian finance ; and his advice was sought by the Government of the day on matters of administration connected therewith. He had been a Director of the East India Company since 1779, and in 1792–93 he acted as its Chairman. Yet, although in spite of these varied claims to enrolment in the peerage he received in the last-mentioned year only the minor honour of a baronetcy, it proved but the first of a series of distinctions attained by a family which, during the last sixty years, has added no fewer than four new titles to the roll of Peers.

Alexander, second son of the first Baronet, was created Lord Ashburton in 1835. Thomas, grandson of Sir Francis, was raised to the Peerage in 1866 as Baron Northbrook, a dignity exchanged in 1876 for the Earldom now held by his son, the distinguished statesman who in the last-mentioned year concluded his term of office as Viceroy of India. In 1885 another of Sir Francis's grandsons, Edward Charles Baring, was created Lord Revelstoke ; and in 1892 his younger brother Evelyn, the subject of this memoir, completed for the present the list of the family honours by his elevation to the Peerage under the title of Lord Cromer.

Evelyn Baring was born on February 26th, 1841, the sixth child of his father Henry Baring's second marriage. From his mother, a daughter of Vice-Admiral Windham, and a woman of high culture, moving in a brilliant literary society of which George Grote the historian and Arthur Helps were members, he himself derived that marked literary bias of which those who enjoy his intimacy are so often and in so many ways reminded. After a year or two at a preparatory school, kept by Rev. F. Bickmore, he was transferred to the Ordnance School at Carshalton, the well-known training seminary for the scientific branches of the Army; and migrating thence, at the age of thirteen, to Woolwich Academy, he in due course qualified himself for a commission, and passed out into the Artillery in 1858, in his eighteenth year.

His military career was as uneventful as such careers could not help being for all those who commenced them after the last of the two great opportunities for active service during the middle years of the century—the Crimean War and the Indian Mutiny—had come and gone. The first ten or twelve years of his life as an Artillery officer seem to have been passed in the usual routine of military duties during periods of peace. Early in the sixties he was stationed at Corfu, where he served as *aide-de-camp* to the last High Commissioner of the Ionian Islands before their retrocession, Sir Henry Storks; and it was through his connection with that official that Baring was subsequently selected to accompany him on his appointment to preside over the Commission which was sent out to inquire into the circumstances of the Jamaica outbreak, suppressed with such memorable controversial results by Governor Eyre.

In the year 1868, shortly after his return from Jamaica, Lieutenant Baring entered the Staff College; and his two years' course of military study in that institution bore fruit in a volume of *Staff College Essays*, published by him in his own name in the spring of 1870. The moment for their publication was not so favourable as it would have been a few months later, when the catastrophic overthrow of France by Germany had set every European nation anxiously studying the new and terrible phenomena of warfare which that tremendous event had thrust upon their view. An awakened interest in military matters generally was, however, already abroad, and Baring's essays deserved, and no doubt obtained, attention on other than the grounds on which he relies in his modest preface. He offered them to the public, he said, with considerable diffidence, "for I am fully aware," he continues, "that they possess little intrinsic merit of their own; the subjects of which they treat are fully discussed by a variety of authors of far greater experience and ability than myself. My chief object in publishing them is to show the public in general, and in particular those officers of the Army who are unacquainted with the Staff College system, the nature of the work that is done at that institution. They do not pretend to anything original; all that I have attempted is to give a clear and concise account of the various military operations discussed, and to add such comments as a study of the best writers on strategy and tactics would seem to suggest."

That he succeeded in accomplishing his "chief object" will not be disputed by any reader of these essays, which in their grasp of principles and mastery of details afford ample testimony to the thoroughness of the system of training which the young officer had just undergone. But their interest and significance for a biographer by no means end here. Their technical accuracy and scientific soundness he must, if a civilian, be content of course to take more or less on trust; or at best he must accept the guarantee afforded by their origin, and by the approval of the authorities to whom they were submitted for approval. But of the form in which their criticisms are presented, of the manner in which their narrative of events is unfolded, and of the intellectual characteristics which they indicate in the writer, the civilian is an even better judge perhaps than the military expert; for the amount of his own original ignorance, and the extent of his subsequent enlightenment, give the true measure of the essayist's abilities, and form the surest criterion of his success. It is no easy matter to make the operations of war intelligible to a reader of this description, while it is an even more difficult task to make them interesting; but both these feats the author of this volume has managed to achieve. The combination of military and diplomatic manœuvres by which

Napoleon checkmated the unhappy Mack, and destroyed the Austrian Army, as he put it, *par de simples marches*, could not have been more lucidly or succinctly set forth ; and it was a curious and, after a sinister sort of fashion, a felicitous coincidence, that the student should have chosen for his theme the greatest capitulation known to military history until that which the world was to witness within six months after the publication of his studies. Strange, indeed, was the irony of fate which drew from a great French strategist the following comment on Mack's surrender : "A general-in-chief should never consent to become the instrument of the destruction of his army. When placed between dishonour and glory, the safety of the State, and the loss of his army, he should be capable of taking a part worthy of himself. Mack, after being shut up within Ulm, might at least have attempted a sortie to follow Jellachich. It is always shameful to capitulate without an effort to escape." What would Jomini have said if he had been told that sixty-five years later Mack's "shameful" example was to be followed almost to the letter by the nephew of his conqueror?

Apart, moreover, from their scientific merits, the essays display in many passages a shrewdness of judgment on men and things, and a reflective habit, which testify to a wider reach of general capacity than is usually to be traced in the professional exercises of the average military student. Take for instance the following acute remarks on the influence of the "personal equation" in warfare :—

"The private character of the men at the head of affairs, their integrity, patriotism, and singleness of mind—in a word their force of character—must always react on the affairs in which they take part. This is self-evident. Take the case of Napoleon himself. We are now well acquainted with his character; we know that his fervid imagination enabled him to grasp great projects, while his vast powers of organization and minute attention to detail eminently fitted him for the direction of the means by which these great objects were to be attained; his imagination and his reason were equally balanced, and it is the resultant of these qualities which forms the man most capable of finding and influencing his fellow-creatures. And we also know that Napoleon often displayed a meanness of character quite unworthy of his undoubted genius. But it will be found that he never allowed his military combinations to be influenced by jealousy or caprice. On the contrary, these were always based on sound strategical grounds; and it is this which render them so instructive, even in those cases in which they failed to accomplish their object. The reputation of a great strategist must ultimately rest on his strategy; posterity—or rather military posterity—takes only a passing interest in the special moral influences which actuated the man. We are concerned with the acts he did and the result of them, and not so much with the train of thought which led him to decide on the committal of those acts, if in that train of thought private influence occupies a conspicuous place. Jealousies such as Benningsen's of Buxhöwden; panics such as the exaggerated fear of Napoleon; caprices, incongruities of character, &c., will recur to the end of time; but they will recur in infinite variety, for the inconsistencies of the human mind are infinite. In the meanwhile it will readily be admitted that no theory for future action can be formed which is based on acts admitted to have been determined by such influences."

The two succeeding years were devoted by Baring to the assiduous study of his profession, and the effects of the German victories are no doubt traceable in the particular direction taken by his studies. Translations of German works on military organization appeared from his hand in 1871 and 1872, and in the latter year his attention seems to have been drawn to the game of *Krieg-spiel*, which was then attracting the notice of soldiers and students of the art of war. An English version of the rules and principles of this game, as formulated in a treatise from the pen of a German officer, was prepared and published by him in 1872. It was in the following year, however, that the event occurred which had the effect of directing his energies and abilities into a new channel, and this in all probability proved the turning-point in his career.

In the year 1873 Lord Northbrook was appointed to the Viceroyalty of India, and Evelyn Baring was invited by his cousin to accompany him in the capacity of Private Secretary. It was, if we except his brief and much less useful experiences in Jamaica with Sir Henry Storks, his first introduction to official life in the civil sphere; and it may reasonably be assumed that he here first disclosed to others, and perhaps first discovered for himself, that, whether or not he was fitted to win distinction as a soldier—as in all probability he also was—he possessed all the varied qualifications for success in the diplomatist's, the administrator's, or the financier's career. There could hardly be a better school of training for service in any one of these three capacities than India, or a better "form" in that school than that to which the confidential assistant of an Indian Viceroy obtains admission as of right. It may well be said that Baring's three years' experience of Indian government, in all its various departments, counted for much in the formation and development of the future Comptroller of Egyptian revenues, the future Finance Minister of India, the future Consul-General at Cairo during the first arduous and troubled years of the British Protectorate in Egypt.

CHAPTER II.

Commissioner of the Egyptian Debt

LORD NORTHBROOK'S Viceroyalty of India lasted but three years. He returned to England in 1876, and in June of that year he married Ethel Stanley, the daughter of Sir Rowland Stanley Errington, the representative of one of the oldest Catholic families in England. In the spring of the year following Baring was appointed English Commissioner of the Egyptian Debt.

The circumstances under which he received this appointment must here be briefly recapitulated. Towards the close of the year 1875 Ismail Pasha, the then Khedive of Egypt, was compelled by financial embarrassments to part with the greater portion of his financial interest in the Suez Canal. His shares were acquired by the British Government for the sum of £4,000,000 sterling. This step was followed shortly afterwards by the despatch of Mr. Cave to inquire, at the request of the Khedive, into the condition of Egyptian finance. Large hopes were built in the sanguine minds of Stock Exchange speculators on the result of this mission, which many of them believed or declared to indicate an intention on the part of Her Majesty's Government to take the entire financial affairs of Egypt under British control; nay, even (it was dreamt by some of the more visionary of the "bull" operators) to guarantee the whole Egyptian Debt. In March, 1876, Mr. Cave's report was received in England, and its publication was followed by the immediate collapse of this stock-gambler's house of cards. It was found that Egypt was financially in a most embarrassed condition, not to say upon the verge of bankruptcy; and that even if the British Government had been meditating any attempt to rehabilitate its credit, they must certainly have already abandoned it. Egyptian stocks fell heavily, and their decline was accelerated by the announcement a few days later of the Khedive having suspended payment of his Treasury Bills.

Meanwhile, and prior to these revelations of the virtual insolvency of Egypt, Ismail Pasha had issued a decree establishing a Commission "for the regular service of the interest of the General Egyptian Debt—including both the consolidated and the floating debt—and for the amortization of such debt." It was to be composed of three special commissioners, nominated by his Highness the Khedive, on the presentation to him of each by the Governments of England, France, and Italy respectively. By this time, however, Lord Beaconsfield's Government, as it happened, were not a little out of conceit with their Egyptian policy. The immediate effect of their intervention had been, apparently, only to precipitate a financial crisis in Egypt, which they could only deal with by taking in hand—at any rate, to some extent, and with some consequences of responsibility to themselves—the reorganization of Egyptian finance.

From this step, however, they shrank back almost in affright. It was not that they regarded the task as an unpopular one; not, perhaps, that they reckoned it a peculiarly dangerous one from the "business" point of view; but they were influenced partly by their recognition of the fact that such a step could never be made perfectly safe except by the assumption of a larger measure of political control over the country, and personal constraint of its ruler, than they were then prepared for, and partly by the less respectable motive of a terror of Parliamentary attack. The Radicals of that day, who to a man were much too innocent to have ever heard before of gambling on the Stock Exchange, were scandalized at the occasionally wild speculation in Egyptian securities, which the movements of British diplomacy, now advancing, now retreating, not unnaturally produced. They taunted the Government with allowing their policy to be influenced by "bondholders," and the Government were weak enough to fear the taunt. The Khedive's proposal to them to appoint an English Commissioner was for the time declined. It was not till nearly a year after, in the spring of 1877, that they consented to it, and Baring took his place at the Board. The Commission consisted in the meantime of a Frenchman, an Italian, and an Austrian.

One of its first acts was to effect the unification of the Egyptian Debt. In June the Egyptian bondholders solicited the intervention of Mr. Goschen for the protection of their sorely imperilled interests, and that eminently capable financier, with whom was associated M. Joubert as a representative of the French creditors, proceeded in the course of the autumn to institute a strict and searching inquiry into the state of the Khedive's affairs. Their investigation bore fruit in November, 1876, in a report and recommendations which Ismail Pasha embodied without delay in a decree. This ordinance, marking, as it may be said to have done, an epoch in the financial history of Egypt, deserves perhaps to be noticed in some detail.

It starts with the appointment of two Comptrollers-General, who are between them to supervise the incomings and the outgoings of Egyptian administration, and define the objects of this step as being to secure (1) the regular payment of the State revenues, whether of those appropriated to the service of the Debt, or those which remain at the disposal of the Government, the two being so intimately connected that it is impossible to dissever their administration ; (2) the due application of these to the purposes for which they are designated, whether by decrees assigning them to creditors or by the budgets ; (3) the establishment of guarantees ensuring that expenditure will be kept down to such a figure as receipts show to be necessary to balance the budget ; and (4) a means of providing these guarantees in such a way as to avoid interference with the administration properly so called." The two Comptrollers-General were to be one English and the other French, and under this arrangement Mr. Romaine and Baron de Malairet were appointed to the two offices in question.

But the article in the scheme which was fraught —unknown to its author—with the most serious consequences for himself, was that by which he created the Commission of the Debt, a body which was to hold permanent authority until the entire extinction of the Debt. The Commissioners were to have the power of remitting the funds received by them directly to the Bank of England, or to that of France. The commodities received in kind, in payment of taxes, were to be directly transmitted to them, and they were to have the sole right of disposing of them without the intervention of the Finance Minister. The Commissioners were to accept no other functions in the Egyptian Administration, and were to remain entirely independent of the control of any other council or committee whatever.

It was to this Commission that on March 2nd, 1877, Major Baring was attached, and he continued to serve upon it for upwards of two years, until March, 1879, when he was succeeded by Sir Auckland Colvin. The period was an eventful one in European history, covering as it does the whole course of the Russo-Turkish War, and of the prolonged diplomatic crisis which terminated in the substitution of the Treaty of Berlin for the Convention of San Stefano ; and it was not without its passages of importance in the affairs of Egypt. At the beginning of the year 1878 the Commissioners of the Debt found it their duty to propose a Commission of Inquiry into the state of the Egyptian finances, and on the 23rd of January the Khedive gave a qualified and limited assent to the proposal, and appointed a Commission with General Gordon as its President. This, of course, was not satisfactory to the Powers ; but it took more than two

CAIRO.

From a Photograph by J. P. Sebah, of Cairo.

months of vigorous diplomatic pressure to procure the required enlargement of his concession. It was not till April 4th that he assented to a full investigation of the financial position, which was forthwith set on foot under the direction of Mr. (now Sir Rivers) Wilson, and in which Major Baring took an active and most valuable part. On August 19th the Commission issued its first report. Its account of the financial position of Egypt was sufficiently discouraging; but that which most forcibly arrested public attention was the indirect evidence which its recommendations afforded as to the extent to which the personal appropriations of the Khedive and his family had contributed to the disastrous result. The Commission announced that it had accepted an offer of Prince Mahommed Tewfik, the hereditary Prince, made on the advice of Nubar Pasha, to surrender all his estates, the annual rental of which amounted to £30,000. Princess Fatmi, daughter of the Khedive, had also declared her intention of doing likewise; and Prince Hussein Kamil Pasha, the Khedive's second son, was expected to follow her example. The mother of the Khedive had also agreed to cede her estates, amounting in value to £30,000, to the Commission.

More, however, was to come. The issue of the Report was soon followed by an announcement of the Khedive's intention, not only to surrender all his private estates to the Commission, so as to reserve nothing from the public resources of Egypt, but to accept absolutely the European system of constitutional government, with its principle of ministerial responsibility; and to appoint a new Administration holding office on this basis, with Nubar Pasha, a man of high ability, at its head, and with European Ministers associated with him in the work of government. Nothing could have been more correct and satisfactory than the Khedive's language. He signified his acceptance of the recommendations of the Commission, and begged Mr. Rivers Wilson to accept his assurance that he did so seriously.

"My country," he said, "is no longer African: we now form part of Europe. It is proper, therefore, to abandon our old ways and to adopt a new system more in accordance with social progress . . . Above all we must not be satisfied with mere words, and for my own part I am resolved to prove my sincerity by my deeds; and to show how thoroughly in earnest I am, I have entrusted Nubar Pasha with the formation of a Ministry. And," he added, "I am firmly determined to apply European principles to the Egyptian administration instead of the personal power hitherto prevailing.

I desire a power balanced by the Council of Ministers, and am resolved henceforth to govern with and through this Council, the members of which will be jointly and severally responsible. The Council will discuss all important questions, the majority deciding. Thus, by approving its decisions, I shall sanction the prevalent opinion. Each Minister will apply the decisions of the Council in his own department. Every appointment or dismissal of higher officials will be made by the President of the Council and the Minister of the department, with my sanction. The officials will only obey the chiefs of their own departments."

A reform of administrative system, especially when described in language of such edifying propriety by the ruler who was submitting to it, could not fail to be received with much gratification in Western Europe. Moreover, the Khedive's undertaking, that he would not be satisfied with mere words, was with commendable promptitude made good. Mr. Rivers Wilson was added to the new Cabinet as Minister of Finance; and M. de Blignières, who had been a member of the Commission of Inquiry, was appointed Egyptian Minister of Public Works, with control over all railways, canals, and ports, except Alexandria. Ismail further pledged himself, as a concession to the mutual jealousies of France and England, that if he dismissed either the French or English members of his Government he would dismiss both.

Meanwhile a summary of the Report of the Commission had been published, and must have convinced the most hesitating of observers that reform had come none too soon. The old system abounded with oppressions, abuses, and even ludicrous absurdities, all of which the Commissioners pointed out with a terseness and vivacity which bordered at times on the epigrammatic. "No tax in Egypt," they say, "is regulated by law. The superior authority asks, the inferior authority demands, and the lowest authority takes just what the Treasury has ordered, and there is no appeal. New taxes are imposed at discretion, and are occasionally quite absurd. For example, when a bridge is built the charge for it is imposed on the boatmen, whose boats are impeded by the bridge, not on the passengers whose journey is facilitated. All who do not own land pay the tax on professions, because not being landowners they might take to professions if they liked.* Egyptians are not allowed to

* This delicious impost, with its still more exquisite reason, can only be paralleled by the posting-tax which was extorted under the fiscal system of the *ancien régime* in France from Tristram Shandy. He had insisted that he owed the King of France nothing but his good-will ; but this did not satisfy the official.

"*Pardonnez-moi*," replied the Commissary, "you are indebted to him six livres four sous for the next post, which, being a post-

own scales because they might evade the weighing-tax ; while the salt-tax is levied according to population, which is never counted, and fixed by an order which is never varied in Egypt. Old Sarum would pay a salt-tax on the consumption of 500 houses. Finally the conscription is forced on anybody who cannot bribe the Sheik, the regulation price for exemption being £80, which an Egyptian peasant can no more save than an English labourer could." These taxes are all levied by "moral pressure," says the Inspector-General ; and the Commission add that moral pressure had been explained to them by other evidence, and meant, in fact, the threat of torture.

This was pretty well for a First Report, and it is not surprising either that the Commissioners, on the one hand, were desirous of prolonging their investigations, or, perhaps, that Nubar

royal, you pay double for the horses and postillions ; otherwise 't would only have been three livres two sous."

"But I don't go by land," said I.

"You may if you please," replied the Commissary.

"Your most obedient servant," said I, making him a low bow.

The Commissary, with all the sincerity of grave good breeding, made me one as low again. I never was more disconcerted with a bow in my life . . .

"Sir," said I, collecting myself, "it is not my intention to take post."

"But you may," said he, persisting in his first reply ; "you may take post if you choose."

"And I may take salt to my pickled herring," said I, "if I choose. But I do not choose."

"But you must pay for it, whether you do or no."

Pasha, who was now nominally responsible for the whole administration, should have preferred to put a stop to its disclosures. He contended that now that the government was in the hands of a constitutional Ministry of enlightened European views, the necessity for this extraordinary inquisition had ceased. He was vigorously opposed, however, by the two European Ministers, whose view ultimately prevailed; and on January 17, 1879, a decree was issued authorizing the Commission to continue its labours, and to propose a project for the definite settlement of the financial difficulties of the country.

Incidentally, no doubt, the inquiries already made had revealed the fact that the appointment of the two Comptrollers two years before had not proved as effective a check upon financial mismanagement as had been hoped. According to the arrangement then made by the decree of November, 1876, one of these two officers was to superintend and check the collection of all revenues of the State, and their payment into the respective Public Chests; and the other, as Comptroller-General of Audit and Public Debt, was to watch the execution of regulations affecting the State Debts, and generally control the Treasury accounts. But they were allowed no voice in the appropriation of the audits assigned by the Budgets to the respective heads of service. Some difference of opinion arose between the two European Ministers as to the expediency of maintaining the institution of the Comptrollership; but Mr. Rivers Wilson, who advocated its suspension, eventually carried his point, and by a decree of December 15, 1878, the functions of Mr. Romaine and Baron de Malairet came to an end.

The situation, however, was not a convenient one, and indeed must, in any case, have sooner or later become impossible. Friction between the European Ministers and their Egyptian colleagues was inevitable; but it was also of course anticipated, and might to a certain extent have been provided for. The Governments of France and England were acting together at this juncture in a fairly cordial fashion, and by agreeing with each other to support the French and English members of the Egyptian Cabinet, whenever these two Ministers concurred in their views, the Khedive could no doubt have been constrained to accept their policy. But friction arising between the Khedive's European Ministers and the diplomatic representatives of the European States of which those Ministers were subjects, was not so easily to be relieved. It was natural enough that an English or French Consul-General should object to having his authority weakened and discredited by the overruling of his advice in favour of that offered by an English or French official not directly responsible to Paris or London; and, indeed, it is impossible to deny that the continuance of such a state of things would have been gravely detrimental to the public service, and injurious to the interests of the two Western Powers in their foreign relations. An international crisis, of a much graver character than any financial difficulties could bring about, might at any moment have arisen in Egypt, when it would have become of the first importance that the diplomatic agents of England and France should have the entire support and confidence of the Government accrediting them.

For the moment, however, it was the authority of the English and French Egyptian Ministers, Mr. Rivers Wilson and M. de Blignières, which was principally suffering. Weakened as it was by the differences of opinion and rivalry for influence which sprang up between them and the diplomatic representatives of England and France, its progressive decline must sooner or later have brought the arrangement to an end. But events precipitated its downfall. The Khedive, who had perhaps hoped that Nubar Pasha, as his Prime Minister, would assist him in quietly counterworking and defeating the attempts of his European tutors to tie him down to the position of a constitutional sovereign, found to his dismay that that astute Armenian statesman had unreservedly thrown in his lot with the two Western Powers. It became a contest for power between Ismail and Nubar, and the former had speedy recourse to the oriental weapon of intrigue. In secret he became the chief of the Opposition. He fomented the disaffection of the Turkish and Arab officials and pashas, whose predominance or privileges were threatened by the new administration, and taking advantage of it he secretly instigated a tumultuous meeting at Cairo of a large body of Egyptian officers discharged from the army without settlement of their long-standing arrears of pay, who mobbed and assaulted the Prime Minister and Mr. Rivers Wilson. He compelled Nubar Pasha, on February 19, 1879, to resign his office. A few weeks afterwards Prince Tewfik was appointed his successor, the Khedive at the same time stipulating for a more active participation in the proceedings of the Cabinet Council. His specific claims in fact were (1) to have the right of summoning the Council and proposing measures to it; (2) to have all measures submitted to him by the Minister before being laid before it; and (3) to preside at all its deliberations.

The last of these demands was strongly opposed by the two European Ministers, who insisted also on the reinstatement of Nubar Pasha, and invoked the interference of their Governments in support of their views. Mr. Vivian, the English Consul-General, advised his Government against the reimposition of Nubar on the Khedive, and eventually the agents of England and France were directed to inform Ismail Pasha that the two Governments would not further press the readmission of the late Prime Minister into the Cabinet, in consideration of its being agreed (1) that the Khedive should not in any case be present at Cabinet Councils; (2) that Prince Tewfik should be appointed President of the Council; and (3) that the two English and French Ministers should possess an absolute right of veto over any proposed measure. These conditions, which were accompanied by a warning almost amounting to a menace of the consequences of refusal, were formally accepted by the Khedive.

It was not, however, in the nature of things that the arrangement thus forced upon Ismail Pasha—diplomatically speaking, at the sword's point—should last long. Its collapse was precipitated by the Second Report of the Commission of Inquiry. Major Baring and his colleagues pursued their investigations with an uncompromising thoroughness which dismayed the old-fashioned officialism of Egypt, and the results of which, at first communicated only confidentially to the Khedive, were of such a nature as to determine him on a last desperate stroke for independence. On April 7 he suddenly dismissed his Ministry, and appointed another under the presidency of Cherif Pasha, while at the same time he brought forward a counter project to that which had been formulated in the Second Report of the Commission of Inquiry for the reorganization of Egyptian finance.

It seemed at first as though the Governments of England and France intended to submit tamely to this *coup d'état* of the Khedive's. In spite of the protest of the European Commissioners of the Caisse de la Dette, and the resignation of nearly every official of high rank connected with the finances of the country, the so-called " National Project " was embodied in a decree ; and the English Government contented itself for the moment with a grave remonstrance against the action of the Khedive, as showing contemptuous disrespect for the Powers who had nominated Messrs. Wilson and De Blignières, and as contrary to the special engagement which he had taken in accepting the terms of the arrangement concluded with him so shortly before.

Nor was there any sign of a disposition on the part of France for more energetic measures. On the 25th of April she joined England in a formal demand for the reinstatement of the European Ministers; but when ten days later the two Powers met with a flat refusal, they seemed indisposed to take any more vigorous measures. A week elapsed without movement on the part of the Powers, and, with a Government so unwilling to move as that which then held office in England, it is even now a question of much uncertainty what turn events might ultimately have taken, had it not been for the sudden appearance of an unexpected *deus ex machinâ* in the person of Germany.

On May 11 Her Majesty's Government was informed by a circular from the German Minister of State, sent through the Ambassador in London. that the German Consul-General had been instructed to declare to the Khedive that "the Imperial Government regarded the decree of April 22, by which a settlement of the Egyptian Debt was arbitrarily made by the Egyptian Government acting alone, so as to involve the abolition of acquired and recognized rights, as an open and direct violation of the international obligations imposed by the judicial reforms; and that the German Government could not therefore admit any binding legal force in the said decree, in so far as it touches either the competency of the Mixed Courts or the rights of the subjects of the empire; and that they held the Viceroy responsible for all the consequences of this illegal conduct." This formal protest was delivered to the Khedive on May 18, and within a month the Governments of the other two Powers had associated themselves with it.

For Ismail Pasha it was the beginning of the end. Both France and England had been thoroughly alarmed by the intervention of Germany. They felt that the Khedive had become impossible, and that to permit his continuance on the throne would simply be throwing down Egypt as a bone of contention to be fought for by the Powers. Having accordingly secured the concurrence of his suzerain at Constantinople for any measures they might find it necessary to adopt, the two Governments directed their representatives to advise the Khedive to abdicate in favour of his son Tewfik. Should he refuse to take this course he was to be told that the Powers would address themselves to the Sultan, in which case he would not be able to count upon obtaining any pension, or on the maintenance of the succession in favour of his son. The German and Austrian Consuls-General made a similar statement four days later. The Khedive hesi-

tated, and asked for time to refer the matter
to the Sultan ; and at the last moment declared
his willingness to submit his whole plan to the
approval of the Powers, and withdraw the decree
against which Germany had originally protested ;
but it was too late. On June 26, by telegram
from Constantinople, the Sultan despatched an
Imperial Iradé, deposing Ismail Pasha and re-
placing him by his son Tewfik, who was
proclaimed Khedive with every sign of general
relief and satisfaction.

CHAPTER III.

The Dual Control

ISMAIL'S successor, Tewfik Pasha, in whose favour as his eldest son the succession had been settled by a firman of the Sultan, assumed the government with a high reputation for integrity and loyalty to western ideas. His habits were simple, and his *entourage* compared very favourably with that of his father, with whom, indeed, he had for some time past been on no very cordial terms. When the report of the Commission of Inquiry was published on August 28, with all its damaging disclosures of the consequences of Ismail Pasha's financial recklessness, and it was pointed out that the surrender of the lands acquired by him and his family was the only means of saving the country from immediate bankruptcy, Prince Tewfik set the example of at once offering the unconditional cession of his own share of the estates. His first act, moreover, on succeeding to his father, was to lower his own civil list from £360,000 to £200,000 a year.

The Porte at first showed a desire to make capital out of the crisis by revoking the firman of 1873, which had practically emancipated Egypt from the control of the Sultan; but the Powers had, of course, no mind to allow the country to be reduced to its ancient state of vassalage to Constantinople. Under strong pressure from them the Porte withdrew its pretensions, and a firman was granted confirming Tewfik Pasha in all the privileges enjoyed by his father. A week or so after it was intimated to Cherif Pasha that his resignation was expected, and on his tendering it, Riaz Pasha, who was regarded as the most liberal of Egyptian statesmen, and who, as a member of the Administration which had accepted the Dual Control, had incurred the greatest odium with the Turkish party, was charged with the formation of a new Cabinet.

Meanwhile active negotiations were going on in Europe concerning the form in which the control of the government of Egypt, which had been gradually assumed by England and France, should be maintained. The introduction of European Ministers in the Egyptian Cabinet had not, as we have seen, turned out an unqualified success. It had led, as it was inevitable that it should, to misunderstandings between the European Ministers and their Consuls-General; the latter claiming, and with technical right, to be the only official representatives of their countries, while the former considered themselves entitled to demand the support of their diplomatic colleagues for all their ministerial proposals, whether approved of at the Agencies or not. More smoothly working machinery for bringing the will of the two Western Powers to bear upon the policy and acts of the Egyptian Government might be found, it was thought, in the reappointment with greatly extended powers of the two Controllers established under the Goschen Scheme. Indeed, shortly before the dismissal of the Nubar-Wilson Ministry in April, 1879, the two Powers had obtained from Ismail Pasha an express undertaking that this step should accompany any material change in the system of responsible government established in the previous August.

Accordingly on September 4 the Dual Control was by decree revived, and Baring, plainly designated for the post by his services in the Commissionership of the Public Debt (in which four months before he had been succeeded by Sir Auckland Colvin), and by the valuable assistance which he had rendered in the inquiry into the finances of Egypt, was appointed English Controller, with M. de Blignières as his French colleague. Their new powers and functions were not defined, however, until two months later, when a decree was issued formally reciting that these powers had been settled by an understanding between England and France, and were as follows :—

(1) They were to have the fullest powers of inquiry into all branches of the public service, and each administration was to furnish them with periodical accounts of receipts and expenditure.

(2) They were *for the present* (and this by the express consent of England and France) not to take part in the business of the public offices, but to confine themselves to making suggestions to the Ministers.

(3) They were to have the rank of Ministers, and a seat and a deliberative voice in the Cabinet; or in other words, were to fill a position analogous to that of an English Cabinet Minister holding no departmental office.

(4) They were to be removable only with the consent of their respective Governments, and were to have full powers of appointing and dismissing all subordinate officials.

The first and most important task before the new Controllers was the construction, on the basis of the Second Report of the Commission of Inquiry of 1878, of a scheme for the general settlement of the financial difficulties of Egypt.

It had been originally proposed to appoint an International Commission of Liquidation, nominated by all the great Powers, for the execution of this work; but this idea, as the time approached for its realization, was viewed with less and less favour by France and England, and the duty eventually devolved upon the English and French Controllers alone. Before, however, any steps could be taken in the matter of the liquidation, the Controllers were confronted by a difficulty curiously illustrative of the conflict of jurisdiction which had been brought about by successive interventions of the European Powers, singly, dually, or collectively, in the affairs of Egypt. Concurrently with the decree defining the functions of the Controllers, another had been issued declaring the lands ceded by the Khedive on the First Report of the Commission to be inalienable and free from legal seizure, except on terms agreed to by Messrs. Rothschild, who had taken them on security for their loan of October, 1878. At the same time it secured the rights of all those judgment creditors who, by registration of those judgments, had obtained priority over Messrs. Rothschild.

The treatment of these creditors and their debtor gave rise, as was indeed but natural, to an irreconcilable dispute between the judicial and the administrative authority. A judgment creditor's right to preference over unsecured creditors is in the eyes of a lawyer sacred; to a Minister of Finance, solicitous only for the credit of the State for which he is acting, and therefore for the strictest possible equality of treatment as between the holders of that State's securities, the recognition of this preference might well seem both unfair and inconvenient.

The Commission of Inquiry of 1878 had openly declared Egypt to be insolvent, and had proposed that a general liquidation should be commenced as upon the bankruptcy of a private individual. Proceeding upon this principle, it would of course follow that all creditors should be put on an equal footing and paid *pro ratâ*, and the insolvency should relate back to the suspension of payment and unification of the General Debt of the decree of May 7, 1876. It was contended, therefore, by the Controllers that it was unjust that those creditors who had obtained the accidental advantage of priority of registration of their judgments upon the Khedival domain lands should be paid in full, while others were only paid a dividend out of the insolvent estates. But the Mixed Courts had by more than one decision refused to admit the right of the Government to override vested rights by financial decrees;

and as far back as 1876 the Court of Appeal at Alexandria had expressly recognized the priority of the claims of registered judgment creditors upon the lands which had been specially appropriated to the settlement of the Floating Debt. It was therefore necessary to obtain the consent of all the Powers, who had been parties to the judicial reforms of 1876, to a law enacting the removal of the attachments ranking prior to that of Messrs. Rothschild. This consent England and France were ready to give, and when Germany and Austria refused to agree, the English Controller and his French colleague were despatched to Vienna to endeavour to persuade the Austrian Cabinet to accede to the view of the Western Powers. The efforts, however, of Mr. Baring and M. de Blignières, though we can well believe that they were energetic enough, proved fruitless. The Austrian and German Governments refused to consent to anything which touched the principle of the inviolability of the decisions of the Mixed Courts.

Most people, we imagine, would now agree in approval of their attitude. The institution of the *privilegium*, or special law, passed for the benefit of individuals in derogation of the settled law of the land, is in no sense a commendable one, nor is it any more to be commended even when the favoured individuals constitute so large

a class as the general body of the unsecured
creditors of a State.   And the blow which it
necessarily strikes at the authority of the legal
tribunals of a country is even more to be deprecated when those tribunals are, as they were in
this case, the creation of Foreign Powers, and
dependent on the support of those Powers for
the maintenance of their authority.

On the other hand, it was not unnatural, for the
reasons above given, that this view of the matter
should fail to commend itself to a Controller of
the Finances.   In a letter addressed to the
Khedive on November 30, the Controllers
openly protested against the decision which had
been forced upon them, and expressed their
deep regret at their inability to overcome the
resistance of the tribunals and of the Foreign
Governments by whom they were upheld.   At
the same time they proposed a plan for diminish-
ing as much as possible the injury done to the
other classes of creditors.

The decree thus framed was at last accepted
by all the Powers, with the exception of Greece;
and on December 19 it was formally announced
to the Courts as having been accepted by all the
Treaty Powers, and incorporated with the codes
of the country.   It now remained to give effect to
it.   Early in January, 1890, a financial report was
presented to the Viceroy.   In it the difficulties of

the situation were in no way minimized; but at the same time no doubt was thrown on the possibility of re-establishing Egyptian credit, if only the Egyptian Government would undertake to "draw a distinct line of demarcation between the past and the future, and to decide that by the enforcement of the new law all claims, prior to its promulgation, should be finally liquidated."

The report of the Controllers was promptly followed by the publication of the Budget, which was generally regarded by those best acquainted with the country as having been framed on a sound estimate of its resources. It certainly offered a great contrast to the Budget of the previous year, the last of the Ismailian *régime*, which was essentially what would be called on the Stock Exchange a " bull " Budget—a financial scheme conceived in the spirit of a "speculator for the rise." In this the revenue had been estimated at nearly eleven millions sterling. Mr. Baring and M. de Blignières were content to budget for eight millions and a half. On the expenditure side the interest on the Unified Debt was calculated at four per cent., at which rate it had been provisionally fixed by the Commission of Inquiry of the previous year. Beyond doubt it was as high a rate as the country at that moment was able to pay; but it is not to be

supposed that the bondholders were prepared
to accept it with cheerfulness or even resignation.
For though the absurd denunciations which were
so incessantly levelled at him in those days by
a certain political party in England were ignorant
and absurd, yet it is nevertheless true that the
bondholder does not take any more kindly than,
let us say, the Radical traders and manufacturers
who used to abuse him in the House of Commons,
to losing any of his expected gains ; for there is
a great deal of human nature in the bondholder,
and human nature is not "built that way." He
strongly opposed the reduction of the interest,
and at one time it seemed as if the Egyptian
Government would give way to him. Baring
and his colleague, however, stood firm, and on
February 24 the President of the Council of
Ministers addressed to them a formal surrender
of the principal points in dispute.

In the President's letter reference was made
to the goodwill with which the recommendations
of the Commission of Inquiry had been carried
out, by the abolition of the poll-tax, the reform
of the salt-tax, and other measures. The
Khedive, the letter went on to show, had
already paid more than a million and a half
of his father's debts to the mortgage creditors,
and was ready to come to terms with the holders
of the Floating Debt. " But," added the Presi-

dent of the Council, "we are stopped by the international principle which prevents Egypt from making her own laws without the consent of fourteen Powers." "Egypt," he went on to say, "contained all the elements of a durable prosperity. The Government has commenced reforms which will enable that prosperity to develop; the most perfect harmony exists between the Controllers and the Ministers. But all these elements of prosperity are paralyzed by the check imposed on our legislative powers by the principle of internationality. A Government cannot live unless it can make laws. Either, therefore, the Egyptian Government must be allowed to make its own laws, or the Powers must agree to make them with her. Egypt is ready to accept either of these solutions. But long negotiations will imperil the vital interests of the creditors as well as the country. If the Government did not know that an International Commission was now being discussed by the Powers a settlement would be at once offered to the creditors."

Riaz Pasha is not perhaps the most enlightened of statesmen, but there was good sense in these words of his, especially in their closing suggestion of a prompt settlement with the creditors of Egypt. The diplomatic jealousies referred to above had been now allayed, and the

Commission of Liquidation was at last appointed on an international basis. It consisted of seven members, England and France being represented by two Commissioners each; Germany, Austria, and Italy by one each; and the other European Powers parties to the Capitulations, agreeing to leave their interests in their colleagues' hands. On July 17 the Report of the Commission was presented to and approved by the Khedive, and a law was at once framed to give effect to their recommendations. Its main provisoes were as follows :—

(1) The privileges of the Railway Preference Loan as fixed by the Goschen-Joubert decree of November, 1876, were maintained, and a further issue of £5,744,000 was authorized. The interest of this stock was secured by the railway and telegraph revenue, and constituted a first charge on the other revenues set apart for the service of the Unified Debt and the revenue of the harbour of Alexandria.

(2) The interest on the Unified Debt was maintained at 4 per cent., to be paid from the aforesaid revenues assigned to it; and, the charge of this debt amounting annually to a little more than two millions and a quarter, it was provided that any receipts in excess of this sum should form a sinking fund, to be applied to the purchase

and extinction of the stock in the open market. At the same time the normal expenditure of the Egyptian Government was fixed at £4,898,000, which sum was to cover the tribute payable to the Porte, the interest due to Great Britain on the Suez Canal shares, and certain other charges.

(3) The property of the Daira Sanieh—the estates surrendered by the Khedive—was formally declared to belong to the State, and the interest on the Daira Loan, to the extent of 4 per cent., was guaranteed by the Egyptian Government, the balance being payable contingently only on the revenue of the estates proving sufficient to provide it.

(4) The Floating Debt was divided into a preference and a deferred stock, holders receiving 30 per cent. in cash and 70 per cent. in preference stock at par. A sum of £650,000 was reserved to meet the claims pending before the international tribunals, and a loan to that amount on the lands belonging to the Egyptian Government was authorized. Certain debts were paid in full cash; namely, the mortgages on the Domain lands prior to the Rothschild mortgage (which had formed, it will be remembered, a matter of international difference in the previous year), together with all the arrears of salaries and pensions, the arrears of the tribute, and certain

other sums which had been diverted by the ex-Khedive.

These proposals of the Commission of Liquidation, and their ratification by the Khedive and his Ministers, gave general satisfaction to the creditors of Egypt. It was on the whole, indeed, a highly satisfying conclusion to the long struggle for the re-establishment of Egyptian credit, in which Baring had taken so active a part. But he did not, officially speaking, live to witness the final result of his labours. The law of liquidation was promulgated on July 17, 1880, and some weeks earlier, on June 22, he had been succeeded in the Controllership by Sir Auckland Colvin, and was himself shortly afterwards appointed to succeed Sir John Strachey as Financial Member of the Council of India.

CHAPTER IV.

Finance Minister in India

THE Controllership of Egyptian Finance was at all times a post of importance, and one requiring both ability and force of character; but it could not of course compare for a moment, either in dignity, independence of initiative, or opportunities of public service and public distinction, with that to which Baring was now appointed. It was, indeed, great promotion for an Artillery officer of thirty-nine. Selections for the office of Financial Minister of the Council for India had heretofore been, and indeed are still, generally made from the ranks of the Indian Civil Service. The appointment of a military man, and of one whose only acquaintance with the country over whose finances he was to preside had been formed during a few years' private secretaryship to a former Viceroy, was an innovation of some boldness; and though it would be affectation in any case of this kind to ignore the operation of political and family interest altogether, it would on the other hand be unjust and unreasonable to lay much stress upon it. No Government can afford to risk its reputation and run the chance of creating countless troubles for itself, both in India and at home, by any appointment which is even so much as doubtful to this important post. It is quite certain that Mr. Gladstone must, either from personal observation or from reports on which he could confidently rely, have fully satisfied himself that the Major of Artillery, who had had two years' experience of fiscal administration in Egypt, possessed abilities which fully qualified him to grapple with the eternal problem of Indian finance.

The undertaking was at this juncture a peculiarly arduous one, since seldom, if ever before, had that problem presented itself in a more formidable shape. During the previous financial year, 1879–80, the chronic difficulties which beset the work of providing for the cost of Indian administration had been cumulated with various acute troubles. The cost of the Afghan War had had to be met; an increasing loss in exchange, produced by the depreciation of silver, had begun to put that severe strain upon the resources of India which has continued to increase in severity ever since; various public works which involved a heavy outlay had already been sanctioned. The returns from certain districts showed that in some parts of the country the effects of the recent famine were still severely felt ; and the financial situation was further aggravated by an increase in the military and other branches of expenditure. The gravity of the crisis was reflected in the Budget of 1879–80, which was actually brought on for discussion in the House of Commons as early as May 22nd, and debated for three nights, instead of getting only as many hours at the fag-end of the Session, and which has been described by a high authority on the subject, the late Mr. Fawcett, as " marking the commencement of a new epoch in Indian finance." The character of the new departure he goes on thus forcibly to describe :—

"The true financial condition of India had never up till this time been officially recognized. Liberal and Conservative Governments had not only persistently denied that there was anything in the state of Indian finance to cause apprehension, but year after year, as the time of the introduction of the Indian Budget recurred, her actual financial condition was depicted in roseate hues, and her future was described in a spirit of increasing hopefulness. So little cause was there said to be for uneasiness or alarm, that the Indian Budget used always to be postponed till a period of the Session when all other important business had been disposed of. When the Budget was considered it was little more than a repetition of an oft-told tale. By classing some branch of expenditure as extraordinary, and by regarding some outlay as exceptional, the Indian Accounts were almost inevitably arranged so as to exhibit a surplus. The public works expenditure was habitually compared to the profitable investment of capital by a wise and beneficent landlord in the improvement of a judiciously administered estate. A most significant change, however, has lately occurred. A large portion of the outlay in public works is now officially admitted to be unremunerative; and the Finance Minister, Sir John Strachey, has been forced to admit that a review of the finances of India for seven years, a period long enough to show their normal position, 'made it plain that we possessed no true surplus of revenue over expenditure to cover the many contingencies to which a great country is exposed.'"

Nor was this the only important point in which, according to Mr. Fawcett, a new departure was to be noted :—

"In order still further to show the striking change of tone recently adopted by those who are responsible for the Government of India, it is particularly worthy of remark that the Viceroy and the Secretary of State now unreservedly accept the conclusion that the limit of taxation has been reached in India, and that it has consequently become imperatively necessary that expenditure should be reduced. In a despatch which has been lately issued by the Viceroy and his Council to the Local Governments, it is declared that 'immediate measures must be taken for reduction of the public expenditure in all its branches.' On behalf of the Secretary of State it has been with equal positiveness announced that the balance between revenue and expenditure must be restored not by the imposition of new taxation, but by a large reduction of expenditure.

The causes which had brought about this serious condition of the Indian finances may—if we dismiss the accidental and temporary demands of the Afghan War — be thus enumerated. First, the necessity, then for the first time recognized, of providing a famine fund out of ordinary revenue; secondly, the increasing loss on exchange; and thirdly, the unremunerative character of a large expenditure on public works.

To meet the demands arising under these three heads, it became necessary in the Budget of 1879-80 to provide a sum of no less than £1,100,000 by increased taxation; and—no doubt, after a careful review of the entire fiscal system of India with the object of ascertaining what new tax could be imposed, or what existing import could be increased with the least hardship to the people—it was determined to raise about two-thirds of the amount required by the imposition of a trade-license tax. As originally levied, this tax was virtually an income-tax of about fivepence in the £ imposed upon all persons earning not less than 100 rupees a year by trade or by skilled labour. Official and professional incomes, from those of the Governor-General and the most successful of Anglo-Indian barristers or physicians downwards, were exempted altogether. Mr. Fawcett's denunciation of this impost was, as might have been expected, uncompromising. After animadverting on its inequality and the severity of the burden which it imposed on men whose income was only £10 a year, he goes on to allege other and more serious objections to it. "Although," he says, writing in 1880, "the tax has been in operation for little more than a twelvemonth, no one can deny that it has already produced a feeling of deep and widespread discontent, and facts can be mentioned which show that this discontent is far more due to the abuses inseparably connected with the levying of the tax, than to the mere amount of the burden which the tax, if it could be fairly raised, would impose upon the people. During many months the Indian papers have contained numerous instances of the tax being assessed at an excessive amount, and of its being levied on classes who were never intended to pay it. These newspapers," he added, "were abundantly confirmed by communications which he had received from persons holding high official positions in the Civil Service of India. He had found it stated on authority which could not be disputed, that in one district in Bombay, out of 25,000 assessments made by one official, nearly one-half were appealed against, and in all these appeals the assessments had to be modified by the Revising Officer; and it was well known," he remarked, "that the cost and annoyance involved in their appeals are so great, that in a vast number of cases people submit to an unjust assessment rather than travel many miles, and thus incur the outlay and the worry of appearing in court to protest."

He complained further that "the indefensible exemption" of the official and professional classes from contributing to the license-tax "converts it into an income-tax in its most obnoxious form," meaning, it is to be supposed, thereby, its most inquisitorial shape, as being confined exclusively to those incomes which, unlike those of the official and in some measure of the professional classes, are matters within the knowledge of the taxpayer alone.   Not only so, but the present license-tax was, he insisted, levied with far more rigour than the income-tax had been when imposed in India a few years before.   " Although the tax was of the same nominal amount, it appears that the license-tax, in spite of its exemptions, enforces a much larger contribution from the mass of the people. . . . When it is borne in mind that the official and professional classes, who are exempted from the licensing-tax, were assessed to the income-tax, and that the net yield of the former tax is estimated to be considerably greater than that of the latter, it seems to be conclusively proved that the license-tax falls with extreme severity upon numerous classes of the very poor who were not reached by the income-tax.   It must, moreover, be remembered that throughout a considerable part of India the burden of this new taxation falls upon many who are only just recovering from the effects of a terrible famine."

Some allowance may have to be made for the unconscious bias of a man who, though scrupulously fair in intention, was always liable to be unconsciously influenced by his strong democratic prepossessions; but the substantial justice of his strictures were tacitly admitted by the Indian Government themselves. On the 14th of November, 1879, the Finance Minister, Sir John Strachey, brought forward at a meeting of the Legislative Council of the Viceroy a Bill for the amendment of the license-tax, which, though it left some inequalities unmodified, introduced many important improvements. A brief description of its provisions will show clearly enough that the author of the measure acknowledged the validity of the most serious of Mr. Fawcett's objections to the tax. The limit of exemption from it was raised from 100 to 250 rupees per annum—a concession which would, it was stated, give relief to not less than a million persons. The consequent loss to the revenue, estimated at about £240,000, was met by the imposition of a uniform tax of $1\frac{1}{2}$ per cent. on all incomes derived from professions and on the salaries of all persons in Government or other employment, with an exemption, however, in favour of all military servants of Government, not in civil employment, whose pay and allowances did not exceed 500 rupees a month, or 6000 rupees per annum, and of all other salaried persons whose incomes did not exceed 100 rupees a month or 1200 rupees a year.

The spirit of this amending Bill is sufficiently obvious ; but, nevertheless, the measure was not regarded as going far enough to satisfy the objectors to the original proposals. It was urged that the lower limit of taxation was still too low, and the Indian Government yielding to these expressions of public opinion, reintroduced their amending Bill with still further modifications ; and Sir John Strachey proposed at a meeting of the Legislative Council to refer it to a Select Committee, with the object of passing it after the next Indian Budget. In its final shape it raised the limit of exemption from 250 to 500 rupees, and, subject to a proviso that the maximum amount to be levied on any person not being an official should be 800 rupees, it imposed a tax of $1\frac{1}{2}$ per cent. on all official salaries without limitation. By the former of these, the raising of the limit of exemption to 500 rupees, it was estimated that no fewer than 1,750,000 persons would in future be freed from all liability to contribute to the tax.

The history of this legislation has been thus reviewed in detail because it affords, perhaps, the best illustration of the gravity of the financial straits to which the Indian Government had been reduced during the years immediately preceding that in which Baring was summoned to undertake his new duties. They had become even more grievous during the financial year preceding his appointment, for, owing to an under-estimate of war expenditure, the Budget of 1880-81, in which the late Finance Minister had estimated for a surplus of £417,000, was falsified to the extent of over six millions by results, and the returns of revenue and expenditure for that year displayed a deficit of £6,269,000. Happily, however, this extraordinary drain on the resources of India was now coming to an end, and Baring was able, in his first Budget, to assume a reduction of outlay to the extent of a little over seven millions, and to calculate on a surplus of £855,000. He had no financial legislation to propose, and his statement accordingly took the simple form of a written minute; but it contains so able and masterly a statement of the bearings of the currency difficulty on Indian finance—a statement to which the years that have since elapsed have given an enhanced significance—that this passage in the minute deserves to be quoted in its entirety. The writer is discussing the proposed application of £750,000, one moiety of the annual charge of £1,150,000 in the nature of a Famine Insurance, and he thus proceeds to examine the question :—

"The disposal of this sum of money raises some difficult questions of principle. Does the application of this money to the reduction of debts, while at the same time the Government still continues to borrow for Productive Public Works, involve the old fallacy of a sinking fund without a surplus? It is this question, on which there may well be two opinions, which has, to a great extent, given rise to those doubts in respect to the discretion of the Famine Insurance policy to which I have already alluded.

"The soundness or otherwise of the policy depends upon the answer which can be given to the question, Is it desirable to convert sterling into rupee debt? The Government is of opinion that within certain limitations it is desirable to effect this conversion.

"The grounds for holding this opinion are as follows :—

"(1) It is essential to a sound condition of State finance that the elements of certainty and stability should prevail to as great an extent as possible. No such certainty or stability can be attained if the State own a large sum of money in a currency other than that in which it collects its revenue.

"(2) It is desirable in years of prosperity to reduce the home liabilities in order that in times of emergency the Government may fall back on the London market and borrow without any aggregate increase in their amount.

"It may perhaps be urged that the object in view will, in any case, only be attained in appearance and not in reality; that it signifies little whether interest is payable in gold or silver, or whether a loan is issued in London or Calcutta, for that in either case the money will be subscribed by investors resident in Europe; and that the so-called 'loss by exchange' depends not on the Secretary of State's bills, but on the cumulated transactions of the Secretary of State and the public.

"If this argument is carried out to its logical conclusion it involves a reversion to the policy of contracting sterling loans, wherever it is possible to obtain money by such means cheaper than by contracting to pay interest in silver. The adoption of this course, although in contradiction to the principles which have been laid down by successive Secretaries of State, is advocated by many high authorities.

"The Government is of opinion that it would be inexpedient at present to revert to the policy of contracting obligations in gold for the following reasons :—

"(1) The best solution of the question would be to obtain money from local investors at the same rate as from residents in Europe. If Government loans are issued in India, and if the interest is payable in silver, we may hope to attract some local capital. If they are issued in London, and the interest is payable in gold, we are almost certain to attract no local capital.

"(2) It is the opinion of those who speak with the authority of long practical experience that the effect on exchange, of the amount which India has annually to remit to England, would not be so oppressive if the bills were more equally distributed between the Secretary of State and the public.

"(3) Any extension of our sterling obligations is in the nature of a speculation, which may prove successful or the reverse, according to whether the value of silver in respect to gold rises or falls.

"Although, however, the advantages of remitting to England, in order to extinguish sterling debt, may be admitted, it is possible to pay too high a price for these advantages. The difference between the value of rupee and sterling stock may be so considerable as to render the transaction undesirable. Further, there are practical difficulties in the way of giving effect to this policy. The amount of the home disbursements is now so large that unless there be a rise in the value of silver, or unless the amount of exports is increased, it may be difficult to remit home £750,000 more than at present. For these reasons the Government cannot give any positive pledge that even when a *bonà fide* surplus of receipt over expenditure is secured it shall be applied to the reduction of sterling debt."

In concluding his statement, Major Baring took judicious occasion to refer to the extraordinary miscalculation of expenditure which had so deranged the Budget of the preceding year. Such a startling failure in the War Estimates had naturally tended to induce a belief that the then financial condition of India afforded ground for alarm ; whereas, as the Minister proceeded to point out, it was merely from the stress of the great war expenditure that India was suffering. Relieved of this, it would be seen, he said, that the actual financial condition of the country was prosperous. The difficulties with which the Government had to deal, considerable though they were, were very different from those which existed in the years immediately following the Mutiny. India was not now in a state of chronic deficit. She could not only pay her way, but could provide a large surplus of receipts over expenditure.

This statement was fully confirmed by the experience of the following year, when for

1882-83 the surplus of £855,000 calculated upon
in the Budget Estimates was exceeded in the
Regular Estimates by £722,000, showing a total
surplus of upwards of a million and a half. This,
too, was by far the most important of Baring's
three Financial Statements, since in it he had
proposed legislation for the reduction of the duty
on salt and for the total abolition of the cotton
duties, two changes involving a loss to the
revenue of no less than £2,619,000.

But before reaching the part of his statement
in which his projected legislation had to be
discussed and explained, the Finance Minister
had to undertake a somewhat detailed and comprehensive examination of a highly contentious
question, on which, perhaps, more nonsense has
been talked and more cant outpoured than on
any other controversy of modern times. I refer
of course to the opium question, which Major
Baring handles in this Budget statement in
admirably straightforward fashion. A great deal
had, he said, been written from time to time as
to the effects of opium, both on the individual
and on the Chinese nation. " I do not think," he
continues, "that anything is to be gained by
discussing this subject at any length. That
opium, when used in moderation for medicinal
purposes, is beneficial; that in China it is very
often used to excess; that when used to excess

its effect is baneful; and that it would be better for the Chinese if they smoked less opium, are truisms which may be generally accepted. The commonplaces on the subject may to some extent be admitted by all parties. Even if it is conceded to the Anti-Opium Society that the effects of the drug are to the full as baneful as they allege, we should, whether from the Chinese or the Indian point of view, be no nearer than at present to the solution of the problem which we have on hand. It is useless to discuss what ideal condition of things would commend itself either to Chinese or to Indian statesmen. The problem we have to treat is an eminently practical one."

Then, step by step, he proceeds to point out that the anti-opium agitator, who professes himself scandalized by the connection of the Indian Government with the opium traffic, must, if he is consistent, aim not merely at dissociating that Government from the traffic in question, but at the total suppression of the trade. For the instant economic effect of that dissociation would be to aggravate the moral mischief against which these agitators protest. China would in that case be simply flooded with the Indian drug. Its consumption in that country would be increased, and the cheapening of it in price would cause the poorer classes of Chinamen who now smoke native opium to substitute Indian opium in its place.

Passing from this point, Major Baring went on to deal with and dispose of the allegations that the Chinese Government had been forced against their will to admit opium by the Treaty of Tientsin, or that they are forced to admit it now. As a matter of fact, they are neither able nor in any effective sense willing to stop the use of opium among their people.

"Numerous edicts, couched in the most peremptory terms, have been from time to time issued to prohibit the use of opium and the cultivation of the poppy. In issuing these decrees the Chinese Government may be credited with a certain amount of sincerity. Without doubt the Emperor of China, his Ministers, and the most enlightened portion of the population of China, deplore the extensive use of opium. If they could afford the loss of Imperial revenue consequent on the importation of foreign opium; if they could exercise any real control over the numberless corrupt officials who earn a livelihood from the use of the native drug; if they thought it were possible to deal with a great social evil of this sort by legislation, and to coerce a large part of the population of a vast empire into a groove contrary to their inveterate habits and the current of their every-day life, it is not improbable that they would gladly see the use of opium abandoned. But whatever are the views which the Chinese Ministers entertain on the question in the abstract, nothing is more certain than that they, equally with the Indian Government, would be embarrassed by the loss of revenue which would be caused either by a cessation of the foreign trade in opium, or by the suppression of the manufacture and sale of the drug in China; that save on rare occasions, when some specially energetic official may have produced a temporary effect, they have up to the present time never earnestly endeavoured to check the use of the drug, and that they recognize both by word and deed their complete inability to do so. A mass of evidence from the consular reports might be adduced in support of these conclusions."

The repeal of the cotton duties was a question on which Anglo-Indian opinion was much more divided, and which needed proportionately more of persuasive power on the part of its advocate to recommend it to general acceptance. Major Baring submitted it to the Council in a speech of marked ability, and the Viceroy, Lord Ripon, lent all the weight of his official authority to the arguments in favour. It was carried, and the cotton duties, together with those payable on all other articles save intoxicating liquors, and arms and ammunition, were for the time abolished. Public opinion in India was rather prepared for than reconciled to the step. The native press were almost unanimous in their condemnation of what they considered to be a needless sacrifice of revenue, and their discontent was no doubt increased by the fact that the license-tax—which they still regarded, even in its amended form, as unjust and unequal—remained untouched, the Finance Minister, though he referred to it as a temporary and not very efficient expedient for raising revenue, pro-posing no change in its amount or incidence.

A Budget in which the repeal of the cotton duties figured as the principal feature was not exactly a popular one, either in India or (out of Manchester) in England, for a Finance Minister to be associated with; but the ability displayed in the construction of the scheme was undeniable, and its author's claim to recognition as a skilled financier was strengthened by the fact that he had approached his task under all the disadvantages incident to convalescence from a serious attack of typhoid fever, which had prostrated him in the early part of the year. Even in exceptional ways, moreover, his activity remained unimpaired by his illness. With a view to obtaining information as to the various methods by which capital could obtain profitable employment, tours were undertaken by some of the members of the Government to various parts of India; and in response to a speech of the Governor of Madras, in which he hinted that that dependency had received too little of the financial attention of the Central Government, Major Baring paid it a visit. He was interviewed by the Madras Chamber of Commerce, with whom he discussed certain public works then in progress or in contemplation, and made inquiries as to the probability of attracting local capital to investments in local railroads.

The Financial Statement of 1883–84 was like that of Baring's first year of office, unaccompanied by legislation, and was therefore not delivered orally in Legislative Council, but presented in the form of a minute. This practice, prescribed by the constituting Act of the Imperial Legislature, which expressly excludes matters of Executive policy from the consideration of that Council, is productive of some inconvenience by depriving the Financial Member of the Council of the advantage of his colleagues' criticisms on the proposals. It has more than once been suggested, as indeed it was again on the present occasion, that the views of the non-official members of the Council might be usefully obtained by means of an unimportant fiscal proposal to be introduced collusively, as it were, and without the intention of proceeding further with it. The suggestion, however, as on previous occasions, was not adopted, and the Statement was introduced in the usual way.

It was of a more humdrum character than that of the preceding year, when, in Baring's words, "a favourable opportunity presented itself for the execution of some very large and beneficial improvements of the fiscal system." The financial situation in 1883, though perfectly sound, was one in which great caution was required. The Government had to look, not only to the circumstances of the immediate moment, but also to the contingencies which might arise in future years. But so treated, the situation was satisfactory enough. " Not only," wrote the Finance Minister, "are we able to balance our revenue and expenditure, but we are able, without any increase of taxation and without in any way starving the public services or checking the progress of public works of utility, to provide an adequate surplus in order to meet any of the numerous unforeseen contingencies which so frequently arise in India."

The Budget was accordingly framed for a revenue of £67,274,000, or £640,000 less than that of the assessed estimates of the preceding year; while the expenditure was calculated at more than a million less than the corresponding figures for 1882 – 83; that is to say, at £66,817,000 against £67,854,000 leaving a surplus of £457,000. Including Provincial with Imperial items of expenditure, an increase was allowed for under the important heads of telegraphs, police, law and justice, medical, education, political and territorial pensions, and subsidized railways. On the other hand, that under the large categories of refunds, frontier railways, irrigation, civil buildings, &c., had decreased.

In his Budget statement of the previous year Major Baring had frankly recognized the evils of the license - tax, and admitted that in its present form it could not be incorporated into the permanent fiscal system of the country. "The Government," he said, "reserved to themselves complete liberty of action in the future, either to propose the abolition of the license-tax, to recast it, or, even should such a course appear desirable when the financial arrangements for 1883–84 came under consideration, to allow it to continue in existence in its present form for a while longer. It was this last course which the Government found themselves, in fact, compelled to adopt. After careful consideration of the whole subject, they saw both general and special reasons for not interfering with this tax for the present. They were, in the first place, influenced by the just reflection that there is nothing more undesirable than to be continually introducing changes in the fiscal system of a country like India. The evils arising from the levy of the license-tax in its present shape were emphatically such as it was better to endure rather than remedy, unless some remedy could be applied with reasonable confidence that no further change would in the immediate future be necessary. Moreover," continued the Finance Minister:—

"There are some special considerations which point to the desirability of making no change in the fiscal system at present. The financial year which is about to close has presented features which are altogether abnormal, and even if this had not been the case, the experience of a year is not sufficient to enable any very correct judgment to be formed as to the ultimate effect of the large fiscal reforms which were carried out in March, 1882. The future of silver and of opium is also very uncertain. On every ground, therefore, the present moment is a time when great caution should be exercised. Under these circumstances the Government, after full consideration, is of opinion that the wisest course to adopt will be to make no changes in the fiscal system for the present, but to allow more time to elapse with a view to watching the effect of those reforms which have already been introduced."

The prospects of the opium revenue were indeed in those years regarded by Indian financiers with almost as great, though as the result has shown with by no means so well-founded, an anxiety as that with which they had begun to look on the continued fall in the value of silver. Opium, in Baring's opinion, constituted the chief danger of the immediate future. For a long time past he said he had been inclined to take a somewhat desponding view of the future of the opium revenue, and recent events had confirmed the view which he had theretofore held.

Considering, he went on to point out, that the crop was singularly precarious, that the indigenous drug of China was daily becoming a more serious competitor with Indian opium, and that the Indian revenue depended in no slight degree on the domestic legislation of a foreign country, China, it could scarcely, in his opinion, be doubted that the yearly revenue which India derives from opium would in all probability show a falling off in future.

This forecast perhaps erred a little on the side of pessimism, but on the whole its substantial accuracy has been justified. The net revenue from opium, which was estimated for that financial year at £7,035,000, did indeed touch a point over eight millions some five years later; but the tendency of falling off has unquestionably manifested itself since then. It was lower in 1892–93 than in 1891–92; lower in '93–94 than in '92–93; and lower in '94–95 than in '93–94, falling in the latest of these years to less than six millions and a half, or in other words, to a sum more than half a million below that at which it was possible to estimate it in this last Budget of Baring's, that of 1883–84.

On the more urgent question of exchange the Finance Minister had to report even more unfavourably. At no period had the inconvenience to India, of having to make a large annual payment in sterling, been more apparent than during the then current financial year. It was, however, not so much of the loss as of the disarrangement of accounts and of the

disturbance of trade that Baring complains in
the following passage :—

"I will not now attempt to discuss whether it is to the
advantage of India that the value of the rupee expressed
in sterling should be low; that is to say, lower than it used
to be when the relative values of gold to silver [silver to
gold?] were as 1 to $15\frac{1}{2}$. That is a subject on which a great
deal might be said. But it is not the fact that the value
of the rupee is, comparatively speaking, low that causes
inconvenience. It would be possible, although it might be
exceedingly troublesome, to adjust the Indian fiscal system
to a rupee of any value. What causes inconvenience alike
to Government and to trade is that the value of the rupee
is unstable. It is impossible to state accurately in Indian
currency what the annual liabilities of the Government of
India are. Those liabilities have to be calculated afresh each
year, according to the variations which take place in the
relative value of gold and silver, and a calculation which
will hold good for even one year is exceedingly difficult to
make."

This difficulty had indeed received a costly
illustration in the very year before.

"In March, 1882, the value of the rupee was taken at
1s. 8d., and at the time this estimate was made it was a
reasonable one, based on the facts of the past and present.
The value of silver was then about 52s. an ounce, which
corresponds with a value of 1s. $8\frac{2}{16}$d. to the rupee. But
since then the value of the rupee has been as high as
1s. $8\frac{5}{16}$d., and as low as 1s. $7\frac{1}{16}$d. The average price
obtained for the bills amounting to £1,184,000 (true
sterling), placed on the market up to March 9, 1883, has
been 1s. $7\frac{13}{25}$d. When it was framed it was thought that
a debt of £1,184,000 (true sterling) would be liquidated
by a payment of 17,020,300 rupees. It has actually cost
17,438,100 rupees to liquidate that debt. It is sufficient

to state these facts in order to show the grave inconvenience to the Government which results from the unstable value of the rupee."

The Budget of that year was framed on an estimate of 1s. 7½d. as the value of the rupee, "an estimate which could not," the Finance Minister remarked, "be considered as erring on the side of optimism." For that date no doubt it was not, but it is indeed melancholy to turn from this to the financial statement of 1894–95 and to note the statement of a Minister, who at the same time declared that he would not waste the time of the Council in "bemoaning" the dwindling value of the rupee ; that on the first considerable issue of Council bills in the previous January a rate of 14⅗d. was obtained, which, however, fell in the course of the next month to 13½d., and had since then recovered to about 14d.

Those dark days, however, were still in the somewhat distant future, and in this, the last Budget he was to introduce, Major Baring was able to take on the whole a tolerably hopeful farewell of the country whose finances he had directed for three years. "I will not venture," he said at the close of his general review of the prospective revenue of the coming year, "to predict what may be the financial situation at the commencement of the year 1884–85.

"All that can now be said on this subject is that we commence the year 1883-84 with a surplus of £475,000 in hand; that the estimates for 1883-84 have been very cautiously framed; that the natural prosperity of the country is increasing, and unless famine should intervene, will continue to increase, with the result that the revenue from excise, salt, stamps, railways, &c., is steadily growing; and lastly, that by the reduction of the salt duty the financial position has been much strengthened and a fiscal reserve instituted which, should the occasion unfortunately arise, can be used in case of necessity. So long as the value of the rupee and the opium revenue continue liable to such fluctuations as those which we have recently witnessed, the financial situation of India must always contain some elements of instability; but I see no reason for taking any despondent view of that situation at present. On the contrary, there is every reason to believe that the country will be well able to cope with whatever financial difficulties the future may have in store."

Even in the hard times which have succeeded, and under the far heavier stress of those financial troubles which have been mainly brought about by the further and most disastrous decline in the value of the rupee, it is likely enough that Lord Cromer would be still prepared to stand by these hopeful utterances of his last Budget speech. Pluck and patience are both of them such salient characteristics of the man, that had he even now the direction of Indian finance, he would doubtless still be "strong and of a good courage." But his own lot in India was undoubtedly cast in happier times than the present. For the due evolution of his powers an able financier needs a financial situation which is neither too prosperous nor too much the reverse. It should neither be one which anybody, nor one which nobody, could successfully deal with, and the condition of the finances of India at the time when Baring took his seat on the Council annually fulfilled that condition.

Slowly recovering from the heavy drain of the Afghan War, they had not yet begun to suffer seriously from the more prolonged and exhausting depletion to which the currency trouble has since subjected them. The Finance Minister could still, as we have seen, describe as a mere inconvenience what has since assumed the proportions of a calamity. India had still breathing-time to prepare for her coming trials, and it was the business of her financial counsellors to turn it to the best account. On the other hand, the season was obviously no opportune one for "brilliant experimentalizing" in any direction. It was pre-eminently a situation calling for treatment by the methods of sound "conservative" finance, and these methods Major Baring in each of his three Budgets scrupulously applied to it. Each, therefore, was in its way a success—a success of the only kind possible under the given conditions and with the available materials; and their author, unlike more than one occupant of that difficult post, undoubtedly left India with an enhanced reputation.   Mr. Gladstone, it is understood, entertained a high opinion of his skill as a financier, and his Indian record was at any rate not otherwise than confirmatory of the judgment formed of him by the highest financial authority of the day.

The last year of Major Baring's official sojourn in India was rendered untowardly memorable in the annals of our great dependency by one of the bitterest disputes which have ever divided English and Anglo-Indian opinion.   It was the year in which Mr. (now Sir Courtenay) Ilbert introduced his Criminal Jurisdiction Bill—a measure by which it was proposed to allow European British subjects throughout India to be tried for criminal offences by native magistrates and judges possessed of certain qualifications. Major Baring supported it in Council, and on his retirement from his post and return to England he defended its principles in a well-reasoned article in the *Nineteenth Century*.   The best proof of its argumentative ability is that it follows a vigorous attack from the pen of the late Sir James Stephen on the democratizing tendencies of the Government, and that even in such trying contiguity with one of the keenest and hardest-hitting controversialists of his day, the writer of "Recent Events in India" holds his own.

On the side of the opponents of the Ilbert Bill and of the Ripon policy in general there was no point more strongly insisted upon than the prematurity and gratuitousness of both. "The present government," wrote Stephens in his usually trenchant style, "of the people of India suits all parties concerned. If it does not, it is for those who feel a grievance to complain of it; but to me it appears like madness to try to train a people who like an absolute government, who are accustomed to it, and who make no complaint of it, into a state of mind which might at any moment produce frightful catastrophes, but is utterly unlikely to produce anything else. Suppose a master and his workmen were going on perfectly well together, the master receiving from the workmen good and faithful service, paying them fair wages and doing them kind offices besides, what would be thought of his discretion if he were to be continually calling meetings to discuss Socialism; if he were to ask them if their wages were high enough; whether they did not think they ought to have shares in the business; whether they had no fault to find with the management of it, and so on?"

It would be difficult to put the case for a Conservative policy in India more cogently than this. Nor, I think, would it be easy to state the only possible reply to it with more lucidity and

skill than in the following passage from Major
Baring's article :—

"It is always difficult in politics to decide whether it is
wiser to anticipate a difficulty, or to await a solution until
the difficulty has become a burning question. Englishmen
generally prefer the latter course, because they are accustomed
to it. The difficulties of parliamentary government are so
great that few Ministers will care to take up a difficult question
until it is forced upon their attention. The consequence is
that reform is often so long delayed as to prevent its producing
a full measure of beneficial results when it is ultimately effected.
As India is necessarily debarred from the benefit of parliamentary institutions, there can be no reason why it should not
reap whatever advantages are incidental to a despotic form of
government ; and one of these advantages is that it is sometimes possible and desirable to anticipate a difficulty and
solve it before it has attained considerable dimensions. I
have, therefore, always thought, in Lord Ripon's words, that it
would be 'wiser to introduce the measure now gradually,
cautiously, and tentatively than to wait till the change is
forced upon us by necessity, and the powers which are now to
be given only to a few men have to be given suddenly to a
very much larger number of civil servants.' *A fortiori* I am
of that opinion now that the question has once been raised."

Arguments of this description had a good deal
more weight with Moderate Liberals of the Baring
type than they possess to-day. After the many
object-lessons on the futility of the policy of
"meeting nationalist movements half-way," which
the past ten years have yielded for statesmen of
all parties, and especially for that to which the hero
of this biography belonged, it is not presumptuous
to suppose that the theories which commanded the
adhesion of Major Baring have lost much of their
influence over the mind of Lord Cromer.

CHAPTER V.

Consul-General at Cairo

HITHERTO the duties which Baring had been discharging ever since his definitive abandonment of military for civil life, had been wholly of a financial character. But now, on his return to England, where his official services of the last three years received Royal recognition in the form of a Knight Commandership of the Star of India, he was about to be selected for a post of even more importance, if not of greater dignity, than any he had before filled. He was appointed to succeed Sir Edward Malet as Her Majesty's Agent and Consul-General at Cairo, with the additional rank of Minister Plenipotentiary in the Diplomatic Service.

It was thus to a country at once familiar and strange, "the same, yet not the same," that he returned. As a financier he knew it and its circumstances well; but as a political agent, as a diplomatic official, as an administrator, nay, as a statesman—for nothing less than that was the part for which destiny was now "casting" him — he had, it may be said without exaggeration, almost to "go to school again to the facts." During his three years' absence in India, catastrophic changes had occurred in Egypt—changes which had at once revolutionized the relations between that country and Great Britain, and those of the European Powers among themselves. The Anglo-French *condominium* had vanished in the smoke of the British guns before Alexandria; and with it the office of the Controllership, which Baring had filled on behalf of England in co-partnership with M. de Blignières as the representative of France, had ceased to exist, and an English Financial Adviser reigned in their stead. The Khedive had been virtually deposed by rebels, and reinstated by British arms. A large British military force was still in occupation of the capital, and Her Majesty's Government had become to all intents and purposes the paramount rulers of Egypt in much the same sense and to the same extent as the Viceroy of India is the ruler of a protected Indian State under the nominal sovereignty of a Feudatory Prince. Sir Evelyn Baring's formal title of Agent and Consul-General has already been given; his true title, if he had realized his position, which at that moment perhaps he did not, or if it had been consistent with diplomatic etiquette to employ it, would have been that of "Resident" at the

THE BRITISH AGENCY (LORD CROMER'S RESIDENCE).

From a Photograph by J. P. Sebah, of Cairo.

Court of His Highness Tewfik Pasha, Khedive of Egypt.

Even this, however, is but a partial account of the immense change which had taken place in the situation since Sir Evelyn Baring exchanged Cairo for Calcutta. The rulers of Egypt were rulers in spite of themselves. It was their poverty of resource and not their will that consented to their assuming the government of Egypt at all. If they could have got out of it on the morrow of Tel-el-Kebir they would gladly have done so; but being there, with the ruins of what was once an Egyptian government all around them, and nothing in the world to take its place except the military force which they had with them, and the civil ability of which they had any amount at command, they could not quite bring themselves to walk straight out of the country and to leave it first to anarchy, and then to whatever other European Power should prove the quickest to step into their place.

But if they had to admit even to themselves that it was impossible for them to evacuate Egypt at once and altogether, there was still one thing always possible to them, and even, to a Government of their way of thinking, attractive. They could revise the definition of the word "Egypt," and limit their responsibilities accordingly. They must of course look after the capital; and this involved protecting and administering the delta which lay between it and the sea. And for so far above Cairo as the country could be protected and administered without any very heavy cost to themselves, they were willing to accept the same responsibilities. But as to extending their authority some thousand miles further towards the equator, beyond the limit of this cheaply-guarded and easily-governed region—as to spending men and money in re-establishing Egyptian authority over distant regions, now the scene of fanatical revolt and savage warfare, and this, too, to no better end than that they might after all have a larger and more troublesome Egypt to protect and administer— to that they strongly objected. If the Soudan was in insurrection, and if the weak and ill-disciplined forces of the Khedive in those regions were, as all the best authorities assured them, utterly unable to cope with the insurgents, so much the worse for the Khedive.

It is an interesting, though no doubt not a very profitable subject of speculation, whether, if the Gladstone Government had from the first recognized the necessity of taking Egyptian policy wholly under their control, they might have preserved the Soudan to Egypt. No doubt they could not have done so without a certain expenditure of English blood and treasure on the work; but these sacrifices we incurred as it was, and without avail. Would it not have been possible for England, if her rulers had acted with ordinary foresight and promptitude, to have prevented Egyptian authority and strength in the Soudan from lapsing into that condition which ultimately rendered the evacuation policy unavoidable? The question cannot now, of course, be answered with confidence; but there is this to be said in favour of the affirmative reply to it, that it was the destruction of Hicks Pasha's army which sealed the fate of the Soudan, considered as an integral portion of the Khedive's dominions; and that if the British Government had from the first controlled the policy of Egypt, it is incredible that such an army would ever have been allowed to start from Khartoum. The very irresolution, the mere timidity that swayed the counsels of the then Administration would have prevented their sanctioning any rash expedition of re-conquest, or probably any expedition at all; while assuredly their military advisers—not to say the ill-fated commander himself—would have told them that the best, if not the only, chance of retaining any of the Soudan was temporarily to abandon its outlying provinces, and concentrate at Khartoum for the defence of the rest.

Mr. Gladstone, however—for we may assume the exercise of his overruling voice in a matter on which more than one of his colleagues must assuredly have seen further ahead—Mr. Gladstone surveyed the situation with that singular lack of imaginative faculty which always characterized his dealings with foreign affairs, and which led him, apparently, to judge of the responsibilities of States and the claims of peoples by analogies applicable only in special circumstances to the pettiest concerns of private individuals. To him no doubt it seemed as easy a matter to divest himself and his Government, by simple diplomatic "notice," of all responsibility for what might happen to Egypt in the Soudan, as it is for a husband to escape liability for his wife's debts by the usual method of an advertisement in the newspapers. The venerable Statesman actually imagined that a Government which we had taken under our tutelage at Cairo might, outside a certain radius from the capital, have its authority shattered and its armies annihilated without our being thereby compelled to take any action on our own account in the matter. Comedy jostles tragedy as we read of the despatches which General Hicks had been in the habit of sending, through Sir Edward Malet, to the Egyptian Government, and which

Sir Edward was strictly charged to deliver to them with a careful disclaimer of any other *rôle* in the affair save that of the postman. The gallant English soldier who was about to be sent forth to disaster and death, showed pretty clearly in these despatches that he knew what was in store for him, and that he thought it desirable that the British Government should know it likewise. But the British Government did not share that opinion. They were apparently not in the least interested in the question, whether the forty thousand Egyptian troops then in the Soudan were or were not capable of re-establishing the authority of the Khedive over the whole or any part of that region ; nor yet in the further question, whether the better way of attempting this was to concentrate all the available strength of the Egyptian Government on the defence of Khartoum and the Central Soudan, or to despatch thence a scratch expedition of hopelessly inferior soldiers into a wilderness overrun by a brave, active, and powerful enemy.

The latter course was adopted, and on September 9th, 1883, Hicks Pasha started from Khartoum. On September 24th he reached El Duem, a point about a hundred miles higher up the river, which he then quitted for the desert, striking off to the westward into

Kordofan. After this no more was heard of him and his doomed army. It was as though the sands of the desert had opened and swallowed them up. Even in that land of mystery no adventure ever came to a more tragically mysterious end. Hicks' objective was known to be El Obeid, at that time the head-quarters of the Mahdi: his force was about 10,000 strong. But it was of wretched material—a mere untrained and chicken-hearted mob of fellaheen. It is probable that Hicks himself foresaw disaster; it is certain that it was foreseen by one at least of the Englishmen of experience around him. " I am writing," wrote the special correspondent of an English journal, "under circumstances which bring me almost as near to death as it is possible to be without being absolutely under sentence of execution or in the throes of some deadly malady . . . in company with cravens whom you expect to see run at every moment and leave you behind to face the worst."

They never completed their march to El Obeid. Months after it was learnt from the few survivors of the force that on November 5th, at Shekan, about two days' journey from their goal, they were surrounded by an overwhelming host of Dervishes and annihilated.

But though it was long before the details of

THE COMMANDANT'S QUARTERS.

From a Photograph by J. P. Sebah, of Cairo.

their destruction came to light, the fact of the great disaster was known in Cairo by the end of November. Sir Evelyn Baring had entered upon his duties as Consul-General on September 11th, and had therefore been little more than two months at his post. It was short notice at which to decide so momentous a question as that which the destruction of Hicks' army had brought from an urgent to a positively acute stage ; and it was hard to have to pronounce, as a first decision, one so thoroughly distasteful to Egyptian feeling as that which the question demanded. But the new Consul-General has never feared responsibility, and has never wavered in the line of duty through solicitude for his own popularity with any man or body of men, from Khedive to fellaheen. His resolution was promptly taken and unflinchingly adhered to. On the 26th of November he telegraphed to Lord Granville as follows :—

"In view of the recent intelligence from the Soudan, I have thought it advisable to obtain the opinion of competent military authorities on the military situation in that Province for the information of Her Majesty's Government.

"Accordingly, General Stephenson, Sir Evelyn Wood, and General Baker met unofficially at my house and fully discussed the subject.

"They were unanimously of opinion that the Egyptian Government will find it impossible, with the force at present at their disposal, to hold the Soudan, and that it will eventually be necessary, after withdrawing the garrisons, to fall back from Khartoum on to Egypt proper. They think that Khartoum should, if possible, be held sufficiently long to allow the more advanced posts and detached garrisons in the Soudan to rejoin."

It is needless, of course, to say that no counsel more acceptable to the nerveless Government then holding power could possibly have been given; and this circumstance does no doubt at first sight appear to constitute a grave presumption against its policy, and a still graver one against its spirit. To the Second Gladstone Administration no advice about Egypt commended, or could commend itself, unless in some form or other it spelt "scuttle." But the particular advice given by Baring in this instance ought not to be unduly prejudiced in historical estimation by the fact that it was acceptable to the Gladstone Government. If we should not refuse to serve God because the Devil bids us, we are not justified in disobeying the commands of discretion because they happen to be echoed by cowardice. The Consul-General's counsels were not, indeed, heroic, but they were sound; and there are cases, and this was one, in which heroism is mere foolhardiness. If concentration at Khartoum had become necessary even before the despatch of Hicks' force, the total annihilation of that force—the shattering, in fact, of the Khedive's last weapon — made even concentration impossible, and, unless the British Government were to come to the military assistance of Egypt, rendered complete evacuation its only substitute.

Theoretically, indeed, it may be said that Sir Evelyn Baring's responsibility was reduced to a minimum. His military advisers at Cairo had certified to the inability of Egypt to hold the Soudan of her own strength; his official superiors at home had signified their fixed determination not to reinforce that strength from English resources. Nothing, therefore, remained but the alternative of withdrawal from the Soudan, and Baring's advice to that effect was (it might be said) the mere irresponsible resultant of the two factors above set forth. And no doubt that was so in theory; but not in practice. In practice, a diplomatic agent "on the spot" is intended by his Government at home—and by no Government was this intention more certain to be entertained than by that Administration with which he had to deal—to be used as a convenient screen for interposition between themselves and the troublesome Parliamentary querist. When, therefore, the Consul-General acquiesced without protest in the announced resolve of the Government to wash their hands of the Soudan; when he hinted, without favouring the suggestion, that it was not at all improbable that the Egyptian Government would request Her Majesty's Government to send English or Indian troops; when, in fine, he wrote, even before the English Government had officially declared for that course: "My own opinion is, that once General Hicks' army is defeated, it would be wiser for the Egyptian Government to accept the fact and to withdraw to whatever point on the Nile they can be sure of defending, although a great impulse would thus be given to the slave trade," he must have been well aware that he personally would be quoted by the then Government as the chief adviser, if not the author of the retirement policy, and that under subsequent Governments, and indeed for an indefinite future, he might well be set down in public estimation as an admirer of that policy, not merely as a *pis aller*, but on its own merits and for its own sake. "How otherwise," he would be asked, "could you have refrained from pointing out at this time to your Government the vital importance to Egypt of the province which she was at the moment too weak to hold, and urging them to reconsider their resolve to deny her that military assistance which would enable her to maintain her grasp?"

Such questions, however, are a good deal

easier to ask to-day than they were in 1883. They are indeed almost as much facilitated by the event as prophecies. It was impossible for Baring to foresee the future of the Soudan for the next twelve years to come. Could he have done so it would, of course, have supplied him with one very powerful argument; for he would then have been in a position to inform the Government that the territory which they were compelling Egypt to abandon would have to be regained for her by a future Administration. Even that, however, would hardly have influenced Mr. Gladstone and his colleagues unless it could have been accompanied by the prophetic information (in this case the reverse of the eventual fact) that the cost and responsibility of regaining the Soudan would fall upon a Government of their own and not of their opponents' party. It is to be feared, indeed, that the most certain foreknowledge of that future which has now become the present, would only, had it been attainable, have confirmed Mr. Gladstone in his resolve.

Sir Evelyn Baring had, in other words, to leave English power and English policy out of his calculations, and to advise that course which was the fittest to be pursued by an unassisted Egypt in the emergency before her. And as has been said, he assumed, no doubt with full consciousness of the responsibility attached to it, the position of an adviser behind whom the then Government would shelter themselves and their policy of surrender, and to whom as their authority for maintaining that policy future Governments would assuredly appeal.

Mr. Gladstone and his colleagues gladly, and let us hope thankfully, accepted the self-sacrifice. Baring was instructed to inform the Egyptian Cabinet that the Soudan must be abandoned with all promptitude, and that any Minister who was not prepared to adopt this programme must go. The Prime Minister, Sherif Pasha, fell at once into this category and resigned office. Riaz Pasha, who had been Minister of the Interior under Sherif, but who had resigned because he was not allowed to hang Arabi, could not be prevailed upon to take the retiring Minister's place, and it was only after prolonged solicitation—and it is said, a threat from Baring that if no Egyptian Statesman would act he would himself come down to the public departments and keep the machinery of State going, provisionally, at any rate, with his own hands— that Nubar Pasha was induced to accept a post to which so unpopular a task was attached. It was a prompt and crucial application of the eminently sound doctrine just laid down, no doubt in reference to this very case, by Lord

Granville. "I hardly need point out," he wrote to Baring on January 4th, 1884, "that in important questions where the administration and safety of Egypt are at stake, it is indispensable that Her Majesty's Government should, so long as the provisional occupation of the country by English troops continues, be assured that the advice which, after full consideration of the views of the Egyptian Government, they may feel it their duty to tender to the Khedive, should be followed. It should be made clear to the Egyptian Ministers and Governors of Provinces that the responsibility which for the time rests on England, obliges Her Majesty's Government to insist on the policy which they recommend; and that it will be necessary that those Ministers and Governors who do not follow this course should cease to hold their offices." This was undoubtedly and unwontedly plain speaking; but one cannot help wondering whether it would ever have been wrung from them by anything but their passion for retreat. Like him whose "honour rooted in dishonour stood," Mr. Gladstone's Government was firm only in flight.

The actual course of events, however, has been somewhat anticipated in the foregoing paragraph. The resolution to evacuate the Soudan was taken by the Government in the latter days of

November, 1883. Sherif's resignation was not handed in until January, 1884, and between these two dates a momentous step of policy had been determined on by the Cabinet in London ; for it was, in fact, at this critical juncture that they arrived at the most fateful, and, indeed, as it proved, the most fatal decision of their career. "Some demon whispered in the ear of their Chief," wrote a political critic a few years after the event, "that the real man for the situation was 'Chinese Gordon,' and the venerable statesman accepted the suggestion as an inspiration from on high. Nothing ever assumed this divine semblance for him so readily as any proposal which promised to save money and to shift responsibility. Then, as always, the point on which his eye fixed was not the situation at Khartoum but the position in Downing Street ; and whether Gordon was the man for the former or not, there was no doubt in the Ministerial mind about his being the man for the latter."

In more favourable circumstances he might well have been the man for both. With full power to choose his own agents and his own methods, with *carte blanche* in the matter of men, material, and, within limits, money, it is possible—though not, I think, probable at that particular stage of Mahdism — that Gordon might have succeeded in pacifying the Soudan. But it must be admitted, in justice to the Gladstone Government, that had he accomplished the feat, he could only have done so by a complete abandonment of all the assumptions with which he set out, and an entire reversal of the policy which he contemplated on his acceptance of his mission. In other words, there is no doubt that when Gordon undertook to retire the Egyptian garrisons from the Soudan, and to rescue its civil population or such portion of them as wished to quit the country, he imagined that he would be able to effect his purpose by means of negotiation. He fancied that the influence of his name, and the prestige of the authority formerly wielded by him in those regions, would enable him to pacify them, at any rate for the period necessary to complete the operation of withdrawal. Hence the language used by him before he reached his destination and discovered the true conditions of his undertaking, lends itself readily enough to quotation by those who have contended at a later date for the policy of leaving the Soudan to "stew in its own juice." Indeed it was actually quoted with that object by Mr. Courtney, in a debate in the House of Commons on the policy of the recent advance into the Soudan. Strange as it may be that a man so familiar with Mahommedan barbarism and its susceptibilities to fanatical impulse should never have suspected the true state of things until he came into actual contact with it, such, nevertheless, appears to be indubitably the fact. It was no doubt not wholly due to such a misconception of racial temperament as we could not ascribe, without extreme astonishment, to a man of Gordon's antecedents and experience, but arose, in part at least, from a more explicable misjudgment of individual character. "I do not," he wrote, "believe in advance of Mahdi, who is nephew to my old guide in Darfur, who was a very good fellow." It is singular that a man so apt to find scriptural illustrations of contemporary phenomena should not have noticed the ironical resemblance between his own reasonings about the false prophet and those of the Galileans about a certain True Messiah. "Is not this . . . the brother of James and of Juda and of Simon?" Whether a prophet's credentials be genuine or spurious, it is equally true that he is likely to be without honour from those who have known him—"among his own kin and in his own house."

Gordon apparently started in the full confidence that he should find plenty of "very good fellows" in the Soudan with whom he could arrange for the peaceful execution of his mission. Had he been right in his calculations it would no doubt have been not only possible to carry out the Ministerial policy of retirement without serious cost or bloodshed, but even advisable, it may be, to leave the Soudan severely alone for the future. And as has been said, it is only fair to remember this in justification of the English Government's subsequently much criticized choice of their agent. The gravamen of their error lay not in sending Gordon on a quasi-diplomatic mission into a distracted region which could not possibly be dealt with by diplomatic methods—for they might well be excused for erroneously believing what their experienced emissary believed himself;—it lay in their obstinate refusal to recognize the rapid development of that quasi-diplomatic mission into a warlike operation; to acknowledge, what was plain to all the world, that their ambassador had become a mere beleaguered soldier fighting for his life against an overwhelming swarm of enemies ; and to undertake, until too late, those plain duties of support and relief which this change in the circumstances imposed upon them.

Yet they could not pretend that they had been left long in ignorance of their new obligation. It was on the 26th of January, 1884, that General Gordon left Cairo for Khartoum, and it was little more than a fortnight later that he arrived, after that picturesque camel ride of his across the desert from Korosko to Abu Hamid, at Berber. Another week saw him at the end of his journey. He reached Khartoum on the 18th of February, and before he had been there eight days his keen eye had penetrated to the very heart of the situation.   He had discovered that a new power of a most formidable kind had arisen in the land over which he had once ruled, and that it was no longer possible for him to conjure with his name. Thus on February 26 he writes to Sir Evelyn Baring : " If Egypt is to be quiet, Mahdi must be smashed up.   Remember, that once Khartoum belongs to Mahdi, the task will be far more difficult . . . I repeat that evacuation is possible, but you will feel effect in Egypt, and will be forced to enter into a far more serious affair in order to guard Egypt."   And again, two months later he writes : " I shall leave you the indelible disgrace of abandoning the garrisons of Sennaar, Kassala, Berber, and Dongola, with the certainty that you will eventually be forced to smash up the Mahdi under great difficulties if you would retain peace in Egypt."

On the very day, indeed, on which Gordon arrived at Khartoum, he took a step which eloquently testified to the rapidity of his awakening.   He made a formal request upon the Cairo

KHARTOUM.

Government that Zebehr Pasha—a man infamous as the largest dealer engaged in the Soudanese slave traffic, and tragically associated with Gordon's past history as the father of the rebel Suleiman, whom the then Governor-General of the Soudan had caused to be executed five years before—might be released from the virtual imprisonment in which he was then held at Cairo, and sent to the Soudan to resume the position of authority which he had lost, together with his liberty, by an unwise visit to the Egyptian capital in 1876. On the very day of his departure from Cairo, Gordon and Zebehr had had an interview, arranged for them by Sir Evelyn Baring at his own house, and the report of this conference, as published in the Blue Book, does undoubtedly show that Zebehr cherished animosity against Gordon, on account not only of the execution of his son, but of the confiscation of his own property as a consequence of his proved complicity in Suleiman's revolt.

We cannot be surprised that in these circumstances the Government found Gordon's request a little startling, and certainly they might have been excused some hesitation to associate with their emissary, even at his own instance, a man whom it was reasonable to regard as his bitterest enemy. Baring himself, in the despatch transmitting Gordon's application, declared that he would be altogether opposed to having General Gordon and Zebehr Pasha at Khartoum together. He suggested that as soon as the former had arranged for the withdrawal of his garrison and the rest of the Egyptian element he should leave Khartoum, and the latter might shortly afterwards start from Cairo. "One of my chief reasons," he adds, "for allowing the interview between the two men to take place was that I wished to satisfy myself to some extent of the sentiment entertained by Zebehr Pasha towards General Gordon. I would not on any account run the risk of putting General Gordon in his power." But this full recognition of the *primâ facie* objections to the appointment lends additional significance of course to the measured but un-doubting approval afterwards given by the Consul-General to the plan. As the point is an important one in any view of it, even if it were not, as Gordon believed, one of cardinal relation to the success or failure of his mission, it would be well to give *in extenso* the material portions of Sir Evelyn Baring's despatch :—

"As regards the choice of his successor, there is, as Colonel Stewart says in his telegram, no necessity to decide at once; but I believe Zebehr Pasha to be the only possible man. He undoubtedly possesses energy and ability, and has great local influence.

"As regards the Slave Trade, I discussed the matter with General Gordon when he was in Cairo, and he fully agreed with me in thinking that Zebehr Pasha's presence or absence would not affect the question in one way or the other. I am also convinced, from many things that have come to my notice, that General Gordon is quite right in thinking that Zebehr Pasha's residence in Egypt has considerably modified his character. He now understands what European power is ; and it is much better to have to deal with a man of this sort than with a man like the Madhi . . . .

"If Zebehr Pasha is nominated, it will be very necessary to lay down in writing and in the plainest language what degree of support he may expect from Her Majesty's Government. I cannot recommend that he should be (as Gordon had suggested) promised the moral support of Her Majesty's Government. In the first place he would scarcely understand the sense of the phrase, and, moreover, I do not think he would attach importance to any support which was not material. It is for Her Majesty's Government to judge what the effect of the appointment would be upon public opinion in England ; but except for that, I can see no reason why Zebehr Pasha should not be proclaimed ruler of the Soudan, with the approbation of Her Majesty's Government. It should be distinctly explained to him in writing that he must rely solely upon his own resources to maintain the position. He might receive a moderate sum of money from the Egyptian Government to begin with. His communications with that Government might be conducted through Her Majesty's Representative in Cairo, as General Gordon suggests."

There was a world of significance in the proviso contained in the words "except for this," as no one probably knew better than the Consul-General. He could not have been unaware of the "effect upon public opinion in England" which was certain to be produced by Zebehr's appointment ; and no doubt he knew his correspondents in Downing Street well enough to suspect that they were not the men to brave it. On February 22 they replied to the above-quoted despatch, that "the gravest objections exist to the appointment by their authority of a successor to General Gordon, and that in any case the public opinion of the country would not tolerate the appointment of Zebehr Pasha." Gordon, however, continued to press for it, and eventually overcame Sir Evelyn Baring's disinclination to allow the two men to meet. On March 4 the latter telegraphed to the Government that in the face of the strong opinion expressed by General Gordon, he was not "inclined to maintain his objection to Zebehr Pasha's going at once to Khartoum." Lord Granville telegraphed back with almost petulant haste on the following day that "Her Majesty's Government saw no reason at present to change their impressions about Zebehr," formed on various grounds, one of which the Foreign Secretary proceeds to specify. He goes on to add in a tone of mild rebuke that he would be glad to learn how the Consul-General "reconciles his proposal to acquiesce in such an appointment with the prevention or discouragement of slave-hunting and the Slave Trade, with the policy of complete evacuation, and with the security of Egypt."

Baring's reply, telegraphed on the 9th, was tolerably effective. The policy of complete evacuation does not, he gravely points out to Downing Street, imply the abandonment of the evacuated region to anarchy and disorder. "I have always contemplated making some rearrangements for the future government of the Soudan, as will be seen from my despatch of the 22nd of December, 1883, in which I said that it would be 'necessary to send an English officer of high authority to Khartoum with full powers to withdraw all garrisons in the Soudan, and make the best arrangements possible for the future government of that country.' As regards slavery it may receive a stimulus from the abandonment of the Soudan by Egypt, but the despatch of Zebehr Pasha to Khartoum will not affect the question in one way or the other. No middle course is possible as far as the Soudan is concerned. We must either virtually annex the country, which is out of the question, or else we must accept the inevitable consequences of the policy of abandonment." On the question of the "security of Egypt," the Government were referred to what General Gordon had already said about it. "I believe," concluded Baring, "that Zebehr Pasha may be made a bulwark against the Mahdi. Of course there is a risk that he will constitute a danger to Egypt, but the risk is, I think, a small one, and it is in any case preferable to incur it rather than to face the certain disadvantages of withdrawing without making any provision for the future government of the country, which would then be sure to fall under the power of the Mahdi."

There is only one point which this otherwise convincing argument overlooks, and that is that the absence of any "middle course" is a matter of no importance to men of the disposition of those whom the writer was addressing, or indeed to anyone who prefers staggering rhythmically from one side of the road to the other. Such an one may be said to make his own middle course —of a zigzag delineation—for himself. In logical theory no doubt you must either retain a country, and with it the responsibilities attached to retention, or abandon it and accept the responsibilities arising from withdrawal. But in practical policy it is quite possible to accept alternately each of these two alternatives, and to decline the responsibilities of either. It was in pursuance of one of these lines of conduct that the Government sent Gordon to Khartoum, and in pursuance of the other that they refused him the means of fulfilling his mission. If the Government had still had a mind to make up about Zebehr on the day when Sir Evelyn Baring penned the despatch above quoted, it would have been made up for

them the day after by Mr. Edmund Sturge and
the British and Foreign Anti-Slavery Society.
On March 10 Lord Granville received a communication from that estimable body protesting
against the appointment of Zebehr, and, while
expressing "no opinion on the policy of a
permanent maintenance of British authority at
Khartoum," intimating at the same time their
earnest hope "that in the event of Her Majesty's
Government making an arrangement for its
independent rule, the conditions will be such
as shall secure the country alike from a reign of
anarchy and barbarism and from that of the slave
trader." In other words, they were willing to
leave it an open question whether the omelette
should be made or not, and would content themselves with entering a solemn *caveat* against the
breaking of eggs. The Government, on their
part, were as firmly resolved as ever to make the
omelette, but were quite willing to give the
required undertaking that no eggs should be
broken in the process. They definitively refused
to sanction Zebehr's appointment, and the matter
fell to the ground. That was on the 5th of
March, and from that moment events moved
rapidly onward to the last act of the sombre
drama. The expedition from Suakin, which, in
his *Life of General Gordon*, Sir William Butler
holds to have sealed Gordon's fate, had been

despatched some time before. General Graham had already, on February 29, defeated the Dervishes at El Teb, and on March 13, 1884, " the door of peace," to quote the same vigorous writer, " was slammed " at the battle of Tamai. From that, if from no earlier moment, all possibility of extricating the Egyptian garrisons and population from the Soudan by the method of negotiation was extinguished.

It was still, however, open to the Government to afford effective military support to their emissary; and it was not till, after having goaded Mahdism to madness by the slaughter at El Teb and Tamai, they refused to co-operate with the man against whom they had let loose these furies of their own raising, that his position became really desperate. The refusal was definitively given in a too famous despatch from Lord Granville to Sir Evelyn Baring, under date of March 28th. It should be read in connection with Sir Evelyn's telegraphic communication of one day's earlier date, to which, indeed, it is a reply, and which once for all relieves the British Consul-General of all responsibility for this the most disastrous of all the decisions at which the Government arrived. The material parts of this despatch must, in justice to the writer, be textually quoted :—

"The question now is how to get General Gordon and Colonel Stewart away from Khartoum . . . Unless any unforeseen circumstances should occur to change the situation, only two solutions seem to be possible. The first is to trust to General Gordon being able to maintain himself at Khartoum till the autumn, when by reason of the greater quantity of water it would be less difficult to conduct operations on the Suakin-Berber Road than it is at present. This he might perhaps be able to do, but it of course involves running a great risk. The only other plan is to send a portion of General Graham's army to Berber with instructions to open up communication with Khartoum. There would be very great difficulty in getting to Berber; but if the road were once open it might be done by sending small detachments at a time. General Gordon is evidently expecting help from Suakin, and he has ordered messengers to be sent along the road from Berber to ascertain whether any English force is advancing. *Under present circumstances I think that an effort should be made to help General Gordon from Suakin, if it is at all a possible military operation. General Stephenson and Sir Evelyn Wood, while admitting the very great risk to the health of the troops, besides the extraordinary military risks, are of the opinion that the undertaking is possible.* They think that General Graham should be further consulted. *We all consider that however difficult the operations from Suakin may be, they are more practicable than any operations from Korosko and along the Nile.*"

To this Lord Granville replied in an elaborate despatch covering several pages of Blue Book. The Government had taken steps to fortify themselves, as it is always easy enough to do, with expert opinions adverse to those on which their "agent on the spot" had relied. They had "very carefully considered the demand for a military demonstration by a British force at

Berber"; they "would not have willingly refused it, coming from General Gordon with the additional weight of your concurrence," but—and here follows the "regulation" objections which had been fully considered by our responsible military advisers in Egypt and, with full recognition of their gravity, overruled. "The distance, the nature of the country to be traversed, and above all the climate, render the march of a British force to Berber at the present season an undertaking so difficult as to be almost impracticable. For a large body of European troops of all arms the military authorities regard the expedition as impossible, while for a small force of cavalry to undertake the expedition without support or communications, in the face of possible opposition by largely superior numbers, would be an extremely hazardous venture, and might in the end prove useless."

The difficulties as regards climate might be thought to suggest the appointment of Indian troops. But no: there were objections, no less considerable, to that — objections of that sort that weigh so heavily against anything that one does not wish to do, and that inclination on the other hand so promptly overrules. But the real, the fatal reason for the Government's refusal of their assistance, is to be gathered from the too pregnant sentences that follow :—

"The condition of affairs does not appear to be such as to call for measures attended by so much risk, and entailing possibly a great loss of life, and certainly large expenditure. There is reason to hope that the successful operations of General Graham in the neighbourhood of Suakin may have wiped away the unfortunate impression produced by the defeat of the Egyptian troops, and may enable the road from Suakin to Berber to be opened by the friendly action of the tribes, without the necessity of further military measures. It is understood that Khartoum is provisioned for six months, and that its present garrison is sufficient for its security during that period from any attack by the Arab tribes, who are without artillery."

Events now moved rapidly to the final isolation of our deserted emissary. On the 9th of April the Bahr el Ghazal Province fell into the power of the Dervishes, and on the 19th all communication with Khartoum was cut off. Three days before Gordon had written that indignant despatch above quoted, declaring his intention, as he had been refused both the appointment of Zebehr Pasha and military co-operation at Berber, "to hold on at Khartoum as long as he could, and if he failed to suppress the rebellion, to retire to the Equator and leave you the indelible disgrace of abandoning the garrisons of Sennaar, Kassala, Berber, and Dongola, with the certainty that you will eventually be forced to smash up the Mahdi under great difficulties, if you would retain peace in Egypt." On May 19th Berber fell, and a veil of darkness and silence, never to be lifted during Gordon's lifetime, descended over Khartoum.

CHAPTER VI.

Gordon and the Government

THE heroic and tragic elements were so predominant in the memorable drama which was enacted in the year 1884, that it was at the time impossible, and is still difficult, for Englishmen to contemplate it with any other feelings than those of pity, admiration, and anger. Their hearts were full of sorrow for the loss of their noble countryman, and of pride in his devotion, and of indignation against those who sacrificed him ; and there was no room for other emotion of any kind. Now, however, when thirteen years have passed away, and one reads again the history of these events in the unimpassioned pages of the Blue Book, it is easy enough to see on what a warp of the grimly humorous the woof of this most moving tragedy was wrought. The very scheme of the *dramatis personæ*, with the characters which it brought together, might seem to have been arranged by the Fates in the most ironical of their moods, and with a direct eye to those collisions of the incongruous to which humour owes its mysterious birth. And there is this amount of truth in the *Tout comprendre c'est tout pardonner* of French proverbial wisdom, that that fuller comprehension of conduct which we gain from humorous appreciation of character and circumstances does in this case enable us to distinguish roughly between wilful eye-shutting and constitutional blindness. That the delays and hesitations which led to the death of Gordon were, in some measure, the result of a voluntary closure of the Ministerial eyelids is no doubt the fact; as it is also, of course, the fact that such deliberate refusals to look at objects of vision which duty and honour plainly enjoin one not for a moment to lose sight of, are among the gravest offences which men or Ministries can commit, and are certainly of those to the commission of which the heaviest responsibility attaches. Nevertheless it would be uncandid to deny that there was that in Gordon's own character, in his peculiar relations with the then Government, and above all in the ludicrously antipodean contrast between them and him in respect of tempera-ment, motives, and ideals, which specially exposed them to the temptation to commit the offence in question. Had the principals better understood the agent he would not have fared so ill at their hands. An ordinary man accidentally entrapped into Gordon's position might very likely have received from them far more efficient support. He suffered, in fact, for his very virtues. It was the unique nobility of his character which, by rendering him unintelligible to them, confounded the policy of these fourteen absolutely unimaginative gentlemen, and left them shilly-shallying till it was too late.

This of course but very slightly diminishes the weight of their responsibility. It was they who selected Gordon for his mission to the Soudan, a mission which they and he at the time believed that he was capable of executing unassisted ; and it was their own fault that they selected a man of so fantastic a chivalry that, once having pledged himself to others to perform a task which turned out to be an impossibility, he held himself bound to persevere in the hopeless attempt at the cost of his own life. Possibly they had persuaded themselves that in the last resort he could be persuaded to look at the situation from their own "reasonable" point of view, and to do what they themselves were prepared to do without any persuasion at all : that is to say, to inform such of the former subjects of the Khedive, civil or military, as were still left in the Soudan, that though the British Government and their emissary would have rejoiced to find it possible to secure their safe transfer from the Soudan to within the new Egyptian frontier, it had become necessary to inform them with sincere regret that this was *not* possible, and that they would, therefore, have to shift for themselves. And it was from the fact that this Government, the readiest to retreat at the cost of honour of all Governments that ever ruled in England, had selected the one man who was the most absolutely certain of all Englishmen to repudiate such a course with indignation, that the grim humour of the situation arose. It was as though Sancho Panza should in a moment of rashness have commissioned Don Quixote to undertake some costly quest of knight-errantry in one of the remote possessions of the Island of Barataria, and had then proceeded to discuss its prospects with him in a long diplomatic correspondence. Honest Sancho would no doubt have dealt more largely in proverbs than Lord Granville did; but the game of cross purposes could hardly have been more complete, or the respective points of view of the two correspondents removed from each other by more miles of moral distance in the case of the knight-errant of fiction than it was in that of the knight-errant of fact.

The writer in Downing Street and the writer in Khartoum sometimes seem almost to be using

two different languages.   Here, for instance, is
a telegraphic despatch from the Foreign Office :—

"Gordon should be at once informed in cypher by several
messengers at some intervals between each, through Dongola
as well as Berber, or in such other way as may on the spot be
deemed most prompt and certain, that he should keep us
informed to the best of his ability, not only as to immediate
but as to any prospective danger at Khartoum ; that to be
prepared for any such danger, he advise us as to the force
necessary in order to secure his removal; its amount,
character, route for access to Khartoum, and time of operation ; that we do not propose to supply him with Turkish
or other force for the purpose of undertaking military expedi-
tions, such being beyond the scope of the commission he
holds, and at variance with the pacific policy which was the
purpose of his mission to the Soudan ; and that if with this
knowledge he continues at Khartoum, he should state to us
the cause and the intention with which he so continues."

This was written on April 23 ; but a fortnight
earlier Gordon, in a quite different dialect, had
already informed Sir Evelyn Baring of the "cause
of his continuing" at Khartoum.   He admits
that he "does not see the fun of being caught
here to walk about the streets as a dervish
for years with sandalled feet; not that (D.V.) I
will ever be taken alive; but," he adds :—

"It would be the climax of meanness, after I had borrowed
money from the people here, had called on them to sell their
grain at a low price, &c., to go and abandon them without
using any effort to relieve them ; and I feel sure that whatever
you may feel diplomatically I have your support—and that of
every man professing himself a gentleman—in private."

What was a Government to do with a man like this? What are "practical politicians" to make of an emissary who drags into a question of official policy such irrelevant considerations as these? One can fancy the painful embarrassment with which this telegram was read at the Foreign Office. The "climax of meanness!" "Every man professing himself a gentleman!" What could it all mean? We almost expect to find in the next page of the Blue Book, "Message unintelligible. Please repeat." No wonder that this communication, transmitted over the wire to Downing Street by April 18th, did not in the least affect the terms of the Ministerial message, above quoted, of April 23rd. "Look here!" that message would have run, if expressed in Gordon's own unconventional style, "there is no use in our talking any more about removing the garrisons and population from the Soudan. The only question now is about *your* removal as soon as things begin to look ugly at Khartoum. How are we to manage that? Can you suggest anything? Just turn it over in your mind, and, indeed, you may give your whole mind to it without troubling your head about the rescue of the population by military measures. We have not the least intention of adopting military measures of any sort. You can't have any

British troops, nor Indian troops, nor Turkish troops—nor, in fact, troops of any kind. And, if now you are sure that you wish to continue at Khartoum, please be good enough to tell us why. We have read your last despatch, in which you say it would be the 'height of meanness' to abandon certain people to whom you refer, and that 'every man professing himself a gentleman' will agree with you. But you can't really have meant to put this seriously forward as an *official* reason for not quitting Khartoum. Kindly provide us with some reason which we can understand and recognize as one which should have weight with practical politicians."

An interchange of communications of this sort—and this is what they virtually amount to when translated into unofficial language—argues a certain incompatibility of temperament between the parties to it. Let us add in fairness, that had the Government understood Gordon better than they did, he would still have proved a trying person to work with. His rapid changes of mind and advice are a little bewildering even to the most friendly disposed student of the Blue Books. It is the fact that during the twelve or thirteen weeks which elapsed between Gordon's arrival in Egypt and the final interruption of communications, he proposed no fewer than five different methods of dealing with the situation in the Soudan. Only a few days after his departure from Cairo, Sir Evelyn Baring learnt, with something like consternation, that he had left behind him a message for Mr. Clifford Lloyd to the following effect:—"Tell Lloyd no panics. It is possible that I may go to the Mahdi and not be heard of for two months, for he might keep me as a hostage for Zebehr." The Consul-General telegraphed at once to him for an assurance that he would on no account put himself voluntarily in the power of the Mahdi. "The question," Sir Evelyn added, "is not a personal one. There would, in my opinion, be the strongest political objections to your risking a visit to the Mahdi." At the same time he telegraphed to the Government for authority to forbid the step. This, of course, was granted; but before it could arrive, General Gordon had sent Baring a despatch from Korosko enclosing a draft of a letter which he had written to the King of the Belgians to urge him to occupy the Bahr Gazelle and the Equatorial Provinces, and to appoint Gordon "Governor of all that country"; and in forwarding this to Downing Street, the Consul-General observed upon it that Gordon seemed "to intend to go straight on" from Khartoum in the direction of these Provinces, an advance which not unnaturally seemed to

Baring to be unadvisable. "I do not think," he concludes, "that General Gordon should be allowed, at all events for the present, to go anywhere south of Khartoum."

Downing Street telegraphed its veto upon this as upon the proposal to go to the Mahdi; but one would have thought that even these early experiences would have put them upon suspecting that the emissary they had chosen was not easily manageable, and that both judgment and firmness would be required in handling him. It is true, of course, that Gordon's somewhat light-hearted suggestion that he might pay a personal visit to the Mahdi was thrown out under the mistaken impression that he still retained his former influence over the Soudanese populations; that immediately upon the discovery of his mistake, he begged for the despatch of Zebehr as a man influential enough in the Soudan to act as a counterpoise to the Mahdi; and that it was only on the refusal of this request that he called for military assistance in the work he had undertaken, such assistance to be rendered according to his various proposals, now by English, now by Indian, now by Turkish troops. But to men not wilfully blind, it must have been obvious from this continual "feeling about" for some new mode of dealing with the situation, that Gordon was in reality at his wits' end; that all his calculations as to his ability to control or even to influence events in the Soudan were disappointed; and that, being the man he was, he would, rather than abandon those to whom, under the aforesaid miscalculations, he had pledged himself, pay the penalty with his life.

And perhaps the Government were not so wilfully blind as to miss all these considerations. It is possible that they appreciated them all— except the last. It is the Quixotism of Quixote, not his illusions, that Sancho has a difficulty in comprehending. The placemen could understand their agent making a mistake; it was a familiar experience of their own. What they *could* not comprehend was the determination of any sane man to suffer death in the last resort for his mistake in preference to evading its consequences at the cost of honour. For the whole art and mystery of the placeman consists in evading the consequences of his mistakes at the cost of anything; and surely—surely any sane man, nay, even any man with only a middle-sized and moderately active bee in his bonnet, would ultimately recognize the supremacy of the great law of self-preservation.

This, and the reliance on the chapter of accidents—that favourite "gamble" of the weak —will amply suffice to account for the inert attitude of Downing Street and its utter destitution of counsels during the first two months of Gordon's sojourn at Khartoum. Why, indeed, should it do anything, or advise anything, or, indeed, forbid anything except what would make trouble, like Zebehr's appointment, for Ministers at home? Gordon had "taken the contract" for securing the safe withdrawal of the Khedive's civil and military subjects from the Soudan. Either Gordon could execute that contract or not. If yes, good; if no, why then as soon as he satisfied himself of the impossibility of executing it, he would come home like a sensible man. The "rescue and retire" policy having proved impracticable, his loyal though futile efforts to perform the former half of that policy would enable him with a quiet conscience to confine himself to the latter. What! refuse to retire *without* rescuing? Die at his post rather? Oh, absurd! "People don't do such things," as is remarked by a notable character in Norwegian drama. And indeed politicians do not do them as a rule; and it was by the nineteenth century politician's standard that the Government habitually judged this stray knight-errant from the middle ages.

It is, in fact, quite probable that before they realized—if indeed they ever did fully realize—that Gordon, being Gordon, would not quit Khartoum if he could, they had arrived at the unwelcome conclusion that he could not quit Khartoum if he would. By what exact date they had thoroughly mastered this most disagreeable fact we shall probably never know; but the Blue Book from the middle of May onwards shows constantly multiplying signs of Ministerial uneasiness. Its very Index is eloquent in its testimony. "May 15. Message to General Gordon. Can delivery be assured by expenditure of money, or communication to be made by means of Zebehr or Hussan Pashas?" "May 16. Messenger to General Gordon. Terms proposed by Zebehr Pasha." The terms as forwarded by Mr. Egerton to Lord Granville were as follows :—

"(Telegraphic). Zebehr will find a man to go to Khartoum for £50 down, and £400 for bringing answer within fifty days. Shall I agree?"

And the answer ran :—

"Her Majesty's Government agree to the proposal, and would be prepared to double the amount offered if the man returned within thirty days. They would, however, wish the messenger to delay his departure until you have received a further message for General Gordon, which will be telegraphed to you."

A further message, which is important, was to this effect :—

"Having regard to the time which has elapsed, Her Majesty's Government desire to add to their communication of 23rd April (the material parts of which have been given above) as follows :—As the original plan for the evacuation of the Soudan has been dropped, and as aggressive operations cannot be undertaken with the countenance of Her Majesty's Government, General Gordon is enjoined to consider and either to report upon, or if possible, to adopt at the first proper moment measures for his own removal and for that of the Egyptians at Khartoum who have suffered for him, or who have served him faithfully, including their wives and children, by whatever route he may consider best, having especial regard for his own safety and that of the other British subjects.

"With regard to the Egyptians above referred to, General Gordon is authorized to make free use of money rewards or promises at his discretion.   For example, he is at liberty to assign to Egyptian soldiers at Khartoum sums for themselves and for persons brought with them per head, contingent on their safe arrival at Korosko or whatever point he may consider a place of safety ; or he may employ and pay the tribes in the neighbourhood to escort them.   Her Majesty's Government presume that the Soudanese at Khartoum are not in danger   In the event of General Gordon having despatched any person or agents to other points, he is authorized to spend any money required for the purpose of recalling them or securing their safety."

There is something grimly comic in the suggestion that Gordon, of all men in the world, should "have special regard for his own safety," as also in the presumption that "the Soudanese at Khartoum,"—the very men whose abandonment Gordon had six weeks before, with an appeal to "every man professing him-self a gentleman," pronounced "the climax of meanness,"—were "not in danger."   And, indeed, the whole telegram appealed strongly to Gordon's sardonic sense of humour, and extracted from him one of those outbursts of irony which render the "Journals" such lively reading. Of the contents of the foregoing despatch as conveyed to him through Mr. Egerton, he writes :—

"Egerton's telegram carefully written in cypher [and equally carefully without date, but which we ascribe to June], respecting the contracts to be entered into with the Bedouin tribe to escort us down ('and be sure to look after *yourself!*'), might as well have been written in Arabic; it would have produced hilarity with the Mahdi."

And again :—

"The pomp of Egerton's telegram, informing me that Her Majesty's Government would (really!) pay on delivery so much a head for all refugees *delivered* on Egyptian frontier, and would (*positively*, it is incredible!) *reward* tribes, whom I might contract with, to escort them down. It was too generous for one to believe. Egerton's chivalrous nature must have got the better of his diplomatic training when he wrote it. The clerks in my divan to whom I disclosed it are full of exclamations of wonder at this generosity! Egerton must have considered that I was a complete idiot to have needed such a permission. I hope he will get promoted, and will not be blamed for overstraining his instructions . . . There is a tone in Egerton's telegram which grates on me: it is, *to me*, as if he said, 'You have got into a mess, and although you do not deserve it, I am willing to stretch a point in your favour and authorize you, &c.' And in the previous part (the author unknown) of the telegram, it is as if I was enjoying this wretched fighting up here. I declare it is Egerton and Co. who made the mess, and would like to hang its fabrication and solution on me: not that I mind the burden, if they did not send such telegrams (the Co. are Malet and Colvin)."

The last fling at the Cairo officials is one of many on which a word or two will have to be said presently, and all that need to be remarked here and now is, that Gordon seems vastly to overrate the independence and initiative of men who were almost as much hampered as himself by orders from Downing Street. It was the Government at home with whose views his own were so hopelessly at variance—how hopelessly, is nowhere brought out more clearly than in the following passage of a despatch from Lord Granville to Mr. Egerton :—

"It appears, moreover, from your telegram of the 12th instant, that you had received an official communication from the Egyptian Government to the effect that the Council of Ministers considering Her Majesty's Government, since the mission of General Gordon, to have taken in hand the retreat of the population and garrison of the Soudan, thought it advisable to ask what course Her Majesty's Government considered should be taken with reference to the population and garrison of Dongola."

Nervously eager to repudiate the suggestion that they had incurred any sort of moral responsibility to these people, Lord Granville goes on to comment on the above official communication from the Egyptian Government in the following terms :—

" Her Majesty's Government have been at all times ready to assist the Government of the Khedive with their advice as to the best means of withdrawing from the Soudan the Egyptian garrisons, and such of the civil population as might desire to retire from these provinces, and for that purpose they consented to the mission of General Gordon."

("Consented" is good. Even so does a drowning man "consent" to avail himself of the help of the straw at which he desperately catches.)

"But the Egyptian Government must bear in mind that the presence of Egyptian garrisons in the Soudan, Equatorial, and Bahr Gazelle Provinces, is in no way due to any act of Her Majesty's Government, and that they cannot hold themselves responsible for the measures which those on the spot may think fit to take with a view to facilitate their withdrawal, or for the consequences of their possible failure to effect that object."

Anything more opposed to Gordon's view of the situation and the duties arising from it, it would be impossible to imagine. He certainly "held himself responsible for the measures" which were to be taken "with a view to facilitate the withdrawal" of the population and garrisons, and among "the consequences of their possible failure" he deliberately contemplated his own death at his post.

Not yet, however, had the Government realized the lengths to which their emissary's devotion would carry them. They were vaguely uneasy about him and his position, but that was all. Throughout the months of May and June their anxiety to communicate with him continued to increase, and on the 10th of the latter month it was greatly intensified by the news of the fall of Berber, which had taken place some weeks before on the 19th of May. On the 18th of

June they are, privately at any rate, no longer exercised by the question so congenial to the subtle mind of the Prime Minister as to whether General Gordon could be more properly described as "surrounded" or as "hemmed in." At all events the Foreign Secretary appears to be clear that a man in either situation is in need of "release." For this word appears for the first time in the Blue Book in a despatch from Lord Granville requesting Mr. Egerton to put himself into communication with Major Kitchener with reference to the employment of the Kabbabish tribe for "the release" of General Gordon. "You will inform him," adds the Foreign Secretary, "that he has authority to offer a large sum of money to their Chief conditionally on his raising the siege of Khartoum or taking such measures as shall enable General Gordon to effect his retreat."

It is unnecessary, however, to proceed further in illustration of this grotesque contrast of characters, this desperate game of cross purposes. So grotesque, indeed, was the one, so desperate the other, that the whole story seemed less like an actual passage of contemporary history than a piece of tragi-comic fairy tale of symbolic legend, which had somehow or other gathered round the half-idealized figures of the Antique Hero and the very "modern" Politician.

THE FIRST CATARACT (THE GREAT GATE).

From a Photograph by J. P. Sebah, of Cairo.

That, at least, was how the matter naturally presented itself to the mind of the political reviewers of this momentous incident while it was yet comparatively recent history; but the subsequent lapse of years enables one to supplement, to modify, and in some degree to rationalize the mythical or even magical element in this account of its coming about. Official secrets are better kept in this country than in any other popularly-governed nation in the world. The immensely powerful restraint of long tradition keeps the main stream of indiscreet loquacity as effectually pent as are the waters of a river behind the massive gates of a lock. But no lock-gates are ever completely water-tight, and through the barrier of secrecy trickle threads of disclosure, which form in the course of years a noticeable addition to public knowledge. The inner history of Gordon's appointment can now be pieced together into a tolerably continuous narrative.

It loses something, as has been said, of the magical, one may almost call it the quasi-diabolical element, which the popular imagination assigned to it. We no longer see the shadow of an evil genius luring a doomed Government to its ruin; but are merely confronted with a half-drowned Minister catching desperately at any straw of expedient by which to extricate himself. There was no evil genius in the affair at all, and the only "demon" who whispered in the ear of Mr. Gladstone was the amiable, the accomplished, the not too energetic, and in this instance, the acutely worried Lord Granville. And *his* demon—and here, let me hasten to say, the word is to be understood in its strictly Socratic sense—was the editor of an evening paper. Lord Granville's "happy thought" was in reality Mr. Stead's bright idea. "Why not send out Chinese Gordon to settle the Soudan business?" asked the enterprising journalist, and "Why not, indeed?" echoed the perplexed statesman, with a sigh of profound relief. Probably in the whole career of a political Micawber, nothing ever "turned up" so precisely in the nick of time.

The realization of the "happy thought" was in itself a beautiful illustration of the method of "go-as-you-please" applied to national policy. Lord Granville's next step was to call together a Committee of the Cabinet, consisting of such of its members as happened to be in town. Lord Wolseley telegraphed to Gordon (who was then in Brussels conferring with the King of the Belgians on the subject of his proposed mission to the Congo) to come to England at once; which he did, arriving in London at 6 a.m. on January 18th, and after a prolonged interview with Lord Wolseley, he attended this Committee of the Cabinet, consisting, it is understood, of Lord Hartington and Lord Northbrook, together with the Secretary of State and Under-Secretary for Foreign Affairs. General Gordon himself has, in a letter to the Rev. J. Barnes, concisely summarised what passed at this interview :—

"At noon, he, Wolseley, came to me and took me to the Ministers. He went in and talked to the Ministers and came back and said, 'Her Majesty's Government want you to undertake this; Government are determined to evacuate the Soudan, for they will not guarantee future government. Will you go and do it?' I said 'Yes.' He said 'Go in.' I went in and saw them. They said 'Did Wolseley tell you our orders?' I said 'Yes.' I said 'You will not guarantee future government of Soudan, and you wish me to go up to evacuate now?' They said 'Yes,' and it was over, and I left at 8 p.m. for Calais."

The colloquy must, of course, have been a little longer than this. Probably some reference was made to the practicability or otherwise of the task which the Government desired to impose upon him. But Gordon, I have no doubt, brushed aside any objections which might have been urged on that score, and pooh-poohed all difficulties. He was at that time, as we know, profoundly convinced of his own influence over the Soudanese tribes, and believed that on his reappearance among them they would desert the Mahdi's standard to rally round him. That was not the opinion at Cairo, and since, as it turned out, the opinion at Cairo was right and Gordon's wrong, the question which has been put by a biographer of Gordon, and which indirectly reflects on the British representative in Egypt, appears to have a pretty obvious answer. "We see," says Sir William Butler, "a desire on the part of the English Government to send Gordon at once to the Soudan when the news of Hicks Pasha's destruction was received. We see the desire repeatedly put forward from home during the ensuing seven weeks, and as repeatedly declined by our Minister in Cairo. Why? Who shall answer?" Well, the Egyptian Government. Their answer was, in fact, given in Sir Evelyn Baring's telegram of December 2, wherein, in reply to a message of the previous day from Lord Granville, inquiring whether, if General Charles Gordon were willing to go to Egypt, he would be of any use, and, if so, in what capacity, the British agent reports that the Egyptian Government were "very much averse to employing General Gordon, mainly on the ground that the movement in the Soudan being religious, the appointment of a Christian in high command would probably alienate the tribes who remain faithful." He added that "he thought it wise to leave the whole responsibility of Soudan affairs to them and not to press them on the subject." It is difficult to see what other course he could properly have taken at that juncture of affairs. If pressure was to be put on the Egyptian Ministers at all in such a matter, it was certainly for the British Government themselves, and not for their representative in Egypt, to apply it.

Applied, however, it was, and from Downing Street. On January 10 Lord Granville again proffered the services of General Charles Gordon—this time with the alternative of those of Sir Charles Wilson—and they were again declined; nor was it till nearly a week later that the objections of the Egyptian Government were overcome. On January 15 the Foreign Secretary telegraphed that he had heard "indirectly" that Gordon was "ready to go straight to Suakin without passing through Cairo." This telegram was (apparently) crossed by another from Baring, to the effect that "the Egyptian Government would feel greatly obliged if Her Majesty's Government would select a well-qualified British officer to go to Khartoum instead of the War Minister." And this telegram was immediately followed by another, replying to Lord Granville's of the previous day, and stating simply that "General Gordon would be the best man." It was immediately on receipt of this that Lord Wolseley's message was despatched to Gordon in Brussels, and that on his arrival in England the interview with the Ministerial Committee took place.

In spite, however, of the hand - to - mouth appearance which the whole of this transaction presents, it is only just to Lord Granville and his colleagues to admit that the mission on which they despatched Gordon was not quite the desperate enterprise into which by his own change of plans it was converted. He left England with instructions to proceed not to Cairo, but to Suakin. There is reason for believing that although he had expressly stipulated against being sent through Cairo, he himself changed his own destination on the voyage; but in any case he would have found it altered for him, though not by the English Government, on his arrival in Egypt. The change, in fact, had been made some days before by the British agent, either of his own motion (that is, of course, after consulting his military advisers), or at the instance of the Egyptian Government. On January 19, the day after receipt of the intelligence of Gordon's appointment, Sir Evelyn Baring telegraphed, expressing his satisfaction at being informed of it; but adding, "I am of opinion that it would be useless for these officers to proceed to Suakin, as General Baker is doing all that can be done in that quarter with the means at his disposal. They should first come to Cairo, and after discussing matters with myself and others, proceed to Khartoum." On receipt of this communication Lord Granville immediately despatched the following telegram to Gordon to be delivered to him by the British Consul at Port Said : "Sir E. Baring gives strong reasons why you should go to Cairo, in which we hope you will concur." At the next Council the Foreign Secretary submitted the new plan to the Cabinet ; and mainly, no doubt, on the strength of Sir Evelyn Baring's recommendation, it was approved.

Having regard to the momentous and ultimately tragic consequences of this change in Gordon's destination, it seems right that its true history should be given, and that the British Government of that day should be relieved of all but the just burden of responsibility—heavy enough in all conscience—that rests upon them. The idea of despatching Gordon to Khartoum by the Nile route was not theirs, and their moral as distinct from their technical and official responsibility does not begin with the first step in the deplorable transaction. But it begins immediately afterwards. For it is not as though the plan which they accepted from others was foredoomed to failure and necessarily fraught with the fate of their emissary. Had that been the case, they might have sheltered themselves to some extent behind the military and other experts in Egypt from whom they took, and, in the circumstances, could hardly have helped taking, their cue. But this was not the case. It was well within their power to have made the Khartoum enterprise, if not successful, at any rate fairly safe; and to the extent to which they neglected or rejected the dispositions by which this was to be effected, they became as responsible for the tragic issue of the adventure as though it was their original suggestion.

On this point it is impossible for any impartial mind to refuse assent to the reasoning of Sir William Butler. This accomplished military critic is a convinced advocate of the Suakin route; and though he admits it to be doubtful whether it was at that moment possible to penetrate from any point on the Red Sea to the valley of the Nile above Abu Hamid, he holds that it would have been better if Gordon had not been deflected from his first purpose, and permitted to make his way as best he pleased without visiting Cairo. But he continues:

"Granted, however, that the route from Suakin to Berber was closed by the Arab revolt, and that it was necessary for Gordon to proceed to Khartoum by the valley of the Nile and the Korosko desert, what was then the right course for the English and Egyptian Governments to pursue? *Simply to keep open this route across the desert from Korosko to Abu Hamid at all and every cost.* That was the one thing to do, and that was the one thing that was not done. Nothing was easier. We held the Nile to Dongola ; Korosko was but a day's steaming above the first cataract ; from thence to Abu Hamid the track lay across a desert which even the Arab cannot permanently live in. Put a post of troops at Abu Hamid ; hold the intervening single well of Murat with a small party of loyal Bedouins, and your line of communication is perfect. Assemble one thousand camels at Korosko to follow Gordon with troops and supplies to Abu Hamid ; reinforce Berber with another battalion of infantry ; hold Abu Hamid with two hundred men, and your work will be done. He will then do the rest. No operation was more feasible than this one, none would have cost so little, none could possibly have been so important. As soon as Gordon reached Khartoum, he began to send away the most helpless portion of the garrison, and in the seven or eight weeks during which communications remained open, not less than two thousand five hundred widows, children, and *employés* reached Korosko from Khartoum, arriving, according to the statement of the officer receiving them at Korosko, 'in an almost perfect state of comfort.' If thus some two thousand four hundred helpless refugees could come down in an almost perfect state of comfort, how easily might half that number of soldiers have been sent to Abu Hamid and Berber by the return camels which had conveyed the refugees from these places. As a military operation, this despatch of a few hundred men to Abu Hamid was at this time as simple as to send them from Malta to Alexandria. The Ababdih Arabs were our firm friends. Hussein Pasha Khalifa, the Egyptian officer in command of Berber, was the sheikh of that tribe ; his men would have gone with alacrity on any service which was in aid of their chief. Abu Hamid was the doorway of the Soudan, the gate of Berber and Khartoum, the one golden key whose possession locked or unlocked the vast prison of that hopeless land. It is really terrible to think that this one cheap, easy, feasible, and absolutely essential precaution should not have been taken, and that the rival authorities in Cairo should during these precious months of grace that were still left to us have been wildly building earthworks at Assouan, sending soldiers to Luxor and Esneh, squandering tens of thousands of pounds in subsidizing Bedouins in the deserts close to Lower Egypt, who are to this day as separated from the Soudan as if they had dwelt in Syria, and that no thought of the real thing to be done appears ever to have entered the head of Minister or General, Pasha, Mudir, or Miralai."

It would be impossible to put more lucidly, concisely, and convincingly the whole case against the Government as it arose and developed between the date of the change in Gordon's destination and the final catastrophe. This is what they might have done, but neglected to do, to protect the life of their emissary, if not to make his mission a success; and this therefore gives the measure of their condemnation.

CHAPTER VII.

Gordon and Baring

CUT off as he was from all regular communication with the Government at home, and indeed almost wholly so with their representatives at Cairo, it is natural enough that a man of Gordon's impetuous temperament should have chafed too sorely at his enforced impotence and inaction to have been able — even if the information at his disposal had favoured the effort — to distribute the responsibility for his position with perfectly equal justice among the various persons upon whom it rested. It would be unfair, not merely to Sir Evelyn Baring, Mr. Egerton, Sir Edward Malet, and others, but to Gordon himself, to lay any stress on the numerous sallies of impatient sarcasm which are to be met with in the pages of the famous Journal at Khartoum. One instance among many will suffice. On October 24 he writes : " I declare that if my telegrams to Baring are made known it will be proved that Baring knew up to the 12th March the exact position of affairs up here ;

and therefore if there was an impression that I did not say 'Send troops (200) to Berber, or you will lose it,' he must have suppressed my telegrams." To this passage Mr. Egmont Hake, the editor of the Journals, appends a footnote, setting out two despatches from Baring to Lord Granville, in one of which the Consul-General, after reporting Gordon's request for 200 British troops to be sent to Wady Halfa, adds : "I agree with the military authorities in thinking that it would not be desirable to comply with this request"; while in the other he expresses his disagreement with the proposal mentioned in Colonel Stewart's telegram, that "a force of British or Indian cavalry should be sent through from Suakin to Berber." It is to be regretted that Mr. Hake should have printed these two extracts alone, because, as Sir Henry Gordon points out in his introduction to the Journals, Sir Evelyn Baring's objection to the latter of these two proposals (the only really practical one of the two) was not by any means intended to apply to *all* relief operations by the Suakin-Berber route. On the 24th March, less than three weeks later, and but ten days after the situation had been modified by General Graham's victory at Tamai, Baring writes :

"I believe that the success gained by General Graham in the neighbourhood of Suakin will result in the opening of the

OSMAN DIGNA.

From a Photograph by Hubert Henry, of Southampton.

road to Berber; but I should not think that any action he can take at or near Suakin would exert much influence over the tribes between Berber and Khartoum. Unless any unforeseen circumstances should occur to change the situation, only two solutions appear to be possible."

The first was to trust to Gordon's being able to maintain himself at Khartoum till the autumn, after briefly discussing which the writer continues :

"The only other plan is to send a portion of General Graham's army to Berber, with instructions to open up communications with Khartoum. There would be very great difficulty in getting to Berber, but if that road were once open it might be done by sending small detachments at a time. . . . Under present circumstances I think that an effort should be made to help General Gordon from Suakin, if it is at all a possible military operation. General Stephenson and Sir Evelyn Wood, while admitting the very great risk to the health of the troops, besides the extraordinary military risks, are of the opinion that the undertaking is possible. They think that General Graham should be further consulted. We all consider that however difficult the operations from Suakin may be, they are more practicable than any operations from Korosko and along the Nile."

On the 25th of March Lord Granville replied to this despatch, definitively declining in the name of the Government to send British troops to Berber by the route suggested; and three days later (on the 28th) the Foreign Secretary wrote an elaborate two-page exposition of his reasons for not entertaining a request which Her Majesty's Government would not willingly have refused, coming as it did from General Gordon "with the additional weight of your concurrence, if the military and other objections to it had not appeared conclusive."

Surely this despatch puts the saddle of responsibility on the right horse; and another, and still longer one, of even date with the above, is yet more instructive on the question of Zebehr Pasha, with regard to which the Journals clearly indicate something more than a suspicion on Gordon's part that Baring had not, or not with sufficient energy, supported his application. Had this been the true state of the case, it certainly would not have been necessary for the Foreign Secretary to fill more than three pages of a Blue Book with a laboured apology for overruling his subordinate. Throughout this lengthy *plaidoyer* Lord Granville treats Sir Evelyn Baring as advocating Gordon's proposals in this particular matter in question without any reserve. "The arguments in favour of employing Zebehr were stated with great force and ability," he writes, "by yourself and General Gordon," and it was with reluctance that the Government put them aside. "The observations," concludes the Foreign Secretary, in the well-known tone of a Minister who is uneasily conscious of having rejected the advice of experts far better informed than himself, "which I have made in this despatch are not intended to imply the slightest blame upon the manner in which you have discharged the arduous and responsible task of advising Her Majesty's Government under circumstances of extraordinary difficulty. It was your obvious duty to communicate your opinions to them in the plainest manner. You have discharged that duty faithfully and well. Her Majesty's Government are deeply sensible of the courage, patriotism, self-sacrifice, and devotion to duty, which actuate General Gordon. They have felt no disposition to criticise in any narrow spirit the suggestions which, with his characteristic frankness, he has made from day to day" (no doubt there is here a touch of veiled satire) "as to the most effectual way of meeting difficulties as they presented themselves to him; but Her Majesty's Government had to decide upon these suggestions to the best of their ability. They are fully sensible of the difficulty of the task, and while they have been unable to agree with General Gordon and yourself upon the question, they are satisfied that the interests of Egypt and of Great Britain could not be entrusted to abler hands."

This is not the language in which they would naturally have addressed an official who had been playing the part which Gordon so often imputes to Baring in the Journals. But in truth one need not seek to go behind the wise and generous words in which the hero's distinguished brother has summed up the matter in the Introduction above referred to. " If General Gordon had known," writes Sir Henry, " how much in unison Sir Evelyn Baring's advice had been with his own, and what support he had received at Sir Evelyn's hands, he would have been eager had his life been spared to acknowledge that co-operation." This surely ought to silence all further injurious talk about Gordon's having been ill-supported at Cairo.

And it must be added that highly as everyone must honour the heroic spirit of devotion which led Gordon to his death, it would argue an utter misapprehension of his character to lay much stress on his judgments of men. His was essentially an impulsive nature ; and in his Journals he responds with perfect *naïveté* to the impulse of the moment. Hence the many bewildering changes in his plans ; hence that multitude of suggestions which, "with characteristic frankness," to quote Lord Granville's words, "he made from day to day"; and hence too the conflicting criticisms on the men around him, which could be so easily collected from his Journal.

Sir Henry Gordon, for instance, has to put in a word for Major Kitchener and the Intelligence Department in mitigation of the severe comments which occur in places throughout the Diaries. With respect to that able officer, now Sirdar of the Egyptian army, and on the high road to yet more distinguished honours, "I am persuaded," writes Sir Henry, "that he did all in his power to get messengers into Khartoum, for just in the same way General Gordon fancied he got them out, and yet how few succeeded in reaching their destination. . . . It is due to Major Kitchener to say that from the time he went to Dongola he certainly kept us acquainted with the position of affairs at Khartoum in a manner most reliable and deserving of much credit."

But Gordon himself supplies, in various other parts of his Journal, the best answer to his own "severe comments." " I like Baker's description of Kitchener," he writes on November 26th. " The man whom I have always placed my hopes upon, Major Kitchener, R.E., who is one of the few *very superior* British officers, with a cool and good head and a hard constitution combined with untiring energy, has now pushed up to Dongola, and has proved that the Mudir is dependable." And again on the same day, "Whoever comes up here had better appoint Major Kitchener Governor-General, for it is certain after what has passed that *I am impossible.* (What a comfort !)" And on the following day, " If

Kitchener would take the place, he would be the best man to put in as Governor-General."

It must, however, be clear to any candid reader of these remarkable self-communings of one of the most remarkable of men, that the very last thing which one should seek in them is anything in the nature of a deliberate and final pronouncement either upon the plot and incidents of the strange and tragic drama in which the writer was playing protagonist, or upon the doings, the motives, or the characters of his fellow actors. The chief charm of the Journal — and what makes it, having regard to the circumstances in which it was written, unique among memoirs—is its absolute spontaneity and its utter absence of self-consciousness. It not only records every thought which occurs to the diarist, but reflects every mood through which he passes, whether grave or gay ; and it adds to one's admiration of this heroic soul to see how continually the gloom around him is illumined by the flashes of his characteristic humour. Indeed, it is the comic aspect of any incident or communication which is frequently the first to present itself, and, as with many another man possessing a strong sense of the humorous, the sally which it provokes from him is often more amusing than just. An excellent example of this is to be found in his comment on Mr. Egerton's inquiry, through Major Kitchener, as to "exactly when Gordon expects to be in difficulties as to provisions and ammunition."

"I am sure," he enters in his Journal, "I should like that fellow Egerton. There is a light-hearted jocularity about his communications, and I should think the cares of life sat easily on him. . . . He wishes to know *exactly*, 'day, hour, and minute,' when he (Gordon) expects to be in difficulties as to provisions and ammunition. Now I really think that if Egerton was to turn over the 'archives' (a delicious word) of his office, he would see we had been in difficulties for provisions for some months. It is as if a man on the bank, who, having seen his friend in the river already bobbed down two or three times, hails, 'I say, old fellow, let us know when we are to throw you the life-buoy. I know you have bobbed down two or three times, but it is a pity to throw you the buoy until you really are *in extremis;* and I want to know exactly, for I am a man brought up in a school of exactitude.'"

There is, of course, nothing unusual in asking the commander of a besieged city how long he expects to be able to hold out, nor does the inquiry imply an intention to withhold relief until the latest possible moment. Nor, again, is "day, hour, and minute" quite a fair gloss upon "exactly," which unlucky word, of course, it was that struck the quickly responsive chord of humour in Gordon's mind. But the apt comicality of the parallel which he draws is irresistible; as also is the remark on the next page that "Egerton is a statistician; he evidently is collecting material for some great work." For "what earthly use," he continues, "can it be to us for Egerton to know exactly our want of provisions when he is 1500 miles away?"

It is in the same ironical spirit that he "wonders what the telegrams about the Soudan have cost Her Majesty's Government. It has been truly a horrid question. There is the *town* El Obeyed and the *sheikh* El Obeyed; there is the Haleman of Cairo and the Haleman of Khartoum. Sanderson must have a hard time of it. 'The *city* moves about.' Why if Haleman is attacked, Cairo must be in danger! Send for Wolseley! Khartoum forces are defeated by Sheikh El Obeyed! Why the town must have moved! Is not El Obeyed the place Hicks went to take? Most extraordinary! Send for Wolseley! . . . Eureka! I have found it out; there is a *man* called El Obeyed and a *town* called El Obeyed. When a movement occurs, it is the man, not the town, that has moved."

Vastly amusing as this is, it can only have been thrown out in pure lightness of heart and as a wholly irrepressible joke. There is not the least reason for supposing that the Foreign Office officials or any of them did ever in fact confound the city with the man. The piece of chaff seems to have occurred to Gordon *à propos* of nothing, and down it went in his diary. He does not spare himself when anything strikes him. " I own to having been very insubordinate to Her Majesty's Government and its officials," he had written just before, " but it is my nature, and I cannot help it. I fear I have not even tried to play battledore and shuttlecock with them. I know if *I* was chief I would never employ *myself*, for I am incorrigible." Mr. Egmont Hake, in his Introduction to the Journals, dwells with indignant emphasis, and, as I admit, with perfect justice, on the mean falsity of the charge, industriously circulated by the Radicals for party purposes, that Gordon disobeyed the orders of his Government. But it is clear from the above quotation that if every entry in his Journal were to be taken *au grand sérieux*, he could be convicted of disobedience out of his own mouth ; and a document cannot be used as evidence for one purpose and rejected for another.

Perhaps, however, the best and fairest way of bringing this question of the responsibilities to a final issue will be to set out in detail Mr. Hake's careful summary of the various points in which Gordon was thwarted in his wishes by the Government ; and to ascertain for which, if any, of these rejections of his demands, or to what, if any, extent in respect of any of them, the British Consul-General can be fairly held accountable. We may be pretty sure that the list of Gordon's just complaints against the Government, seeing by how ardent a partisan it has been framed, is exhaustive, and that we have in it, therefore, a statement of the whole case of those who have sought to include Baring in the condemnation so deservedly pronounced by the country upon the dealings of Mr. Gladstone's Administration with Gordon during the spring and summer of 1884. Mr. Hake thus formulates his charges:

(1) Gordon wished to visit the Mahdi if he thought fit, but Sir E. Baring gave him a positive order *from Her Majesty's Government* that he was on no account to do so.

(2) Gordon proposed to go direct from Khartoum to the Bahr Gazelle and Equatorial Provinces, but Her Majesty's Government refused to sanction his proceeding beyond Khartoum.

(3) Gordon desired 3000 Turkish troops in British pay to be sent to Suakin, but Her Majesty's Government, *advised by Sir E. Baring, who disapproved of the measure*, declined to send these troops.

(4) Gordon, being convinced that some government was essential for the safety of the Soudan, suggested the appointment of Zebehr as his successor, and gave the most cogent reasons why it was absolutely necessary for the accomplishment of his mission that the appointment should be made. He reiterated his request over and over again from February to December. Her Majesty's Government would not permit the Khedive to make the appointment.

(5) Gordon requested that in the interests of England, Egypt, and the Soudan, he should be provided with a Firman

which recognized a moral control and suzerainty over the Soudan. This was peremptorily refused.

(6) Gordon asked for Indian Moslem troops to be sent to Wady Halfa. They were refused him.

(7) In March, Gordon desired 100 British troops to be sent to Assouan or to Wady Halfa. In making known this desire to Her Majesty's Government, *Sir E. Baring said he would not risk sending so small a body*, and the principal medical officer said the climate would exercise an injurious effect on the troops. These troops were not sent.

(8) Gordon, for the sake of everything and everybody concerned, showed that the Madhi's power must be smashed. Her Majesty's Government declined to assist in or even to countenance the process.

(9) Gordon, in a series of eleven telegrams, explained his difficulties, and said that if Her Majesty's Government would not send British troops to Wady Halfa, and adjutants to inspect Dongola, and then open up the Berber-Suakin route by Indian Moslem troops, they would probably have to decide between Zebehr or the Madhi; and he concluded these telegrams by saying he would do his best to carry out his instructions, but felt convinced he would be caught in Khartoum. *Sir Evelyn Baring, in his reply to these telegrams, recommended Gordon to reconsider the whole question carefully, and then to state in one telegram what he recommended.*

(10) Gordon telegraphed, "The combination of Zebehr and myself is an absolute necessity for success. To do any good we must be together, and that without delay"; and he supplemented this by another telegram, saying, "Believe me, I am right, and do not delay." The combination was not permitted.

(11) *Sir Evelyn Baring telegraphed to Lord Granville that General Gordon had on several occasions pressed for 200 British troops to be sent to Wady Halfa, but that he (Baring) did not think it desirable to comply with the request.*

(12) Gordon desired a British division at Berber, but *Sir Evelyn Baring replied that there was no intention to send an English force to Berber.*

(13) Gordon, foiled on every point, telegraphed a graceful adieu to Her Majesty's Government. Then came the fall of Berber, upon which Sir Evelyn Baring at once telegraphed to Lord Granville that it had now become of the utmost importance not only to open the route between Suakin and Berber, but "to come to terms with the tribes between Berber and Khartoum"; and Lord Granville telegraphed to Sir E. Baring that "General Gordon had several times suggested a movement on Wady Halfa, which might support him by threatening an advance on Dongola, and under the present circumstances at Berber this might be found advantageous."

A glance through the Blue Book in which all these wishes and suggestions of Gordon stand recorded will conclusively show that in none of these instances, save perhaps the first two, was Sir Evelyn Baring responsible for the rejection of any one proposal. As to the first, it is difficult to treat it seriously, and one rather wonders how Mr. Hake could have brought himself, as he apparently has done, to give it serious entertainment. The facts which have been given above, but which may here be more conveniently recalled, were as follows: Gordon before quitting Cairo on his southward journey left a message for Clifford Lloyd in these terms, "Tell Lloyd no panics. It is possible I may go to the Mahdi and not be heard of for two months, for he might keep me as a hostage for Zebehr." Upon this (and no wonder) Baring telegraphed, doubtless of his own motion, to

Gordon: "I hope you will give me a positive assurance that you will on no account put yourself voluntarily in the power of the Mahdi. The question is not a personal one. There would, in my opinion, be the strongest political objections to your risking a visit to the Mahdi." The prohibition was approved from home, and no doubt it may be said that what Mr. Hake calls the "positive order from Her Majesty's Government" really emanated from the Consul-General. But surely it cannot be gravely contended that this sudden proposal on the part of the British emissary to put himself into the hands of his savage and fanatical enemy for two months, should or could under the circumstances have met with anything but an instant if provisional veto; or that its refusal in any degree affected the success of his mission.

The same remark applies to (2), of which by the way Mr. Hake does not give quite a complete account. Gordon did not propose *simpliciter* to "go direct from Khartoum to the Bahr Gazelle and the Equatorial Provinces." What he did was to write a letter to the King of the Belgians, urging that sovereign to "occupy the Bahr Gazelle and the Equatorial Provinces, and to appoint him Governor-General of all that country." This, it is evident, involved political considerations, which clearly left a diplomatist in

Baring's position with absolutely no alternative but peremptorily to forbid the step. For political reasons it was his duty to oppose Gordon's extraordinary suggestion (3) with all the influence at his command.

As to (4), the solicitation for the appointment of Zebehr, it has already been fully dealt with in the foregoing pages ; and the last-quoted despatch of Lord Granville, showing as it does that he regarded Gordon and Baring as *solidaires* on the question of Zebehr's appointment, is conclusive. The refusal of Zebehr to Gordon was the work of Downing Street, and—if, that is to say, we exclude the unofficial influence of Exeter Hall— of Downing Street alone.

The refusal of the Firman (5) is obviously a step which could not be taken by the Consul-General on his own authority. There is no evidence to my knowledge that he either supported or opposed Gordon's application ; nor any proof that, if it had been entertained, it would in the slightest degree have influenced results.

Mr. Hake does not allege that Baring was responsible in respect of (6).

Similarly we may dismiss (8) from consideration. Nobody clearly can be responsible for not "smashing the power of the Mahdi," still less for "declining to assist in, or even to countenance the process," but Her Majesty's Government.

(10) This has already been disposed of under (4).

(12) and (13) refer to the fall of Berber, the responsibility for which has been discussed already. It has, moreover, been already pointed out that Sir Evelyn Baring on March 24 pressed the Government to send a portion of General Graham's force to Berber, to open up communication between that city and Khartoum.

There remain (7), (9), and (11), which may conveniently be considered together. Mr. Hake makes much of Gordon's "eleven telegrams"— there were, in fact, twelve — and prints his summary of Baring's reply in contemptuous italics, followed by a scornful note of admiration. But really all our respect for Gordon's nobility of character and faculty of command must not deter us from admitting that this fire of messages to Cairo—the whole round dozen despatched within four days, and the series commencing little more than a week after his arrival —show what seem to be unmistakable indications that Gordon had temporarily lost his head. " I cannot," he says, in substance, on February 27, "remove the Egyptian *employés* from Khartoum without leaving the population helpless, and with no course open to them but to submit to the Mahdi. The removal of the sick, etc., might be managed easily enough, and in fact this may be considered to have been already effected ; but unless you are satisfied with the 'partial evacuation' you must act by Indian Moslem troops from Wady Halfa, and do so at once by sending detachments of troops to Wady Halfa." On the next day he telegraphs : " There is just a chance of enticing the Mahdi's troops over to me by money. Shall I try it? Will you find the extra funds ? " His next telegram, sent the following day, begins : " Should you wish to intervene send 200 British, ' not Indian Moslem,' troops to Wady Halfa, and Adjutants to inspect Dongola, and then open up Suakin-Berber route by Indian Moslem troops. This will cause an immediate collapse of the revolt. Whether you think it worth while to do this or not you are of course the best judge." The last telegram runs : " *Re* policy. I maintain firmly policy of eventual evacuation, but I tell you plainly it is impossible to get Cairo *employés* unless the Government helps in the way I told you."

Baring's reply, which Mr. Hake has so contemptuously summarized, but which seems to me a model of patience and loyal solicitude for Gordon's safety and success in his mission, is as follows :—

"I have received your eleven telegrams of the last four days on matters of general policy. I am most anxious to help and support you in every way, but I find it very difficult to understand exactly what it is you want. I think your best plan will be to reconsider the whole question carefully, and then to state to me in one telegram what it is you recommend."

I cannot see anything in the last sentence to justify Mr. Hake's note of admiration. It was quite possible to state all these recommendations in one telegram, for Baring proceeds to do so tentatively himself.

"If I understand rightly, your main ideas are as follows: First, you wish the policy of eventually evacuating the Soudan, including Khartoum, to be formally maintained; secondly, you see clearly that anarchy may ensue on the withdrawal of the Egyptian Government, which may affect Egypt proper; thirdly, you see special objections to the immediate withdrawal of the Egyptian *employés*. The remedy which you recommend to prevent anarchy, so far as is possible, is to hand over the government to Zebehr as your successor, who would receive for a time at least a subsidy from the Egyptian Government, in order to enable him to maintain an armed force. Have I correctly interpreted your views? I have again pressed on Her Majesty's Government the desirability of allowing Zebehr to succeed you with a temporary subsidy, and have to-day received an answer asking me whether it is urgent to make an arrangement for your successor at once. I should be glad of your opinion on this point . . . You may, I think, regard the question of Zebehr as still under discussion, and not finally settled. As to the Egyptian *employés*, I am not sure that I understand what you propose. In your written report of the 8th February you speak of the Egyptian Government nominating Mudirs; but in all other documents, especially your telegram of the 18th, you condemn any interference from Cairo, and such interference is obviously inconsistent with the policy of eventual evacuation. There can, of course, be no objection to any Egyptian *employés* remaining if they wish to do so, or if Zebehr, or whoever takes over the government, wishes to retain their services.

As regards some other points mentioned in your recent telegrams, you asked me on the 28th whether you should endeavour to entice the Mahdi's troops over by money. I cannot give instructions on such a point as this. You are in a much better position to judge than I am. In your telegrams of the 26th and 29th you recommend sending 200 British troops to Wady Halfa. I should not be prepared to send so small a body so far from supports; but I have authority, if I think necessary, to send British troops to Upper Egypt, and am about to consult with authorities here as to what should be done. The consideration of the question has been allowed to stand over until the result of Graham's operations was known. British troops will probably not go south of Assouan. Two battalions of Woods' army have already been sent there. As regards the proposal made in your telegram of the 26th to send an officer to Dongola under pretence of looking out quarters for troops, I cannot say I like it, as there is no real intention of sending troops to that place. As regards your proposal to open out Berber-Suakin road by Indian Moslem troops, I am not at present prepared to recommend such a measure. Now that Graham has gained a victory, could not Hassan Khalifa open the road? As regards money, I explained to you in Cairo that your £100,000 was only on account. It is of course desirable to spend as little as possible. The financial difficulties here are very great, and one of the objects of an evacuation is to relieve the overtaxed people of the country, to whom the Soudan by reason of bad government has been a constant drain; but if you really want more money when the £100,000 is spent you can have it."

Sir Evelyn Baring might well afford, I think, to risk his case on this despatch alone, for a more complete answer to the charge of having failed to support any reasonable demands of Gordon, so soon as it could be ascertained what they were— which, as is shown by the above, was not always an easy task—it would be impossible to imagine.

CHAPTER VIII.

The Last Act of the Tragedy

IT is unnecessary, and within the limits of this volume it would be impossible, to rewrite the sombre history of those nine months which elapsed between the final investment of Khartoum and the death of Gordon. On the other hand, a recapitulation of what may be called the official incidents of that period is unavoidable. The fatal tragedy which was advancing step by step towards its climax during those months has left so deep an impression on the minds of the English people, their grief at the loss of their national hero was so intense, and their shame at the national failure to support and rescue him has been so lasting, that no English public servant in any way connected with that melancholy drama can afford to neglect the duty of clearing himself, if that be possible, of any responsibility for its tragic close. Thus, though the sad but splendid story has been told again and again in more or less worthy and adequate forms, and though it is scarcely possible to do more here than to give a dry and bald recital of the facts, it is necessary once again to set them forth. For though such a narrative may well show that "someone had blundered," or even that there were more blunderers than one, it will nevertheless appear, even from the briefest exposition of them, that no efforts which zeal, goodwill, and forethought could suggest for promoting the success of the rescue expedition was wanting on the part of Her Majesty's representative at Cairo.

Let us for a moment recall one or two incidents and dates. It was on the 19th of April, 1884, that communication with Khartoum was finally cut off, and it was precisely on the same day a month later that the fall of Berber extinguished the last possibility of adopting what all the most competent authorities agreed in pronouncing the most hopeful scheme of relief. The position of Gordon had already given rise to anxiety in the House of Commons, a feeling which it is not unfair to say was sensibly reinforced by the eagerness of Lord Randolph Churchill and his little party of *frondeurs* to give effect to their views as to the duty of an Opposition. As early as March 16th, the member for Woodstock endeavoured to induce the House to refuse its assent to the Third Reading of the Consolidated Fund Bill before "receiving further information as to the military operations in the Eastern Soudan, the position of General Gordon at Khartoum, and the policy of Her Majesty's Government in Egypt Proper." In the course of his speech on the matter, the noble lord asked which "of the two policies were the Government going to adopt—the 'rescue' or the 'retire'?" and added the following significant words: "There was one rescue which the Government, if they did not adopt it very soon, would be compelled to adopt, or they would have to make way for other people —the rescue of General Gordon. He did not believe that hon. members who were in favour of a pacific policy carried to an extravagant degree, would object to strong measures being taken without delay for the rescue of General Gordon. If the matter were left to chance, and General Gordon were sacrificed owing to the neglect and indifference and callousness and heartlessness of the Government, then they would not keep their seats for twenty-four hours after the news were known in England."

For the next five or six weeks the Government were plied almost nightly with questions as to the position of Gordon and the nature of the advices which they received; and on the 21st of April, two days after communication with Khartoum had been finally cut off,

Mr. Gladstone, in answering a question from Mr. Bourke, drew one of those distinctions for the surpassing subtlety of which he is so justly famous.

After describing the condition of Shendy and Berber, as reported to him in the latest despatches from Cairo, the Prime Minister said that with regard to Khartoum itself the information contained in their last telegram from General Gordon was, so far as the question of Gordon's position was concerned, in complete concurrence with what had reached them from Sir Evelyn Baring, "the general effect being, according to the expression used, that he is hemmed in ; that is to say, that there are bodies of hostile troops in the neighbourhood, forming more or less a complete chain around it. I draw a distinction between that and the town being surrounded, which would bear technically a very different meaning." Whether, however, there was much practical difference in the meaning would depend (though I need not say I am not quoting Mr. Gladstone's words) upon whether the "more or less complete chain" of hostile forces round Khartoum was, as a matter of fact, a "more" or a "less" complete one. And as such matter of fact, we know now at any rate that it was complete enough to prevent any effective communication with Gordon for the next nine months, and indeed until the eve of his death at his post.

On the following night, and again a week later, the Government were interrogated as to their adhesion to their opinion that the position of " General Gordon is one of security at Khartoum," and with the same unsatisfactory result. On May 1, the Prime Minister was asked in so many words whether he was able to state to the House when the Government intended to send an expedition to the relief of General Gordon. Mr. Gladstone replied that he had no statement to make on the subject. On the following day Sir Michael Hicks - Beach gave notice of a motion expressive of the regret of the House to find that "the course pursued by Her Majesty's Government has not tended to promote the success of General Gordon's mission, and that even such steps as may be necessary to secure his personal safety are still delayed." The debate upon it opened on March 12, and it was in the course of Mr. Gladstone's reply to the speech of the mover that he uttered the memorable and often-quoted declaration, that an attempt to put down the Mahdist movement in the Soudan would be a " war of conquest against a people rightly struggling to be free." Here also he referred to the " well-known case of Cambyses " as illustrating the difficulty of carrying on military operations in the Soudan, and finally—pleaded for delay. It was the duty of the Government to ask Gordon's "advice and opinions" (the advice and opinion of a man who had been nearly two months cut off from all communications) "as to the best mode and circumstance and form and time of affording him succour should the necessity arise." The motion was defeated by the comparatively small majority of twenty - eight ; and it is probable enough that from that moment the Government recognized that whatever their own individual prepossessions or collective differences on the question might be, Parliamentary, supported by national, pressure would eventually compel them to take action.

Yet they still delayed even the definite announcement of their willingness to do so. On May 27 Mr. Gladstone parried with generalities a question put to him as to whether any actual preparations had been made up to that date to organise an expedition for the relief of General Gordon. Lord Hartington's contribution to the discussion was a little more reassuring, but not much. In answer to an ironical suggestion of Lord Randolph Churchill's, that the Government would begin in October to think what measures of relief could be taken, the Secretary for War said : "The Government are thinking now, and have been long thinking, what measures they could take for the relief of General Gordon."

On July 11 the Government were again questioned; and on July 18 they were pressed to say whether they "still considered it inexpedient to take active steps for the relief of General Gordon," but in each case without effect. And up to the very last day of the session of 1884 their replies were in the same strain. They contented themselves with taking a vote of credit for the purpose, as Lord Hartington put it in answer to a question addressed to him on August 11, of "putting themselves in a position if necessary to adopt measures for the relief of General Gordon," and at the present time, added the Secretary for War, they were "taking active measures in discharge of their responsibility." Not till after Parliament had risen did it become a matter of public knowledge and assurance that a relief expedition was to be sent out, and the second week in August had expired before the precise nature and character of these active measures was announced to the world.

For it was one thing to settle the question whether Gordon was "surrounded," or merely "hemmed in," or even to reach the further conclusion that in either case a military expedition would be required to extricate him, and quite another thing to determine of what strength and composition the expeditionary force should be, and what route it should take. The last question in particular was the most contentious of all, and months were spent in debating it. It was by railway from Suakin to Berber, said one set of advisers, that Khartoum must be relieved. "Impossible!" cried another set; "that route has many mountains, and the passes are three thousand and four thousand feet above sea-level, and for distances of eighty miles there is not a drop of water along the proposed line, and the Arab enemy swarm at Suakin and at Berber. It would take two campaigns and two years' labour to complete such a line." "No," they continued, "the true route of advance is the one which nature points out. The Nile, in its long reaches of open water, gives easy transport for men and stores, and even in its worst cataract it yields that first necessary of desert warfare—water."

For many precious days and weeks the dispute went on. The question of route was no doubt one of high importance—higher perhaps than any other question save one, of which, however, it was unfortunately allowed to take precedence. A man may quite legitimately debate with himself whether he shall make his way to a railway station by cab or omnibus, and he may indeed debate the question at any length he chooses consistently with his allowing himself sufficient time to catch the train by which he desires to travel. This condition Her Majesty's Government unhappily neglected to observe. It was not until August 12 that the plan of a boat expedition, put forward by Lord Wolseley several months before, and often urged by him in the intervening period, was at last sanctioned. A vote of credit for the expenses of the expedition had been obtained a week earlier. On the 26th of the same month Lord Wolseley was formally appointed to its command.

It was not, however, till nearly a month later that the boats destined to carry the men and food over the cataracts were beginning to arrive at Alexandria; while the troops intended to form the desert column, which was to cross from Korti to Metemneh, had not yet left England. On September 10, the very day when the ill-fated Stewart and Power started up the Nile in the *Abbas* with Gordon's despatches, the first steamer of the relief expedition was setting out from our shores. It was on the 21st of the month that Gordon first received authentic news of a relief expedition being on the road, and on the 30th he despatched his armed steamers to Metemneh to await the arrival of the troops. Three weeks later he received the news of the loss of the *Abbas*, the slaughter of Stewart and

Power, and the capture of his papers. Among them unluckily were some which gave the fullest details of all stores and food remaining in the city up to September 9, with the exact strength of the garrison and population still surviving. It became possible for the Arabs to calculate to a day how long the place could hold out, and from that time forth the siege, which had been slack of late, was now closely pressed.

Meanwhile the expedition had got no further than Wady Halfa. On the 21st of October they were still struggling with difficulties of transport, lack of coal, and administrative "hitches." Two hundred boats had reached that point, but were still waiting at the foot of the Second Cataract; and it was not for another fortnight that the first company of infantry was embarked for Khartoum. November passed amid prospects steadily darkening for Gordon and the beleaguered garrison. On the 12th the Dervishes opened a resolute attack upon Omdurman, and one of Gordon's two remaining steamers was hopelessly disabled by shell-fire. He calculated his stores of food at a thirty-days' supply; but believing as he then did that the expedition had already arrived at or near Metemneh, he no doubt counted them sufficient. The English forces, however, were still at Ambukol, two hundred miles further off. December came and brought with it no fresh news of the expedition. On the 10th of the month Gordon wrote in his diary, "Truly I am worn to a shadow with the food question. It is our continued demand." There was then not fifteen days' food in the whole town. "During this time," writes Sir William Butler, from whose condensed but masterly narrative of the last days of the siege I have selected most of the details given above, "there is a daily lessening supply of food given out, and then actual starvation begins; everything that can keep the light of life flickering a little longer in their wretched frames is tried—rats and mice, the leather of boots, the straps and plaited strips of native bedsteads, gum of mimosa, the inner fibre of the palm-tree, have all been eagerly devoured. Fifteen thousand of the townspeople have been sent out to the camp of the Mahdi. Great numbers have died; there are only some fourteen thousand inhabitants now remaining in the city. Daily and nightly the enemy presses the attack. Omdurman has fallen, the circle of the Arab leaguer is clasped tighter around the famished garrison, and many among the Egyptian officers and officials are clamouring for surrender. These particulars we know from the collected accounts of soldiers and slaves who escaped the final catastrophe. We learn too from the accounts of these men, that through all the terrible time the heart of

Charles Gordon never wavered, and that up to the very brink of the last scene he stood the sole stay of the defence, the head and front of the defending, refusing all idea of surrender, still toiling to the last, still ' doing his best for the honour of the country' which he thinks has forgotten him in his agony, but which would now willingly give her best blood and spend her last treasure to save him."

On December 14, the day when he was writing the last entry in his Journal, the leading troops in boats and on camels reached Korti, the point at which the caravan route crosses the desert to Metemneh. Here a halt of sixteen days was necessary for the concentration of troops and supplies ; and on December 30, just about the time when the food supplies of the garrison were exhausted, the march was resumed. But the rate of advance was painfully slow. Short of baggage animals as it was, the expedition was forced to move forward its men and stores in detachments, halting its first body of troops at Jakdul, little more than half the way to Metemneh, and forming a depôt there, while the camels were sent back to Korti to bring on another detachment of men and stores. When at last the entire column was concentrated at Jakdul on January 12, the camels were exhausted by their triple journey, and a rest of sixty hours was necessary before the march could be resumed.

On the evening of the 14th the column moved forward from Jakdul, and from that place onward it had to make its way with the sword. On the 17th it fought the Dervishes at the wells of Abu Klea; it engaged them a second time near Metemneh on the 19th; and on the evening of the same day the Nile was reached at Gubat. By the night of the 20th the entire column was collected on the left shore of the river, about three miles south of Metemneh; and on the morning of the 21st Gordon's four steamers were sighted, and communication was at last effected between the expedition and the garrison. Three days passed before the steamers left with the relief force for Khartoum, and for this delay Sir Charles Wilson, who had succeeded to the command of the column on the death of Sir Herbert Stewart, slain at Abu Klea, was at the time severely criticised. In his published narrative of the march from Korti to Khartoum he defended his dispositions, and repelled the hostile criticisms with much ability and to the satisfaction, at any rate, of many competent and impartial judges of the matter. With the merits, however, of the controversy on its strictly military side we are here in no way concerned. Whether a tactical or strategical error was or was not committed on a specific occasion is a question which experts may reasonably enough insist on discussing, apart from the question of what or whether any disastrous consequences resulted from the alleged blunder. In other words, Sir Charles Wilson and his supporters, even though they may believe that the game was lost on the 21st of January, and that no movements, however prompt, could have saved the life of Gordon or averted the fall of Khartoum, are yet quite justified in persistence with their contention that no unnecessary delay occurred. No military commander accused of negligence or blundering could condescend to what lawyers call a plea " in confession and avoidance "— could, in other words, admit expressly or by implication that he *was* negligent or that he *did* blunder, and merely urge that the result was unaffected thereby. But to the purposes of an endeavour, such as is here made, to trace the causes of a tragic failure, the question of Sir Charles Wilson's military conduct is irrelevant, and the question of its results all-important. We have simply to ask ourselves whether the three days' delay, avoidable or unavoidable, was the proximate cause of the death of Gordon and the fall of Khartoum.

It is contended by Gordon's latest biographer, Mr. D. C. Boulger, that it was. But his contention was promptly challenged and searchingly examined by a correspondent of the *Times*, who showed a complete mastery of the facts; and Mr. Boulger's reply to his adversary appears to me to be conspicuously inadequate. It would have been possible, urged Gordon's biographer, for Sir Charles Wilson by a desperate effort " to have snatched the chestnuts out of the fire, and converted the most ignominious failure in the military annals of the country into a creditable success." To this his opponent replied by recalling the military situation to which a series of blunders had committed the desert column. " Round Khartoum there were some 40,000 Mahdists. In Khartoum there were some 30,000 people in the last stages of starvation." He continues :

"I believe in enterprise as much as anyone. I also believe implicitly in the fighting qualities of the British soldier. But I do not believe that the appearance of twenty heroes in red coats and a handful of gallant bluejackets would have sufficed to raise the siege of Khartoum. The relatively insignificant Dervish forces which held Metemneh could not be dislodged by the whole available fighting strength remaining to the desert column, although they had been heavily defeated at Abu Klea and Gubat. Yet we are actually asked to believe that the appearance of a subaltern's guard before Omdurman would have sufficed to cause the instant retreat of the whole Mahdist army. Even in Mosaic times I cannot recall such a remarkable achievement as this, the possibility of which we are coolly asked to accept. But even supposing that this great miracle was worked, what would have become of the starving people of Khartoum, and by what date could food have been conveyed to them either from the desert column itself, in face of an undemoralized enemy, or from the river column struggling amid unknown rapids hundreds of miles to the rear? A second miracle would evidently have been required."

He recalls another consideration, to the weight of which not only many of Gordon's despatches, but many entries in his since published Journal abundantly testify:

"Gordon, we know, would never have left his post of duty. Are we therefore to understand that Sir C. Wilson's party had orders to kidnap him and bring him away by force? And if this feat had been accomplished, Gordon's hapless charges at Khartoum being massacred, would history have recorded a creditable success?"

Mr. Boulger's rejoinder is not very forcible. He had asked, he said, for neither the miraculous nor the impossible. What he had stated was, first, that Gordon had "begged three months before the force reached Metemneh for '100 men, or even 50.'" Three months before! Had there then been no change in the situation in that time? Three months before the attack on the town was not being pressed; the Mahdi was still far away in Kordofan, and his lieutenants, the Sheikh el Obeyed and Wad el Nejumi, kept their investing forces some miles back from the outworks. It was still easy to reach Shendy, one hundred miles north, even by land. Desertions were going on among the black troops of the Dervishes; the store of grain and provision in the town was still ample; the spirit of the garrison was fairly good. Three months before the hapless venture of Stewart and Power had not been attempted; the *Abbas*, with Gordon's despatches, informing them of the condition of Khartoum, had not fallen into the Mahdist's hands; the iron ring had not been drawn close round the beleaguered city. "Considering Gordon's position," says Mr. Boulger, "I think the public will agree with me that every effort should have been made to comply with his demand." Assuredly they will, and they would bitterly blame Sir Charles Wilson for not complying with it, if it were possible for him to do so. But again it must be said the question is not whether Sir Charles Wilson is to be blamed for what he failed to do, but whether the doing of it would have saved Gordon's life.

On that point Mr. Boulger's contention is that though the arrival at Khartoum of fifty men on the 24th or 25th of January would not indeed have "raised the siege," or "caused the instant retreat of the whole Mahdist army," it would have enabled the one solitary man, on whom the whole burden of the protracted defence had fallen, borne down by physical exhaustion and constant watching, to hold out for the few days or weeks longer until larger reinforcements could arrive. In plain words, the fifty men would,

humanly speaking, have saved Gordon's life, and
fed the 30,000 people in Khartoum for the days
or weeks—it would certainly have been weeks—
until the river column could have come up!
Surely Mr. Boulger must see that the two undertakings between which he seeks to distinguish
as between the possible and the impossible were
in fact identical.   To rescue Gordon and the
garrison *meant* to compel the Mahdists to raise
the siege of Khartoum straightway.   The
feasibility of the one feat depended on the
feasibility of the other.

And there is no doubt that on the 24th or 25th,
if not on the 21st of January, and probably by a
much earlier day than any of the three, the feat
had become impracticable.   " By an extraordinary
chance," says Mr. Boulger's critic, " it became
possible to persuade the large portion of the
public which does not trouble itself with facts,
that an expedition which was more than two
months too late had missed success by a few
hours.   It is surely time that this precious fiction
was dealt with as it deserves."

It is impossible, I think, for any unprejudiced
student of these events to withhold his assent
from this judgment.   Not at Gubat in January,
1885, but at Westminster in the summer of 1884
was the doom of Gordon sealed.   The unwilling-
ness of the Government to admit that any relief

expedition was needed, their doubts and hesitations as to its character and route, their long and disastrous delay in equipping and despatching it—to these causes and to no other was the final tragedy due; and its sad and shameful *dénoûment* was already written in the book of fate before a single camel knelt on the desert sands to receive its burden, or a single boat was launched on the waters of the Nile.

Let us hasten to the conclusion of the miserable tale. On the morning of the 24th of January two of the steamers started for Khartoum, carrying Sir Charles Wilson and a small detachment of English soldiers of the Sussex Regiment. The distance to be traversed was about one hundred miles, but about midway in that interval the Sixth Cataract begins, and the Nile flows for twelve miles through narrow, rock-beset channels. To continue in the words of Sir William Butler's spirited narrative:

"It was nearly midday on January 28 before the boats, having cleared the cataract, approached the north end of the Isle of Tuti, from whence Khartoum can first be seen on the level point of land between the Blue and White Niles. As the steamers drew slowly on into the broad water, which still shows the unmixed current of the two rivers, every glass was fixed upon the palace—that large square building, whose flat roof raised high above other houses was conspicuous over all. There was no flag flying. Another half-hour passes; the boats are now abreast of the centre of the island; the city is in full view. Still no flag waves on the palace roof; no sign of welcome comes from a long-expected garrison; but hostile guns are opening fire upon the steamers, and the crackle of musketry is spreading further along the shores until, reaching the houses of the city that are nearest the water, it completes the circle of the enemy's shot around the approaching boats. On the shores of the mainland, and over the sandy point below the town, crowds of men wearing the strange uniform and waving the battle-flags of the Mahdi are visible; and between the roar of cannon and the rattle of small-arms ten thousand shrill shouts of Arab triumph tell that all is over in Khartoum.

"This is what had happened. Three hours before daybreak on January 26 the Arabs made a final assault upon the lines. Of the details of the attack we know very little. We know that the sight of the wounded from the battle of Abu Klea, who had been brought to the camp of the Mahdi, produced a profound effect upon the Baggara and other fighting tribes of the army. These men, inflamed at the appearance of their stricken comrades, loudly demanded to be led at once against the city. The attack, delivered under a chosen leader in the darkest hour of the early morning, was directed against the lines near the gates of Bourré and Mesalamieh. On this morning of Monday, January 26, the moon, just past its first quarter, set at one o'clock. From that hour until the earliest dawn profound darkness wrapped the dying city and the hostile camps. It is certain that the Arabs as they approached the ramparts were met by the feeblest resistance. Hunger had now brought to the lowest point the spirit of a garrison never strong; but whether actual treachery added its black help to famine, or whether the wretched soldiery fell back from the parapets in panic before the first onset of the enemy, will probably never be accurately known. Once the lines were gained by the enemy the city lay at the mercy of its assailants. Shortly before daybreak they appear to have advanced cautiously into the town, and as the winter dawn was breaking they reached the neighbourhood of the palace. Here, certain that the entire city was now in their possession, they gave vent to those shrill shouts of triumph with which the soldiers of

THE PALACE,
KHARTOUM.

Islam celebrate victory. It was at this hour—just as day was breaking—that Gordon, roused from one of those short and troubled slumbers which for months had been his only rest, quitted the palace, and moved at the head of a small party of soldiers and servants towards the church of the Austrian Mission. This building lay to the east of the palace, from which it was separated by an open space of ground. Some months earlier the church had been made the reserve magazine of the town ; the surrounding houses were cleared from its vicinity, and it had been silently selected as the spot where a last desperate resistance might be maintained if ever the final moment of the defence of Khartoum should arrive.

That supreme moment had now indeed come. Walking a few yards in advance of his party, which did not number more than twenty men, Gordon drew near the church. The short and mysterious dawn of the desert was passing into broader day—over the palm-trees on the edge of the Blue Nile the eastern sky was flushed with the red of the coming sun. From the lost town still lying in shadow to the right the shouts of a victorious enemy, and the cries of a perishing people, rose in deeper volume of sound. Ere yet the little band of footmen had crossed the open space between palace and church, a body of Arabs issued from a neighbouring street. For a moment the two parties stood almost face to face, then a volley of musketry flashed out at close range, and the bravest and noblest soldier of our time was no more."

A few days afterwards his gory head was thrown with fierce exultation by the Mahdists at the feet of Slatin Pasha—for ten long years afterwards a prisoner in their camp—to convince him that the English hero had indeed been slain.

CHAPTER IX.

The Financial Crisis

BEFORE quitting this too memorable episode in the history of British policy to
return to the main course of Anglo - Egyptian
affairs, a few, but only a few, words are necessary
to wind up the account of Baring's connection
with the drama of Khartoum. To all practical
interests and purposes it ceased at the time when
communications with Gordon were finally cut off.
For it was in that same month of April, 1884,
from which Gordon's isolation dates, that Baring
was summoned to England for the consultation
on financial matters, which will be hereafter
referred to ; and in England for the next four
or five months he remained.

It was not till about the beginning of
September that he returned to Cairo ; and on
the 17th of that month he forwards one of those
messages from Gordon which show him in the
most incalculable of his moods, and upon all the
representations of which it would have been
impossible for anyone either in Cairo or in

London to take action. It contains nine paragraphs which, summarized, are to the effect that English troops must be at once sent to the Soudan; that Zebehr Pasha must be appointed, with assistance and with a salary of £8000 a year; that on the arrival of the English troops the Egyptian troops should return to Egypt; that if the Sultan would send 200,000 of his troops the Soudan would be handed over to him; that if no part of the scheme is carried out, and if the rebels attack the people of the Soudan and kill them, "you will be responsible for their lives and all their salaries"; that, reckoning expenses and pay of the soldiers in the Soudan at £1500 a day, "you have already become responsible to them for £300,000"; that he hoped shortly to take Berber, in which case his troops would be ordered to remain in it fifteen days, and then to burn it and return to Khartoum; that if the Sultan's troops come, they should come by Dongola and Kassala, and should be given £300,000; and lastly, that "Mahommed Ali Pasha is the only person in the Soudan on whom I can rely and who can replace me."

But by this time Baring's official concern with the situation in the Soudan, if it cannot be said to have been determined altogether, had at any rate become of a far less intimate and responsible kind than before. The expedition in relief of Khartoum had by that time at last been resolved upon, and Lord Wolseley had been appointed to its command. The affair, in short, had passed out of diplomatic and into military hands; and Baring's *rôle* now became virtually that of a mere intermediary between the British Government and the commanders of the expeditionary force.

With the fall of Khartoum, and the return of our baffled troops from the scene of their unmerited failure, the Consul-General's advisory function revived; and he was called upon, at the instance of the Government, to consider the following important question with regard to our future policy in the Soudan:

"The question of establishing some administration for the Province of Dongola being mainly a military one, I consulted Lord Wolseley and General Buller on the point mentioned in your Lordship's telegram of the 9th instant. I have now the honour to enclose a copy of the reply I have received from Lord Wolseley, who thinks that if the railway were completed to Hannek the province might be held by a small force of good black soldiers with four armed steamers, until the Mahdi can make an attack in force; that when he does so, Dongola will fall into his power; the defence of Dongola might be attempted with a British battalion at the end of the railway at Hannek, supported by the Egyptian battalions, to hold the railway and Wady Halfa. Lord Wolseley thinks this experiment embraces dangers, but might be worth trying, as preferable to handing over Dongola to the Mahdi and anarchy."

Then followed an opinion of hardly less weight than Lord Wolseley's :

"Sir R. Buller has sent me two telegrams on the subject, copies of which I have the honour to forward herewith, the first being a statement of the facts on which his opinion, as given in the second, is formed. Your Lordship will see that General Buller thinks the extension of the railway to Hannek at this moment would be a waste of money ; that no force of blacks which we can get would be sufficient to hold or reconquer the Province of Dongola, and that no reliance can be placed on them ; that the Mudir Emir Ezzam will occupy Merawi the day after our troops leave . . . In a subsequent telegram (also enclosed) General Buller says his opinions might be materially altered, and the whole condition of things changed, by a great misfortune, such as a crushing defeat at the hands of Sheikh Osman Merghani happening to the Mahdi, an event which might occur at any moment."

It did not occur, however, and General Buller's opinion may therefore be considered apart from the unrealized contingency. Other authorities were equally emphatic.

"I have also consulted General Stephenson, Nubar Pasha, Abd El Kader Pasha, and Colonel Watson on this subject. We are unanimous in the opinion that to endeavour to establish any government at Dongola, if the English troops were withdrawn at once, would be quite useless. In view therefore of the decision of Her Majesty's Government, we think that instructions should be given to General Buller to send down all troops, arms, and ammunition, and as many of the civil population as wish to leave, to Wady Halfa, and that the English rear-guard should be the last to leave."

Then follows the most significant observation :

"Your Lordship will understand that we make this recommendation only because we consider it to be the necessary consequence of the decision of Her Majesty's Government to abandon the Province of Dongola at once; but that it must in no way be taken to imply our agreement in that decision."

Their unanimous opinion — the opinion in which all the array of authorities, military and civil, English and Egyptian — was, in fact, summed up in one pithy sentence of Sir Redvers Buller's: " I have already said that I believe we are withdrawing as the fruit is falling into our hands; possibly the fruit was not worth remaining for. It has been so decided." Not very pleasant reading this, at a time when we have just had to despatch an expedition, with infinite labour and at no little cost, to gather up again the lost fruit which thirteen years ago was falling into our hands.

"Anyhow," continued Sir Redvers Buller, " I do not believe that when we leave Dongola anyone else here can keep the Mahdi out." No one could or did keep out the Mahdi's successor. Dongola, city and province, fell early into the hands of the Khalifa and his marauding hosts, and the results of their twelve years' mastership of it were only too miserably apparent last autumn, to our re-entering forces, in the ruined bazaars and deserted streets of what was formerly one of the most flourishing and prosperous of the cities of the Upper Nile.

It is time, however, to have done with this ill-starred military enterprise and its immediate sequel, and to resume the thread of our diplomatic history in Egypt. To do so we must go back some months to the anxious summer of 1884, when the summons of the home Government withdrew Sir Evelyn Baring from his post at Cairo. For some years past it had become apparent that the finances of Egypt must again be taken in hand by the Powers. The country had to meet the heavy liability of the Alexandrian Indemnities, as well as to clear off the debts due to the rebellion and the war in the Soudan. The arrangements, moreover, as to the distribution of the revenue between the Government and the bondholders were crying aloud for a readjustment. Wise as it was confessed to be by all well-wishers of Egypt to give her solvency the foremost place in their consideration, it was possible to carry that provident policy beyond its legitimate limits; and when it appeared that the administration was being starved in order to provide the public creditor with superfluous security for his dividends, it was felt that that limit had been overpassed. During the year 1883 the revenues assigned to the Debt produced so large a surplus, that after full payment of the interest it was found possible to redeem £800,000 of the capital. Yet in this very year the revenue assigned to administration fell short of the expenditure by more than £E 1,600,000. To cover the deficit Egypt was obliged to borrow on short loans at high rates, while at the same time she was paying off debts bearing no higher interest than four or five per cent.

Such a state of things was clearly intolerable. It was the finance of an Irish squire of the days before the Encumbered Estates Court, raising loans at fifty or sixty per cent. on personal security to pay the interest on old mortgages contracted in days when the borrowing power of the land was not only unexhausted, but fresh. Yet neither of these two necessities—neither the need for more money, nor the need of a more provident application of existing funds—could be met by Egypt of her own mere motion. The Law of Liquidation, under which the public creditor starved the Government, could not be modified without the consent of the Great Powers. To raise a new loan required the consent not only of the Great Powers, but of Turkey. As a first step towards procuring these consents the British Government appointed a Committee, consisting of Sir Evelyn Baring, Sir Rivers Wilson, Sir Reginald Welby, and Sir James Carmichael, to examine and report upon the finances of Egypt, and the Consul-General left Egypt towards the end of April in order to serve upon it. The inquiry of this singularly strong body of financial and administrative experts was conducted with great ability, and extended over several weeks. In their report, which was presented on the 28th of June, they estimated the total expenditure of Egypt at £4,667,000 for administrative purposes and £3,920,000 for debt, or a total of £8,587,000, and the revenue at £8,855,000. To this expenditure, however, it was necessary to add the interest and sinking fund on a loan of £8,000,000, which it was sought to raise with the permission of the Powers, for the payment of the Alexandrian Indemnities and the extinction of the floating debt; and further, the costs of the army of occupation. By these additions the expenditure would be raised to the sum of £9,231,000, thus converting the surplus into a deficit of £371,000.

The Committee thus conclude their report: "Our task is now completed. It only remains for Her Majesty's Government, in consultation with the other Powers interested in the subject, to decide on the measures which are to be taken to restore the financial equilibrium. There are, however, a few points to which before we conclude we wish to draw attention.

"The fact is that it must be especially borne in mind in considering our figures that we have made no difference between assigned and non-assigned revenues. We have assumed that the surplus on the assigned revenues will be devoted to administrative expenditure and not, as heretofore, to the purchase of Unified Stock in the market"; *i.e.*, to the redemption of debt. "If this be not assumed the result would be to increase heavily the normal deficit, and also the floating debt, to the end of 1884.

"Secondly, we wish to state that in our opinion no financial settlement will be satisfactory which, upon the estimates which we have framed, does not leave an excess of revenue over expenditure amounting to about £3,150,000.

"Thirdly, we are of opinion that measures should be desired to exercise such a check over the Egyptian Government as will for the future effectually restrain them from exceeding the limits assigned to their expenditure."

The most important of these recommendations was the first. Indeed, the main object of the efforts then being made for the rehabilitation of Egyptian finance was to free the revenue from the undue pressure placed upon it by the bondholders, and to enable its progressive increments to be devoted not to the reduction of the Debt, but to the development of the resources of Egypt.

This report, together with a counter proposal

drafted by M. de Blignières, were discussed in detail by a Conference of the Powers which met in London in the early autumn of 1884, and the sittings of which Sir Evelyn Baring and his colleagues were invited to attend for the purpose of explaining and justifying their scheme. The mere fact, however, that France, our former partner in the Condominium, had put forward through her former representative in the Dual Control a rival scheme, sufficed of course to defeat the hopes of any definitive result. The Conference broke up without coming to any agreement; and Egypt was left face to face with the gathering difficulties of her position under the Law of Liquidation.

Before any further step could be taken for the remedy of these evils by regular diplomatic methods, the course of events brought the Powers into the field in an unforeseen and far from agreeable way. Upon the failure of the Conference of London to agree then and there to any readjustment of the finances and financial system of Egypt, the Government despatched Lord Northbrook in September, 1884, as High Commissioner to examine into and report upon the situation. The starvation of the Egyptian administration had by that time reached an acute stage. Money was wanted on all hands for the public service of the country; yet, though the coffers of the Caisse de la Dette were overflowing with the surplus which remained to them after meeting the engagements of the country to the national creditor, the hard-pressed administrative departments were unable, under the Law of Liquidation, to touch a single piastre. Never had a Treasury so undeniably earned for itself the description of *magnas inter opes inops*. Nothing short of a financial *coup d'état* could meet the desperate urgency of the case; and Lord Northbrook had the courage to recommend one. Acting on his advice, the Egyptian Government instructed the heads of the Customs and Railway Administration and the Mudirs of the Provinces, whose revenues were allocated to the service of the Debt, to pay the balance of their receipts for the current half-year direct to the Treasury instead of to the Caisse de la Dette. This step, it is hardly necessary to say, was a direct infringement of the Law of Liquidation, which had been passed with the assent of the Powers, and could only be justified, if justifiable at all, on the plea of necessity. Still, apart from the technical illegality of the proceeding, it was perfectly defensible as a financial, and indeed, it may be said, as a political, expedient. The Caisse, as has been said, had already money enough and to spare for the payment of the then maturing coupons of the Debt, and the sums intercepted by the Treasury would simply have gone to swell the Sinking Fund; and, from the financial point of view, it would have been absurdly improvident on the part of Egypt to devote large amounts to the reduction of her Funded Debt when she was at the same time obliged to borrow on short loans at a much higher rate of interest, and even with such borrowing could not meet her current expenses. Politically, again, it was undoubtedly preferable to the alternative of suspending payment of the tribute to the Sultan, which would have caused grave political complications, or to that of stopping the pay of the Government officials, which would of course have thrown the whole mechanism of administration out of gear. Moreover—and this is a point of high importance in its bearing on the moral as distinguished from the technical justification of the act — the Powers had been unanimous at the abortive Conference of London in admitting the necessity of suspending the Sinking Fund, although they had not been able to agree to any definite scheme.

It was with arguments of this description that the Egyptian Finance Minister endeavoured in a letter to the Commissioners of the Caisse to defend his irregular action, and the British Government did their best to support him in their diplomatic communications with the other Powers. But they failed to persuade. The answer which they received was, that even admitting a suspension of the Sinking Fund to have been inevitable, the arbitrary manner of carrying it out struck a blow at the faith of international compacts, and was calculated to destroy public credit in the integrity of the Egyptian Government. Alike in Paris, Berlin, Vienna, and St. Petersburg had the representatives of the British Government to submit to this rebuke, which was further embodied by the Consuls - General of the four Powers in an identic note addressed by them to the Egyptian Government in the last week of September, 1884.

A worse indignity, however, was in store for them and for us. On October 4 the Commissioners of the Caisse applied to and obtained from the Mixed Tribunal a writ of summons, calling on the Prime Minister and the Finance Minister and the Mudirs of the provinces to answer to the law, the former for having issued, the latter for having obeyed, the illegal order. There was nothing for it but submission. The Egyptian Government "bared the neck to the smiter, explained piteously that if it had sinned it had done so only under the gravest compulsion, and pointed out that the regular payment of the assigned revenues to the Caisse had already been resumed." The Commissioners, however, proceeded implacably with their action, and on December 18 the Court of First Instance pronounced judgment against the Ministerial and Official Departments. The Government appealed, with the object probably of gaining time rather than of reversing the decision; for time at this juncture had become important. Though the recommendations of Sir Evelyn Baring and the Committee had borne no fruit in the Conference of London, yet, supplemented by the suggestions of Lord Northbrook on his return from Egypt, they had been embodied in a definite scheme; and the negotiations which were then going on between the British Government and the Powers, on the basis of these proposals, bore fruit eventually in an International Convention, which naturally deprived the dispute between the Caisse and the Egyptian Government of further practical importance. The proceedings were accordingly allowed to lapse.

Not, however, that the result was reached without much diplomatic difficulty and a protraction of negotiations, which in itself was a source of grave detriment to our position in Egypt. At the beginning of the year 1885,

Baring had to report to the British Government
that the delay which had taken place in arriving
at a settlement of the monetary claims had
exasperated public opinion, and shaken the confidence of the Egyptian public in the power, if
not in the integrity, of England. " Intrigues,"
wrote the Consul-General, " of all descriptions
are rife; the suffering caused by the non-pay-
ment of the Alexandrian Indemnities is very
great; trade is very slack; and commercial
transactions, as far as they are based on credit,
are almost at a standstill." Lawsuits against the
Government on account of the recent deductions
from the coupon were still pending, and sooner
or later another financial crisis seemed inevitable.

The urgent necessity for a settlement was no
doubt appreciated by the British Government;
but it found its proposals of the previous year
obstructed by the determined opposition of
France, while Prince Bismarck at the same time
made hardly any secret of his intention of availing himself of English difficulties in order to put
pressure upon her in favour of the objects of
German colonial policy in Africa. However, by
the middle of January, after a delay of seven weeks,
France submitted a series of counter proposals,
which opened the way for fresh negotiations. In
these proposals the view that the Egyptian
revenue was sufficient to cover the normal ex-

penditure was reaffirmed, and it was suggested that a Commission of Inquiry should be appointed to examine into the matter. But as inquiry meant delay, the French Government expressed themselves willing to assent to a tax of 5 per cent. on the coupons of all the debts, to be repaid if the revenues were found sufficient. As to the new loan, it was suggested that it should be for the sum of £9,000,000, issued at the rate of $3\frac{1}{2}$ per cent. under the collective guarantee of the Powers, the amounts required for service of the Debt being at the same time made a first charge upon the Egyptian revenue. The proposal of the English Government to tax foreigners was agreed to ; but objection was taken to our scheme with reference to its treatment of the Daira and Domain lands and loans.

At the time these counter proposals were put forward the British Government was also indirectly made aware of the fact that during the interval of delay France had been negotiating with the other Powers, and had already obtained the adhesion of Germany, Austria, and Russia. In reply to this communication from the French Government, Lord Granville signified his willingness to accept the substitution of an international guarantee for this new loan, and withdrew that part of the scheme relating to the Daira and Domain lands and loans. He declined, however, to consent to the appointment of a Commission of Inquiry, and suggested that the new arrangements should have a two years' trial before any step of the kind was resorted to. This counter proposal was accepted by the French and other Governments, and on February 8 M. Waddington delivered a detailed statement as to the mode of carrying out the scheme. After some weeks further negotiation the Convention above referred to was signed by the representatives of Great Britain, Germany, Austria, Hungary, France, Italy, Russia, and Turkey on March 18, 1885. The financial arrangements embodied in it made provision, through a somewhat complicated way, for the application of the surplus revenue to the expenses of administration; and for the payment of the Alexandrian Indemnities and other purposes it sanctioned the raising of a loan of nine millions sterling.

It was in connection with this last transaction that Baring rendered one of the most valuable of his many important services to the prosperity of Egypt. Eight millions of this new loan was applied, as has been said, to the liquidation of the Indemnities and to wiping out the deficits of the three previous years; it was the ninth million that gave the Consul-General his opportunity. How it did so is eloquently told by Sir Alfred Milner, whose account of it is as follows :—

A VIEW BELOW THE FIRST CATARACT (ABOVE ASBOUAN).

From a Photograph by J. P. Sebah, of Cairo.

"The history of that million is one of the most marvellous chapters seen in the romantic history of Egyptian finance. The old saw recommends 'a hair of the dog that bit you.' The million in question was to all appearances a remedy quite as illogical. That a country which had been ruined by excessive expenditure and reckless borrowing should borrow once more in the very moment of insolvency, and should do so not merely to clear off existing liabilities, but actually to plunge into fresh expenditure, seemed contrary to every manner of financial prudence. There were not wanting critics of the highest repute who were vehemently hostile to the proposed new outlay. And in principle they were entirely right. Not in one case out of a hundred would such a policy have been justifiable. But Egypt, the land of exceptions, supplied just that hundredth case. It was life and death to her to put the great central works upon which the irrigation of the Delta depended into proper working order. To do so required a capital expenditure which was beyond the means of the annual Budget of the Public Works Ministry. This extra million just provided the necessary capital. It saved the irrigation system, and with it the finances of Egypt. It has brought in cent. per cent. Of all the extraordinary contrasts of which the history, and especially the financial history, of Egypt is so full, there is none more striking than that of the countless millions borrowed by Ismail and this single million for irrigation ; the former raised with ease in the heyday of fortune, the latter only obtained after a hard struggle, when Egypt's borrowing powers seemed almost extinct ; the former squandered with so little benefit to the country ; the latter of such incalculable value in the re-establishment of her prosperity."

There is scarcely any passage, I am able to say, in the whole of his Egyptian career to which the Lord Cromer of to-day looks back with such pride and satisfaction as he does to this. And certainly with abundant reason ; for not only was his work a beneficent one, but it was achieved under circumstances of signal difficulty. It was, indeed, one of those most difficult of all human feats which men have to accomplish in the face not only of their opponents' criticisms, but often also of their own misgivings. To determine on so bold a policy of expenditure at such a time, and to carry it through against the opposition of colleagues, required a rare combination of nerve, firmness, and foresight. The brilliant success of the policy, as entrusted to the master-hand of Sir Colin Scott Moncrieff and his able staff of Irrigation Inspectors to carry out, is a sufficient proof of Baring's eminence in the last of these three qualities. It is only in the privacy of councils that the other has found its proper field of display. But in that sphere they must have been severely tested. We may take it as pretty certain that but for the Consul-General's steady tenacity of purpose, and his courageous confidence in his own cool judgment, this great and wise measure of financial and economic policy would never—or certainly not at that critical moment—have been resolved upon.

But Egypt was in other respects also beginning to feel the benefits of the British occupation. It was during his visit to London in connection with the financial difficulty, and indeed on the very day on which he and his colleagues signed their report on the subject, that Sir Evelyn Baring addressed one of his most important despatches to the Foreign Office with reference to the progress of reforms in Egypt. The despatch was not intended as a detailed review of all that had been done in every branch of Egyptian administration, but was written simply to combat the view that British intervention had been "barren of result so far as the welfare and prosperity of the Egyptian people are concerned."

"By far the most important reform effected since the British occupied Egypt has been the partial suppression of the use of the courbash. I say the 'partial suppression' because I am not prepared to say that even now the courbash may not be occasionally used; but I am convinced that its use is now comparatively rare. It used to be very frequently employed for two main objects, viz. (1) the collection of taxes and (2) the extortion of evidence. I think I may say with confidence that the use of the courbash as a general practice in connection either with the collection of taxes or the extortion of evidence has ceased. The use of the courbash was always illegal, but the great change which has recently taken place consists in this, that the people now know that it is illegal."

And in illustration of this Sir Evelyn goes on to relate, on the authority of a very trustworthy witness, an English officer, the following anecdote :—

"Shortly after the decree was published abolishing the use of the courbash, a fellah was brought before a Mudir accused of being implicated in a murder. On refusing to answer the questions which were addressed to him he was threatened with the courbash, and the implements generally used for securing the men when they are flogged, and for flogging them, were brought into the room. The man, however, still refused to speak, and told the Mudir that he was fully aware that he could not be flogged. Moreover, as a matter of fact, he was not flogged."

"To anyone, adds the writer," who is acquainted with the submissive character of the people of Egypt, the fact of a simple fellah daring a Mudir to commit an illegal act is very eloquent."

Another reform of great importance was the establishment of the new native tribunals; and in criticizing the organization of these bodies, Baring lays an unerring finger on a defect which was not destined till some time afterwards to reveal its full gravity, and to necessitate a modification of the original scheme.

"So far as I have been able to judge, the new tribunals have worked quite as successfully as could with any degree of reason have been anticipated. It may be an open question whether it would not in the first instance have been wiser to have adopted the English rather than the French system of criminal procedure. Under the former the Mudir would have taken the place of the English magistrate, and would have been charged with the preliminary investigation of criminal offences. Under the French system the duty is confided to the Procureur-Général and his deputies. A very powerful check is thus exercised on any act of oppression and illegality on the part of the Mudir. On the other hand, the transition from the old state of things, under which the Mudir was practically supreme, to the present system, under which all judicial power has been taken away from him, involved a change of the most radical description. It may be doubted whether the English system, inasmuch as it involved a less rapid transition, would not have been more suited to the actual condition of society in Egypt.

"The subject is one on which a good deal of difference of opinion exists. Nubar Pasha, who throughout his career has advocated the substitution of judicial, as opposed to arbitrary power in Egypt, is, nevertheless, of opinion that under existing circumstances some well-considered measures must be taken to maintain the authority of the executive officers of the Government in the provinces by associating them to some extent with the administration of justice . . . . I will not, however, attempt to discuss this subject at length. I will only say that the question of whether under proper safeguards some additional power may not be entrusted to the Mudirs, is now under the consideration of the Egyptian Government."

Later on it will be seen how fully these criticisms were justified, and how imperative became the necessity of correcting the error which was committed when these provincial governors, instead of being merely controlled, as they should have been, in the exercise of their authority, were deprived of it altogether.

No less acute was the prescience of another subsequent reform of the judicial system which Sir Evelyn Baring displayed in the following remarks on the constitution of the new tribunals :—

"One of the main obstacles to the introduction of any reforms into Egypt is the great difficulty of finding suitable agents to carry them into effect. The Egyptian Government almost invariably finds itself in this dilemma, that it must either employ a number of Europeans, a course to which there are obvious financial and political objections, or that it must employ Egyptians, whose training and experience of the special subject concerned is generally defective. This difficulty was brought prominently forward in connection with the establishment of the new tribunals. The number of Egyptians who have received any judicial training is very limited. On the other hand, the Egyptian Government could not bear the expense of employing a large number of European judges. Moreover, Europeans are often ignorant of the language and the customs of the country. Under these circumstances, although the services of a limited number of Europeans (principally Belgians) were secured, the majority of judges are native Egyptians. Many of these latter have not had any special legal training. Under these circumstances it may readily be admitted that the composition of the tribunals is not everything that could be desired. As time goes on it will no doubt improve. In the meanwhile it may be said that the judicial system, as it now exists, is a great improvement on anything which has heretofore existed in Egypt."

Six years after these words were written these courts were still so far below any satisfactory standard of efficiency that it was found absolutely necessary to strengthen them by a larger infusion of the European element, even though it cost the resignation of an Egyptian Prime Minister to get the indispensable changes carried into effect.

After reviewing further the excellent work done in the Public Works Department by Colonel (now Sir Colin) Scott Moncrieff and his able assistants, by whose efforts water had been provided for the cultivator in greater quantity than before, and much had been done to check the notorious abuses which occurred in its distribution ; and after a brief reference to the improvements which had taken place in prison discipline and in sanitation, Baring continues :—

"Besides these and other minor reforms to which I might allude, I maintain that a new life has been breathed into the spirit of Egyptian administration and into the Egyptian people. The people are beginning to learn that there is such a thing as justice as between man and man."

For the first time in how many thousand years !

"I am very far from saying that mistakes may not have been committed. It would, indeed, have been strange, considering the difficulties of the situation, if this had not been the case. These difficulties have been very great. The events of the last few years, beginning with the abdication of the late Khedive, have profoundly shaken the authority of the Government in Egypt. Broadly speaking, it may be said that the principal reforms which were required in Egypt took the direction of imposing some check on the abuse of power by the governing classes. The very difficult problem, therefore, presented itself at every turn of imposing these checks, and at the same time of maintaining to a sufficient extent the legitimate influence and authority of the Executive Government over a people long accustomed to purely arbitrary and personal rule. It was natural enough that under these circumstances the official classes should generally be opposed to reform. The fact that reforms were advocated, and to some extent executed, by an alien race tended to enhance the opposition ; while recent events in the Soudan, where the wild schemes of territorial extension conceived by the late Khedive have received a fatal blow at the hands of the Mahdi, have imported an element of religious fanaticism into the settlement of Egyptian questions to a greater extent than might otherwise have been the case. Simultaneously with this combination of affairs the political position occupied by the British Government in Egypt has led to a recrudescence of those international, jealous, and petty intrigues which have at all times been rife in Egypt."

And he concludes with a plea for patience, which at the time no doubt was urgently needed, though the progress made during the next decade was so rapid as to diminish to a very considerable extent the original demands upon that "magical" virtue.

"Under these circumstances it can be no matter for surprise to those who, like myself, are exceedingly sceptical of the possibility of affecting beneficial reform with rapidity in an Eastern country, that no greater degree of progress has been made. Rather is it a matter for congratulation that so much has been done in so short a while. Englishmen have no reason to be ashamed of the work which has been done in Egypt. The present situation, with all its difficulties, is of better augury for the future well-being of the Egyptian people than the crushing despotism which existed when I first went to Egypt seven years ago. . . . The abuses of the Egyptian administration are of long standing, and cannot be reformed in a few months or even years. Many of them, indeed, cannot be wholly eradicated until by the slow progress of education some impression has been made on the habits of thought of the population. But if we are contented with such slow progress as can alone, in my humble opinion, produce really beneficial results; and if we bear continually in mind that we must reform such customs as exist in the past rather than endeavour to supplant them suddenly by the importation of Western practices and habits of thought, I see no reason to take a gloomy view of the future of internal reform in Egypt. Some allowance must in fairness be made for the very difficult position in which the Khedive and his ministers are placed. I feel sure that both His Highness and some at least of the leading Egyptians are really desirous of availing themselves of European assistance to introduce these reforms of which the country stands so much in need. But many of these reforms are no doubt unpopular with the influential classes, while the ignorant peasants, whom it is intended to benefit, naturally fail in the first instance to realise their significance. The European adviser, however able and well-intentioned, is liable to error from want of local knowledge and from ignorance of Oriental habits of thought. Unless, moreover, he acts with great tact and judgment, the result is that the native minister appears before his own countrymen as a mere cypher, a position which the latter naturally resents. Without European assistance, however, very little progress will be made. This I believe is fully recognized by the Khedive and the Egyptian Government.

"On the other hand, it must be borne in mind that the progress of reform in Egypt depends quite as much on the judgment and discretion which the Europeans employed in the service of the Khedive bring to bear on their work as on any particular systems of administration which they may advocate."

I have thought it well to quote thus copiously from the foregoing paper, not only because it contains so comprehensive and informing a survey of the progress made by Egypt under English administration, but because I am disposed to regard it as the last important official document penned by Sir Evelyn Baring before what may be described as the close of the purely financial and administrative phase of his career.

At this point, or so it seems to me, he takes
a new and more commanding position in the
history of our empire—a position which, bringing
with it even larger problems and higher responsibilities, widened the imperial outlook of the man
upon whom they had devolved, and gave him a
clearer and loftier view of the mission and the
destiny of England in the land of the Pharaohs.
But this final merger of the financial expert and
administrative reformer in the diplomatist and
statesman may be more conveniently described
in the ensuing chapter.

CHAPTER X.

The Consul-General as Financier

IT may at first sight seem presumptuous on the part of a biographer to undertake to indicate what is called a turning-point in a public career which, being still incomplete, might hereafter exhibit such phases or enter upon such passages as would bring that biographer's conclusions to nought and turn his forecasts into foolishness. Yet, even at the risk of such future discomfiture, I shall make bold to affirm that the Baring who quitted the Council Chamber at Calcutta for the British Agency at Cairo brought with him a widely different conception of his mission from that which animates the Lord Cromer of to-day; and that it was during his first two years' tenure of his new office that, whether consciously or unconsciously to himself, this momentous change began.

Let us take a momentary retrospect of the new Consul-General's past official history. He had from 1877 to 1880 filled two posts of a financial character in Egypt—one of them, the Commissionership of the Public Debt, exclusively financial; the other, the revived Controllership (which, however, he held for less than a year), associated with a certain undefined amount of political authority. Since then he had served for three years in an exclusively financial capacity in India, and during his absence the Egypt of his acquaintance and its relations with England had been wholly transformed. When he left that country it was under Anglo-French tutelage, limited by a certain, or rather an uncertain, right of European interference; when he returned to it, England was to all intents and purposes the *de facto* ruler of Egypt. Our right of controlling its policy and of directing its destinies, even temporarily, might be and was questioned, but our power of doing so was unquestionable. It could be resisted only by warlike action on the part of any objector, and was limited only by our reluctance to provoke that action. No one, even of those who had taken an active part in the suppression of the Arabi rebellion, and had more fully realized the utter collapse of native authority in Egypt than could have been possible to a spectator of these events from Calcutta, was in those days able to form anything like a correct estimate of the time it would take to re-establish a strong and settled government in the country. Most people estimated the period of our occupation not by their knowledge of facts, which was nowhere abundant, but by their wishes, of which there is always a plentiful supply. Those who, like the Radicals, had actively opposed our intervention in Egypt, or, like the majority of the Liberals, had viewed it with passive dislike and distrust, were all convinced by the persuasion of their preferences that our stay in the country should not or need not be a long one; and though men of a military training are seldom political partisans of a very pronounced type, it is not unreasonable to presume that Sir Evelyn Baring, who had received his first introduction to official life from a kinsman who had been a Cabinet Minister in a Liberal Administration, leaned rather to the Liberal view than its opposite.

If this presumption be well founded he must have entered upon his Consul-Generalship with the expectation that the duties of that office would bear a far closer resemblance to those which he had discharged in 1878–80 than proved to be the case.

In all probability he was then under the impression that his work would be consultative rather than constructive, and that it would consist rather in keeping financial watch and ward over the government of Egypt in the hands of native administrators than, as it turned out to be, in superintending the instruction of Egyptians by

European officials in the very rudiments of the administrative art.

Indeed it is pretty plain, from the elaborate report on Egyptian affairs which he drew up at the suggestion of the Government shortly after his arrival in England in the summer of 1884, that this was, in fact, his conception of the situation. For the keynote of this interesting and, for our present purpose, self-revealing paper is the necessity of economy—an excellent text for a mere financial adviser, but not the last word of a constructive statesman. He admits, of course, that the Egyptian Government had been called upon to perform impossible feats of economical administration by the European Powers, and that the Law of Liquidation must be modified. As a member of a Committee then sitting for the express purpose of determining what amount of relief from the less stringent terms of the law should be granted to the Egyptian Government, Baring could hardly say less than this. But he proceeds :—

"While recognizing that certain exceptional and, it may be hoped, temporary causes tend to render the position of the Egyptian Treasury abnormally bad for the time being, at the same time it is essential to bear in mind that in order to give any hope of finality [to the projected financial resettlement], it is important to guard against the acceptance of unduly optimist estimates of revenue and expenditure. I am, moreover, convinced that no confidence can be entertained in the stability of any financial arrangement which may now be framed unless a powerful check be exercised over the expenditure of the Egyptian Government. I believe that the opinion which I have thus expressed is shared by every authority who has had actual experience of the working of the Egyptian administration. Experience has proved the necessity of a rigid financial supervision over expenditure, and that supervision must be mainly, if not entirely, exercised through the agency of Europeans rather than through that of native Egyptians."

His conception, it will be seen, of the duties of the Europeans who are to assist in the work of government is still mainly a financial one. When he thinks of European officials he clearly thinks of them not as men associated with the native heads of departments for the purpose of instructing them in the principles of zealous, upright, and orderly administration of the affairs of an Oriental people, but rather as men sitting by these departmental chiefs for the purpose, not so much of directing into the channels of efficiency their efforts at government, but simply of taking care that they did not draw too heavily upon the Treasury in their struggles. He continues :—

"During the brief period of prosperity which ensued immediately after the Law of Liquidation was passed, the expenditure of the Egyptian Government was largely and often very unnecessarily increased. Everyone who has been concerned in the working of a financial department knows how difficult it is to keep down expenditure, even under a thoroughly well-organized system of control. The difficulty of enforcing economy in Egypt is exceptionally great. There are indeed several zealous and able officials employed in the Financial Department of the Egyptian Government, and I can testify to the fact that they have done their utmost to keep down expenditure. But the power possessed by the Egyptian Financial Department is inadequate. It possesses relatively to the Spending Department of the Government far less power than that which is vested in the Treasury in England, or in the Financial Department with which I was associated in India. Again, Eastern Ministers submit with great reluctance to the irksomeness of financial checks on expenditure. They often fail to see the necessity of rules which from the point of view of Western administration would be considered essential to the enforcement of economy and to the preservation of financial order. The temptation to which every Oriental Minister is exposed to increase his establishment in order to provide places for friends, relations, or adherents is very great."

That there are legitimate demands upon some at least of the Egyptian departments for additional expenditure, Baring goes on to admit; but the admission is hardly made in the tone of one who was himself but a few months to make the wise but daring demand upon a Government "in liquidation" for an advance of no less than a million of money to be expended under one head—that of public works. "It is to be borne in mind," he says, "that although the tendencies of Egyptian Ministers themselves are generally the reverse of economical, they are by no means wholly to blame for the increase of expenditure which has taken place in the past."

"They are often subjected to great pressure from without to spend money. The nature of this pressure has undergone a considerable change since I was first connected with the Egyptian Government some seven years ago. At that time the Egyptian Treasury was exposed to frequent assaults from Europeans who wished to obtain concessions, contracts, &c., of different descriptions. The employment of a number of high-class European officials, whose advice in such matters is perfectly disinterested, has without doubt been very beneficial to the Egyptian Government, in so far as it has enabled it to offer an effective resistance to projects and claims of this sort, which would have been detrimental to the interests of the Egyptian Treasury. But in the place of this pressure to which I have alluded another has sprung up which, if directed to more laudable objects, is hardly less costly than that which formerly existed. The Egyptian Government is being constantly pressed to spend more money on public buildings, prisons, sanitation, education, improved justice, &c. Very valid arguments may be adduced in favour of expenditure of this sort, and the Financial Department is not sufficiently strong to enforce the lesson that however desirable administrative reform may be, it must be carried out with due regard to the fact that the first essential requisite to the well-being of any State is that it should not spend more money than it receives."

The main point, he again insists, the root of the matter, is to establish an "effective check upon Egyptian expenditure," though it is important, he admits, to bear in mind that sufficient elasticity should be given to whatever institutions are created to enable the amount of expenditure to be modified periodically with reference to the financial situation, and to the requirements of the country for the time being. Even here, how-

ever, the " financial situation " came first and the
" requirements of the country " second ; and the
order in which they are placed meant more, we
may fairly suppose, than the mere truism that you
cannot lay out money if you have no money
to lay out.   One can hardly doubt of its implicitly
containing the much wider proposition, that
even when an Egyptian Treasury has money to
the good its English advisers should not recommend its outlay on the requirements of the
country, unless it was certain that this could be
done without committing the Government to
administrative engagements which could by any
possibility affect for the worse its financial future.
And this, it is needless to say, is not the principle
which Baring was to apply himself a few months
later, or upon which our work in Egypt has been
since carried out with such beneficent effect upon
the prosperity of the country.

But how far the Consul-General then was—in
common, it may be admitted, with every other
English observer of Egyptian affairs — from
realizing the extent of our undertakings in
connection with Egypt appears still more clearly
from the following instructive passage :—

"Another important consideration with which we have to
deal is, that Her Majesty's Government is—most wisely in my
opinion—not prepared to assume the government of Egypt,
whether permanently in the form of annexing the country, or
temporarily in the form of establishing a Protectorate.

"The British interests in Egypt, over which Her Majesty's Government are bound to watch, may, I conceive, be summed up in a single phrase. They consist in keeping open the highway to the East, the freedom of which would be compromised if Egypt fell into the hands of any other Power. At the same time Her Majesty's Government have shown by the proposals they have made in your Lordship's circular to the Powers of the 3rd of January, 1883, that they desire to arrange that the Suez Canal shall remain open in peace and war to all ships, whether of war or commerce, of all nations. Under these circumstances it is desirable in British interests that Egypt should be so reasonably well governed as not to afford any justification for the serious interference of any foreign Power in its internal administration. Unless the finances of Egypt are in fairly good order, Egyptian affairs must always constitute a source of disquietude to Europe, and of special anxiety to England."

Here, again, the insistence on the purely financial character of our concern with and control over Egyptian affairs is very marked. And the next sentence is still more significant, as showing Baring's leaning in those days to the policy of "internationalizing" this exercise of authority in Egypt—a policy which, considering how that authority was then supposed to be limited, had much to say for itself.

" As Her Majesty's Government does not intend to assume the government of Egypt, there can be no reason why the insidious and unpopular task of checking expenditure should be undertaken by the British Government exclusively. The matter is one of international concern, and the check would naturally be exercised by an international body. Moreover, the attempt to exercise the check exclusively through British agency would excite the jealousy of foreign Powers without any countervailing advantage. Actuated by these considerations, I suggested to your Lordship before any communications had passed between Her Majesty's Government and the French Government, that the Commissioners of the Public Debt should be entrusted with a certain degree of supervision over the expenditure of the Egyptian Government. I now proceed to examine the extent of supervision which may without objection be confided to the Commissioners."

This examination starts from a retrospective review of the arrangements subsisting at the time of the Dual Control, and proceeds to the consideration of the question to what if to any extent it would be possible to revert to them. The Controllers appointed with the enlarged powers of 1879 had, by virtue of their right to be present at all meetings of the Council of Ministers, a genuine and effective power, not only over the financial policy of the Egyptian Government, but in other directions also. "M. de Blignières and myself," says Sir Evelyn Baring, "without any attempt to usurp functions which did not belong to us, were consulted, not only on financial matters, but on almost all matters which came before the Council. We kept carefully in the background, but we took a part in the government of the country to an extent of which the public at the time were scarcely aware." There would, however, be grave objections to a re-establishment of this system on an international scale, as, indeed, there would be to any modification of it which should go the length of enabling the Commissioners of the Public Debt to exercise any such powerful check over the expenditure of the Egyptian Government as would make them actual rulers of the country.

The question remained whether it would be possible to limit their powers to such an extent as to avoid " the evils of an international government." Baring thought it would be. The desired object might, in his view, be attained, not, indeed, by giving the Commissioners such powers over the details of expenditure as are exercised by the Treasury in England and by the Financial Department in India, but by clothing them with authority of a more general kind, which he then proceeds to describe :—

"It has been proposed that the Commissioners of the Public Debt should have a " voix consultative " in the preparation of the Budget : that is to say, that the Budget before it is adopted by the Government should be submitted to the Commissioners, who would have a right to make any observations or suggestions upon it which they might consider desirable. The Egyptian Government would without doubt attach great weight to the views of the Commissioners, but I do not understand that it is intended to place them under any legal or diplomatic obligation to follow their advice. I think that a power of advice in the preparation of the Budget within the limits I have indicated may be conferred on the Commissioners, not only without objection, but with great advantage to the interests of all concerned."

Moreover, except in cases of urgent contingency, which should be explained and justified to the Commissioners, no expenditure should be incurred during the currency of the year in excess of the Budget, unless with the previous sanction of the Commissioners of Public Debt. This, of course, was not to preclude the Egyptian Government from making any change in estimates, but only to prevent them from incurring an expenditure in excess of the total figures of the Budget. Then, after carefully providing for a certain addition to the powers of the Commissioners "when the British occupation ceases," and remarking that they should of course be, in the meantime, debarred from exercising any sort of control over the cost of the British Army of occupation, "the payments for which should be regulated between the British and Egyptian Governments," the despatch thus concludes :—

"The plan which I have sketched above appears to me to guard sufficiently against the danger of undue interference on the part of the Commissioners of the Public Debt with the details of the Egyptian administration, while at the same time an institution will be created which cannot fail to exercise a check on the expenditure of the Egyptian Government."

Qualis ab incepto. The despatch begins and ends with the proposition that the first and last word of English diplomacy in Egypt is "keep a tight hand on the purse-strings," and if the

English hand alone is not tight enough, to invite the grasp of all the other European Powers as well. Strengthen the control of the Commissioners of the Debt. How little could Baring have foreseen when he wrote these words how obstructive an agency this control would become, and how vexatiously it would afterwards be employed to thwart the policy which the Lord Cromer of the future was to recognize afterwards as the only one in true conformity with the administrative genius and mission of England, and in which he was to throw himself heart and soul.

Let us look back a little at the history of the Caisse de la Dette, as reviewed in the pages of a writer whose account of this object of Baring's solicitude in 1884 is all the more valuable because he is an ardent admirer of the Consul-General himself.

The Commissioners, to begin with, were little more than receivers of certain revenues which had been specially assigned to the service of the Debt. They were representatives not so much of the Powers as of the creditors, the British Government refusing, as we have seen, in the first instance even to go the length of proposing a British Commissioner. It had consisted originally of three members—a Frenchman, an Austrian, and an Italian, appointed as early as 1876, so that nearly a year elapsed before they

were joined at the Board by an English colleague
in the person of Evelyn Baring. But though
their functions were originally as specialized
and limited as this, they have been so extended
by successive changes—some of them, as appears
from the foregoing despatch, expressly approved
by Baring himself—that these receivers of revenue
on behalf of creditors have acquired also the
position of guardians, commissioned by the
Powers to watch over the execution of the
complicated series of agreements, decrees, con-
ventions, declarations, protocols, which constitute
in their totality the international compact regulating the finances of Egypt. In that capacity they
even possess a certain legislative power, and
many decrees recite in their preamble the
adhesion of the Caisse to the provisions which
they contain. The Commissioners of the Caisse
are, it is true, appointed by the Khedive, and are
in theory Egyptian officials. But in reality they
are almost as much foreign representatives as the
Consuls-General themselves, while their influence
in the administrative work of the country is even
greater than the majority of these functionaries.

Thus the Egyptian Government cannot, for
instance, adopt any general measure for the relief
of taxation without the approval of the Caisse,
inasmuch as such reduction must necessarily
affect the receipts of the provinces specially

assigned to the bondholders, and those revenues cannot be reduced without the consent of the Commissioners. Again, it cannot raise a loan even for the most legitimate purposes, such as the construction of irrigation works, without their consent; and when the loan is approved and the money raised, it is once more the Caisse which will be charged with the disbursement of it, and with the duty of seeing that it is applied to the specified objects.

But the full extent of its authority is only realized when we come to consider the singularly commanding position which was assigned to it under the Law of Liquidation of 1879, and which Sir Alfred Milner thus lucidly describes :—

"The Powers, as we have seen, stepped in to save Egypt from bankruptcy [by their assent to the financial arrangements embodied in that law], but in return they put her into a strait waistcoat of the severest kind. The revenues of the State were divided into two nearly equal parts, of which one was to go to the Caisse for the benefit of the bondholders, and the other to the Government to defray the expenses of administration. There were thus practically two Budgets, but the principles applied to them were very different. If the Budget of the Caisse showed a deficit the Government was bound to make good that deficit, whereas if the Caisse had a surplus, however large, the Government had no right to share it. On the other hand, if the Government had a deficit the Caisse could not be called upon to make up the deficiency, while if the Government had a surplus the Caisse had certain contingent claims thereon."

The inequitable terms of the schoolboy's wager, known as " Heads I win, tails you lose," have never perhaps been illustrated before or since on so dignified a scale. But though this was bad enough, proceeds the writer quoted, this was not all.

" For the Caisse might have a claim on an imaginary surplus of the Government which did not exist at all. This sounds nonsensical, but in matters Egyptian it would be rash indeed to take no account of a thing because it sounded nonsensical. That is rather a reason why it should exist. And as a matter of fact this particular arrangement, though in my humble opinion unwise, was not so absurd as it looks at first sight. The explanation is that the Law of Liquidation fixed an ideal figure for the national expenditure—a sum which in the opinion of the Powers Egypt ought not to go beyond. If the revenues of the Government exceeded this sum then the Government was to be regarded as having a surplus, no matter what its real expenditure might have been ; and in that surplus the Caisse might, under certain circumstances, have a claim."

We have already seen how the intolerable inconvenience of the arrangement actually drove the Egyptian Government within a few weeks of the perusing of Sir Evelyn Baring's despatch into a technical breach of the law ; and it is a curious illustration of the inability of even this sagacious and farseeing observer to forecast the future relations between that Government, under his guidance, and the Commissioners of the Caisse, that he should have shown himself at this period so much more solicitous to strengthen the

THE BARRACKS - KASR-EL-NIL.

From a Photograph by J. P. Sebah, of Cairo.

controlling hands of the latter than to enlarge the administrative freedom of the former.

But a brief recapitulation of the principal views enunciated by him in the despatch above quoted will better enable us to define the position which he then occupied, and thus to measure the distance to which he was soon to advance beyond it.

(1) He was at that time evidently contemplating only a temporary and probably a not very protracted prolongation of British military occupation of Egypt and British direction of her civil affairs. In this spirit he congratulates Her Majesty's Government on their being—most wisely in his opinion—"not prepared to assume the government of Egypt, whether permanently in the form of annexing the country, or temporarily in the form of establishing a Protectorate"; and he discusses the financial arrangements that should be made against the period "when the British occupation ceases."

(2) While admitting that "it is desirable in British interests that Egypt should be so reasonably well governed as not to afford any justification for the serious interference of any foreign Power in its internal administration," he goes on in his next sentence to reveal his implied assumption that this is only another way of saying—and means no more than—that the

finances of Egypt must by English supervision "be kept in fairly good order."

(3) As a corollary of this assumption he insists by implication that the principal, if not the sole task of England in Egypt, would be to check the tendency of the Egyptian Government to extravagant expenditure, and he suggests as a means to that end that it would be well to strengthen the powers of an international body of officials who were simply trustees for the public creditor, and, except in so far as the interests of that *cestui que trust* were involved, had no direct concern either in promoting the just and equal government, or even (save as aforesaid) in advancing the prosperity, of its people.

In other words, Sir Evelyn Baring had, it is evident, by no means yet realized that over and above the duty of maintaining the solvency of Egypt, the work which then lay before her English guardians included a thorough purification of her judicial tribunals, a complete reorganization of her central and local administrative system, a remodelling of her constabulary, a radical reform of her methods of tax-collection, and an unexampled development of her material wealth and the comfort of her cultivators by a liberal and well-directed outlay on irrigation.

In fine, he had not yet embraced the conception that the enterprise to which events had called his country was not the mere patching up of an old Egypt, but the creation of a new one. Still less one fancies did he foresee that in that great achievement, one which for brilliancy and rapidity deserves to rank beside the greatest of our administrative triumphs in India, he was himself destined to play so memorable a part.

CHAPTER XI.

The Struggle for Reforms

EVENTS were not long in convincing Baring by their resistless logic that a great extension of the preconceived scope of his mission was inevitable. The Egypt to which he returned in September, 1884, was in the throes of the severest crisis through which it had passed since the rebellion of Arabi. The policy of the English Protectorate was on its trial, and things, it must be admitted, were looking rather black for it. Had we only come into Egypt to make confusion worse confounded? Or had we at any rate only put down military disorder to create civil anarchy in its place?

Such were the questions which were being asked on all hands, and not in Egypt alone, throughout the years 1883 and 1884, and which in the autumn of the latter year became clamorous and importunate indeed. It is hardly an exaggeration to say that Great Britain at that moment possessed neither the goodwill of any single European Power as regards her Egyptian policy, with the doubtful exception of Italy, nor the confidence and support of any class of the Egyptian community, unless it were the creditors of the impoverished fellah. The official caste, the Turkish pashas and Levantine adventurers, to whom Egypt had long been the "happy hunting ground" of *bakshish*, had of course no liking for the intrusion of English probity and providence into the administration of the country ; and even the few statesmen that Egypt possessed, the half-dozen or so of trained administrators who were capable of ascent to the conception that the government of a country means something more than filling the pockets of its governors, had little cause to be satisfied with their experiences of these blessings. England had been willing enough to employ their experience and local knowledge as instruments for the direction of Egyptian policy, but she had not stood by her servants. Again and again she had counselled measures which brought them into sharp collision with the European Powers, and then when the inevitable conflict occurred, instead of backing them up in resistance, she had advised an ignominious capitulation. She had induced, or rather compelled, the Khedive to renounce the sovereignty of the Soudan, yet at the same time she had taken no effective steps to assist him in carrying out that policy without a cruel and disgraceful abandonment of military garrisons and civil populations (for whose plight their rulers at Cairo were, of course, directly responsible) to a barbarous foe. All these humiliations and rebuffs rankled deeply in the minds of the leading men of the Egyptian official class ; they were not unfelt, as we know, by the ablest among them, and the best disposed towards the English Protectorate, Nubar Pasha; and the minor officials naturally took their cue from their superiors. In any case the working of the new system recommended by Lord Dufferin must to a certain extent have irritated and embittered them. The introduction of Englishmen into high posts in the various departments—though an essential condition of all effective reforms—involved the further necessity of bringing personal pressure to bear upon the native officials. They had to be told that it was no longer permissible to them either to neglect their duties or to feather their nests, and the information was most unwelcome. Nevertheless, with the pliability of the Oriental they might have adapted themselves more rapidly and easily than was in fact the case, had it not been for the diminished influence and prestige of the British Government. Months before this, Lord Dufferin had warned us at home that unless men like these were convinced " that we intend to shield and foster the system we have established, it will be vain to expect the timid politicians of the East to identify themselves with its existence." Why, indeed, the harassed official may have asked, should he work cordially, at the cost of his own pocket and popularity, with the organizers of a new-fangled *régime* who are here to-day and gone to-morrow? The power, and not only the power but the popularity, of England in Egypt has always varied directly with the degree of general belief in the permanence of English control. During the year 1883–84 that belief had declined to its weakest point. "There was no conviction of the permanence of anything. There was no general feeling of tranquillity, but on the contrary, perpetual unsettlement, incessant alarms from without, incessant rumours of change within—all eagerly seized upon and exaggerated by the European, and especially the French Press," which, as within the "internationalized" sphere of Egyptian life, lay entirely beyond the control of the Government.

Nor were the "dim common populations"— the men for whose rescue and redemption, if for anybody's, the English in Egypt were toiling at their seemingly desperate undertaking—any better satisfied. They were suffering from the reaction of disappointment—from the failure of the hopes excited in their breasts during the months of revolution. For the cultivator of the Nile valley the military rebellion of Arabi had no terrors. It threatened him with nothing in his humble plot, but his creditors with much. During the brief interregnum of anarchy in 1882, the usurers to whom he was bound had mostly taken to flight. But now they were all back and insisting on the fulfilment of their legal obligations, a demand against which the Government could not have protected them even if it would, for the restoration of order had restored the authority of the Mixed Courts, and these tribunals would insist on payment in full of the fellahs' debts to these foreign creditors of his, even if his Government might have been willing to force them to accept a composition. Profound then as was the discontent of the official classes, it was not deeper—while from the greater ease of their position it was less vehement and acute— than the dissatisfaction of the fellaheen.

Even the commercial classes, such as the European traders in Alexandria, much as they owed the Power which had put down disorder and restored the reign of law and the security of property, were at this moment little better affected towards English rule. Apart from their special grievances—the delays in the payment of the Indemnities for the damages caused by the bombardment and subsequent conflagration—the continuing depression of trade had bitterly dis- appointed them. They had cherished the illusion that the mere planting of the British flag in Egypt would have given an instantaneous and most powerful stimulus to commercial enterprise, and caused an immediate influx of capital into the country. They had not realized the truth of Sir Robert Peel's often quoted observation, that " confidence is a plant of slow growth," and that capital is only another name of timidity. It did not occur to them that some time must elapse before men of reasonable prudence would be prepared to risk any large stake in a country which had only just been rescued from anarchy by the armed intervention of a European Power, whose intentions, whether of continued occupation or of more or less sudden departure, were from year to year, if not from month to month, uncertain. And without this large influx of fresh capital which was not forthcoming, it was impossible that a country which was already taxed to the utmost of its taxable capacity, and whose material wealth had so greatly declined through the neglect by a long-embarrassed Government of those great Public Works which are the main factors in its fertility, should as a whole be prosperous.

Such was the condition of the country over which Sir Evelyn Baring was, not nominally indeed or formally, but in a very real and practical sense, appointed to preside ; and such were the formidable difficulties with which at this very outset of his consular career he had to grapple. True to his instincts as a financier and to the principles above laid down by him for the guidance of our policy in Egypt, his first attack was upon the problem of Egyptian finance; but in this very process he found himself called upon, as we have seen, to take a step which to any financier would have been most distasteful, and which, to a man who was a financier and nothing else, would have been impossible. In the very act of proposing the large loan which was necessary to restore financial equilibrium to the bankrupt country, he was confronted with, and he manfully recognized, the necessity of drawing upon its heavily-burdened Exchequer for that "irrigation million," which was employed, as related in a previous chapter, with such magically reviving effects upon the prosperity of the country.

Nevertheless for some time to come the principal part of Baring's work—a part so great indeed as almost to divert his energies exclusively into that one channel—consisted, as he had virtually predicted, in the stern supervision of Egyptian finance. Two or three annual Budgets had to be framed, and the expenditure of two or three years had to be provided for, before the stability of Egyptian solvency could be regarded as assured; and it was only through the inflexible firmness of the control exercised by Baring during these years in the face of the most powerful native opposition, and at the cost of the sharpest diplomatic conflict, that the haunting spectre of bankruptcy was finally laid. What made his task in this respect so extraordinarily difficult was the fact that every step in his progress with it generated continually increasing friction between him and the ablest of Egyptian statesmen—Nubar Pasha. The abilities, and indeed the patriotism of this eminent man—if the latter quality can be predicated of an Armenian Christian administering an alien country of the Mahommedan faith—are admitted on all hands ; but his temperament, his training, and the peculiar bent of his political genius alike unfitted him to acquiesce in the limitations which British tutelage imposed upon the exercise of his power. A reformer at heart, he was too sagacious not to recognize the immense advantage which the presence of the English gave to the cause of reform. But though he was in sympathy with our spirit, he could not bring himself to love our methods. No financier himself, he chafed against the restraints which the British Minister of Finance—Sir Edgar Vincent—with the loyal support of the Consul-General, was obliged to impose upon his administrative projects. "Fully recognizing the necessity of British troops, he was doubtful about the utility of British officials. 'I am in favour of the Occupation,' he was in the habit of saying, 'but not of the Administrative Occupation.'" What he wanted, as Sir Alfred Milner acutely remarks, "was our support without our guidance."

Clearly, however, he could not have the one without the other. The principle laid down in the memorable despatch of Lord Granville still held good. The responsibility which for the time rested on England still "obliged Her Majesty's Government to insist on the adoption of the policy which they recommended"; and in the last resort it would still be "necessary that those Ministers and Governors who do not follow this course should cease to hold their offices." It was or might have been foreseen from the first that if Nubar Pasha, able and well-intentioned as he was, was ever to change his attitude of passive obstruction for one of active resistance to British policy, this alternative of *se soumettre ou se démettre* would at once arise.

It has been said that it was the methods rather than the aims of British administration which were distasteful to him, and one of his main objections to these methods arose from the fact that they occasionally scandalized him by their irregularity. The objection may seem strange enough in an Oriental statesman, but Nubar had been brought up, in common indeed with many of his subordinates, in the pedantic school of French bureaucracy, and was imbued with its traditions. It was this which brought him into collision with the Director of the Irrigation System, Sir Colin Scott Moncrieff. His Gallic leanings towards excessive centralization were offended by the large freedom of hand which had been allowed to the English local inspectors of irrigation, and he pressed for the imposition of greater Ministerial restraint on their executive powers. Sir Colin Scott Moncrieff, however, wisely refused to make any concessions on this point to the Egyptian Prime Minister. He saw that unless these officers were allowed considerable liberty of action, unless they were clothed with authority to decide for themselves in urgent cases, and to give prompt effect to their decisions, it would be impossible for them to discharge their duties efficiently. And, indeed, it must be clear even to those not specially conversant with the matter, that if every landholder threatened with the deprivation of his unjust privileges in the matter of water supply could have delayed justice by an appeal to a Ministerial Department in Cairo, the great end of equitable distribution, which the inspectors were appointed to secure, would in many cases never have been attained at all.

Nubar's differences, however, with Sir Colin Scott Moncrieff were of a slight and transient character as compared with the sharp and standing conflict in which he was involved with his English Financial Adviser. And not with him alone, but rather with the whole body of European counsellors who were associated with him. This body, the Committee of Finance, which was called into existence early in 1884, consisted of, besides the Finance Minister, two Englishmen, an Austrian, and a Frenchman, and was a very potent instrument for the restraint of arbitrary expenditure. It contained the highest financial authorities in the country, and was representative of all that was most respectable and influential in the European official world. If the Finance Committee protested against any new item of expenditure as extravagant and unnecessary, it was very difficult for the Council of Ministers to overrule its decisions, and supported by it Sir Edgar Vincent's recommendations became practically decrees.

The divergence of view between him and the Prime Minister was radical and fundamental, and went down to the very roots of financial policy. It was indeed little less than a difference of opinion as to whether the solvency of Egypt in the years 1885 to 1887 was or was not assured. Vincent held the affirmative of this proposition,

Nubar the negative. The former believed that she could pay her way on the basis provided by the Convention of London, the latter held that she could not. The English Financial Adviser was persuaded that when the two years relief granted to the country by that Convention, in the form of a slight reduction of interest on her debt, expired, she would be able to resume and to continue payment in full to her creditors. The Prime Minister was convinced that this was impossible, and that at the close of this period Egypt would once more have to appeal to the Powers as a bankrupt, "on her own petition," so to speak, and apply for a revision of the arrangement. Neither of them, it may be, deprecated this contingency less earnestly than the other. It was simply that the Egyptian Minister took a more desponding view of the future than his English colleague, and being more tenacious of his opinion on this point than his judgment on financial matters warranted, he thought himself justified in opposing economies which could only operate to check the beneficent work of administrative reform, without eventually staving off the inevitable future of financial collapse. Vincent, on the other hand, perceived that the difficulties which caused Nubar to despair were, though formidable in their dimensions, essentially temporary in their character. For the moment Egypt was still suffering from the accumulated effects of a series of disasters—the rebellion, the destruction of Alexandria, the cholera, the loss of the Soudan. But if she could only tide over the effects of these calamities, her great recuperative powers, and the large reinforcement of them which was to be expected from Sir Evelyn Baring's judicious outlay on Public Works, would render her future financial position secure.

Animated by these convictions, the Financial Adviser applied himself vigorously to the work of retrenchment, and by exercise of the severest economy he succeeded in resuming the full payment of interest in 1887. The sacrifices, however, which this policy compelled him to demand from Nubar Pasha were felt by that Minister as intolerably irksome. He resented being compelled to refuse the money for which, in the name of efficiency and improvement, the different departments were clamouring. He had the Oriental magnate's contempt for small savings and his toleration for little jobs. On the other hand, he was especially desirous of effecting an immediate reduction of the land-tax, which not only pressed heavily on the fellah, but cut deeply into the income of his own—the landowning—class.

Moreover, it would have been a policy as

popular as Vincent's remorseless cheeseparing was unpopular; and popularity was a commodity with which the Egyptian Premier, associated as he was with the abandonment of the Soudan and the "bad times" which had followed it, could hardly afford to dispense with. Why should his natural wish to acquire it be thwarted by an English financier's insistence on a policy which in Nubar's opinion could only avail to postpone, and was powerless to avert, the evil day? Why should he continue to make himself odious by pinching and screwing on the expenditure of a nation which after all would sooner or later have to make another composition with its creditors? Under the influence of the irritation which these to him unanswerable questions excited in his mind, he drifted at last into an attitude of fixed hostility to the Financial Adviser. And to assume this attitude towards the Financial Adviser was to assume it towards the Consul-General; for Baring had full confidence in Sir Edgar Vincent, and the policy which Vincent was carrying out was, as has been seen, identical with that which Baring had represented to the English Government as indispensable to the rescue of Egypt. He accordingly supported Vincent in his struggle with Nubar with that quiet firmness which is part of his nature, and thereby came soon to be regarded by the Prime Minister with the same feelings of bitter dislike which he cherished towards the Financial Adviser.

In the year 1887 matters came to a crisis. Nubar found his position no longer endurable, and resolved upon a bold stroke for liberty. On the ostensible plea that it was necessary for him to obtain the assent of the Powers to certain administrative reforms, he visited England in the hope of inducing the English Government to free Egypt from what he described as the intolerable domination of the Financial Adviser and the British Consul-General. Possibly he may have hoped something from the recent change of Government in the country. Baring's, it may have occurred to him, was a Gladstonian appointment, and a Unionist Government which had just been returned to power with an overwhelming majority, might not be displeased at an opportunity for substituting " their own man." Such a calculation would be eminently likely to commend itself to an Oriental politician partially, but not thoroughly, acquainted with the English party system, and therefore unaware that there is still one department of our policy which English statesmen, and especially English Conservative statesmen, have always striven to keep outside the sphere of its pernicious influence. Nubar in all probability did not fully realize the strength of the obligation incumbent on any high-minded and

THE ABASSIEH BARRACKS.

From a Photograph by J. P. Sebah, of Cairo.

patriotic English Minister to extend his loyal support to any public servant of the Crown, by whatever Government appointed, who has faithfully and ably represented the nation and upheld the national interests abroad. Or if he did realize this, he overrated his own power of persuasion. Lord Salisbury upheld the Consul-General, and Nubar returned *re infectâ* to Egypt.

When relations are thus strained to breaking-point, the final rupture cannot be long delayed. Early in the following year it happened. The death of Baker Pasha had created a vacancy in the office of Chief of the Police, and Nubar seized the opportunity of proposing such a reorganization of the force as would enable him to get rid of the English officers. The police were once more to be placed entirely under the Mudirs, even for purposes of discipline, and the central office at Cairo was to be abolished. To this proposal, however, Sir Evelyn Baring opposed an inflexible resistance. He insisted, and rightly, that whatever changes might be introduced into the organization of the police, an Englishman should again be appointed to the chief command.

The struggle between the Consul-General and the Prime Minister was sharp but short. Nubar, relying upon the Khedive's special need of his services at a juncture when the intrigues of Ismail

Pasha at Constantinople were causing no little alarm and uneasiness to his son and successor, threw himself upon Tewfik's support, and at first found an ally in his master. The Khedive was assured that, if only the Egyptian Government took up a firm enough attitude in the matter, the British Government would throw over its representative ; and the Prime Minister seconded these assurances by despatching an agent to London on his own account to make express complaint of Baring's conduct as tending to reduce the Khedive to a nonentity, and to render British influence unpopular. The result of this singular but not unimportant little conflict is related by the author of *England in Egypt* as follows :—

"It was a last trump, boldly played, but it failed to win the game. The British Government saw through the manœuvre. It knew its agent too well to suspect him of any leaning to excessive meddlesomeness. It had too much reason to be grateful for the skill and patience with which he had so far steered his way through the maze of Egyptian politics to dream of sacrificing him. Nubar's emissary met with no better success at the Foreign Office than Nubar himself. A strong hint was given to the ruler of Egypt that if he expected England to support him against external enemies, he must listen to English advice on vital questions of internal policy. And the warning had its effect. The Khedive saw that in siding with his Minister he was running into the very danger from which he had looked to that Minister to protect him. The fact once realized, the choice was made. The question of the command of the police was without more delay decided in accordance with the views of Sir Evelyn Baring."

More, however, was decided than the command of the police. The incident had constituted, if not the first, at any rate the most significant and conspicuous application of the principle enunciated by Lord Granville at the time of and with reference to the abandonment of the Soudan, namely, that in all important matters the advice given by the British Government must be followed.

Nubar's defeat was fatal to him. It did not, indeed, destroy his official life at once, but it wounded his authority to the death. Though he remained in office yet another year, he never recovered his position and prestige; and in June, 1888, on some minor and now forgotten question, the Khedive dismissed him. He was succeeded by Riaz Pasha, a man of not inconsiderable ability, if of somewhat less than Nubar, but in most respects his polar opposite. It will be convenient, however, to delay the course of my main narrative for a brief space in order to recount the history of a highly important episode.

The years 1885–1887 are memorable in the annals of the British occupation of Egypt as constituting a period during which that occupation came nearer to being determined than it has ever been before or since, or possibly than it ever will be again. In the summer of 1885 Lord Salisbury, who had then recently acceded to office, conceived the hope of arriving at such an understanding with Turkey as would allay the intense and growing jealousy of the Porte at our presence in Egypt, and diminish the hostility of France. It might, he thought, be possible to conclude an arrangement which, while providing for the maintenance and development of the reforms which we had set on foot, should at the same time reduce the amount and duration of British interference in the country.

In pursuance of this purpose, and also, it should be added, with the object of acknowledging the obligations of the Conservative party to one of the most energetic of its members, Sir Henry Drummond Wolff was despatched to Constantinople as Envoy Extraordinary and Minister Plenipotentiary to the Sultan, "on a special mission having reference to the affairs of Egypt," and in October, 1885, succeeded in concluding a preliminary Convention with the Turkish Foreign Minister, which was ratified in the following month by their respective Sovereigns. This Convention provided that an Ottoman and an English High Commissioner should be sent to Egypt whose business it should be, in concert with the Khedive, to reorganize the Egyptian Army, and to consider what changes might be necessary in the civil administration. The Ottoman High Commissioner was also to take counsel with the Khedive as to the best means of tranquillizing the Soudan by pacific measures, the English Commissioner being kept informed of the course of the negotiations, while any steps decided upon in this direction were to be adopted and executed in agreement with him, " as forming part of the general settlement of Egyptian affairs." But by far the most important clause of the Convention was that which stipulated that as soon as the two High Commissioners should be assured of "the security of the position, and the good working order and stability of the Egyptian Government," they should present reports to their respective Governments, who would then "consult as to the conclusion of a Convention regulating the withdrawal of the British troops from Egypt in a convenient period."

The two High Commissioners sent to Egypt under the terms of this Convention were Mukhtar Pasha on behalf of Turkey, and on behalf of England Sir Henry Drummond Wolff himself. Their joint inquiry lasted rather more than a year, at the end of which time the Turkish High Commissioner addressed a long report to his Government, while his English colleague returned home to render in person an account of his mission. In the course of the twelve months during which they had pursued their inquiries, two changes of Government and two general elections had taken place in England. Lord Salisbury's

First Administration had been ousted by an adverse vote on the Address in January, 1886; Mr. Gladstone had succeeded, had introduced and failed to carry his first Home Rule Bill, had appealed to the country with a result of overwhelming discomfiture, and Lord Salisbury was once more at the Foreign Office, as desirous as ever, apparently, for the success of the diplomatic policy which he had launched the year before. Not much had as yet been done towards its realization. A special envoy had been despatched by the Khedive to the Soudan to enter into communication with the insurgent tribes, but nothing had come of it; and beyond this and the formulation by Mukhtar Pasha of an unworkable scheme of military organization, which his British colleague had been obliged to reject, the two Commissioners had little or no fruit to show for their labours.

Above all they were no nearer to a settlement of the troublesome question as to the withdrawal of British troops, and to this the Foreign Secretary at once directed his attention. The instructions with which he once more despatched Sir Henry Drummond Wolff to Constantinople form, as has been justly said, "a landmark in our Egyptian policy no less important than Lord Granville's despatch of January 3, 1883, of which indeed they constitute the natural development." "The Sultan," wrote Lord Salisbury on January 15, 1887—

"is pressing the Government of Great Britain to name a day for the evacuation of Egypt, and on that demand he is avowedly encouraged by one, or perhaps two, of the European Powers. Her Majesty's Government have every desire to give him satisfaction upon this point, but they cannot fix even a distant date for evacuation until they are able to make provision for securing beyond that date the external and internal peace of Egypt. The object which the Powers of Europe have had in view, and which it is not less the desire of Her Majesty's Government to attain, may be generally expressed by the phrase, 'the neutralization of Egypt,' but it must be neutralization with an exception designed to maintain the security and permanence of the whole arrangement. The British Government must retain the right to guard and uphold the condition of things which will have been brought about by the military action and large sacrifices of the country. So long as the Government of Egypt maintains its position, and no disorders arise to interfere with the administration of justice or the action by the Executive Power, it is highly desirable that no soldier belonging to any foreign nation should remain upon the soil of Egypt, except when it may be necessary to make use of the land passage from one sea to another. Her Majesty's Government would willingly agree that such a stipulation should, whenever the evacuation had taken place, apply to English as much as to any other troops ; but it will be necessary to restrict this provision as far as England is concerned to periods of tranquillity. England, if she spontaneously and willingly evacuates the country, must retain a treaty right of intervention if at any time either internal peace or external security should be seriously threatened. There is no danger that a privilege so costly in its character will be used unless the circumstances imperatively demand it."

This claim of a recognized right on the part of Great Britain to defend the *régime* of her own creation does not seem a very unreasonable one, nor was it regarded as inadmissible by the Turkish Government. They consented, though not of course without a struggle, to recognize a British right of reoccupying Egypt in case of internal disturbance or external dangers ; and after four months of debate at Constantinople a definite understanding was arrived at between Sir Henry Drummond Wolff and the Turkish representatives, and embodied in a Convention signed by both parties on May 22, 1887.

According to this agreement the British troops were to be withdrawn from Egypt at the end of three years, unless at that date the appearance of external or internal dangers should necessitate the postponement of the evacuation, in which case they were to be withdrawn as soon as the danger had disappeared. Two years after their withdrawal the general supervision exercised by Great Britain over the Egyptian Army was to cease. Thenceforward Egypt was to enjoy *sûreté territoriale*, or in other words, the inviolability of Egyptian territory was to be recognized and guaranteed. Nevertheless, the Convention continued, the Imperial Ottoman Government will make use of its right of occupying Egypt militarily if there are reasons to fear an invasion from without, or if order and security in the interior were disturbed, or if the Khediviate of

Egypt refused to execute its duties towards the Sovereign Court or its International obligations.

On its side the Government of Her Britannic Majesty was authorized by the Convention to send in the above-mentioned cases troops into Egypt, which will take the measures necessary to avert these dangers. In taking such measures, the commander of these troops will act with all the regard due to the rights of the Sovereign Power.

The Ottoman troops, as well as the British troops, were to be withdrawn as soon as the causes requiring their intervention should have ceased.

A further article provided that Great Britain and Turkey should invite first the great Powers and then all the others who had made or accepted arrangement with the Khediviate of Egypt to give their adhesion to the Convention; and annexed to the main document was an important declaration by the English Plenipotentiary, that in case during the three years allowed for the withdrawal of the troops any of the great Mediterranean Powers should not have accepted the Convention, Great Britain would regard the state of things as an "external danger," justifying the postponement of the Convention.

To this Convention all the European Powers save, perversely enough, that one which is most jealous of our position, were ready to agree. France offered it a most strenuous resistance. Her Ambassador was directed to expostulate in strong and even threatening language with the Porte, and he was backed as usual by his Russian colleague. Together they worked with such effect on the mind of the Sultan that in spite of the counter advice of the representatives of Austria, Germany, and Italy, he could not be induced to ratify the Treaty which his Ministers had signed. For nearly a month after the date fixed for the ratification the British Plenipotentiary in vain awaited the return of Abdul Hamid to a wiser and more independent frame of mind ; and at last, his continued stay in Constantinople having ceased to consist with the dignity of the Government by whom he was accredited, he was, on July 15, 1887, recalled to England.

Few regrets of course were felt in this country for the failure of the Convention. An evacuation within three years would have been extremely hazardous to the peace and security of Egypt, and the further agreement that within two years thereafter all British control over the Egyptian Army should come to an end would have added materially to dangers against which our reserved power of re-entry would have but very imperfectly provided. France, even from her own suspicious and unfriendly point of view, would have done well—or so it has always struck foreign critics of her policy— to accept the Convention. But it suited her to attack and defeat an arrangement by virtue of which if it had been concluded we should have evacuated Egypt nearly seven years ago; and in so doing she has morally lost the right—-which, however, as a matter of fact she is continually claiming to exercise—of protesting against the prolongation of our stay in the country. It is as well to remind those who are apt to lend too ready an ear to French complaints on the subject, that France, and France alone, is responsible for the continuance of the British occupation. It is nearly ten years since " perfidious Albion " attempted to free herself from her entanglement in Egyptian affairs by an effort so vigorous, not to say violent, that its success would in the opinion of many high authorities have endangered the durability of her Egyptian work. In our haste to conciliate those who objected to the English scaffolding around the edifice of reform, we were prepared to run no inconsiderable risk of bringing the whole structure to the ground. That may not have been good policy, but it was certainly pretty strong evidence of good faith.

CHAPTER XII.

Reforms Accomplished

THE fate of Nubar Pasha may be said to mark the close of the first and most urgent stage of the great undertaking in which our representative in Egypt was engaged. The country was at last materially prospering. Its finances had been reduced to permanent order; the sources of its industrial wealth had been reinvigorated; its executive departments had been purified and rendered efficient; its fiscal system had been regularized and simplified, made humane and equitable; its Army had been set in the path of improvement, and was steadily developing into a trustworthy instrument of national defence; its police had been reorganized and redisciplined; and all this good work had, by Baring's firmness, been secured against any attempt to undo it. One thing more remained to be accomplished before the English guardians of Egypt were entitled to say that they had done all that could be done for their ward, and that the rest must be left to time. That one thing was the reform of the judicial tribunals.

This was also the one portion of the English work which, owing to a variety of competing circumstances—the untoward quarrels of certain English functionaries, the overwhelming pre-occupation of Baring with other and even more pressing duties, and the necessity of making some concessions to the most powerful and capable of Egyptian administrators—had been turned over to Nubar Pasha. As himself the creator of the mixed tribunals he had just pretensions to high authority, and it would have been hardly possible in the troubled days of 1884 to dispute his claim to superintend the working and determine the composition of the native courts for himself. For three years accordingly he retained the almost undivided control of the Egyptian judiciary, and the results of his management of the business proved to be profoundly unsatisfactory. At the moment which he unwisely selected to try conclusions with the British Consul-General in a pitched diplomatic battle, his failure to perform the work which he had undertaken had become conspicuous and notorious to the Egyptian, no less than the European, community. The courts were manned from top to bottom with his nominees, and when, therefore, complaints of the corruption and incapacity of the judges became general, when nothing was heard on all hands but criticisms of the cumbrous procedure of the courts, of the costliness and delay of litigation, and of the doubtful nature of the results, it was of course Nubar whom people held responsible.

Ever since the last year of his ministry the attention of the British representative and his colleagues had had to be more and more closely directed to the crying evils connected with the administration of justice, evils which arose not only from the incompetence of the native courts, but from the arbitrary proceedings of the so-called Commissions of Brigandage, which in respect of a large class of crimes had been substituted by Nubar Pasha for the regular tribunals. It was the prevalence of brigandage which had broken down the new native courts at the very outset of their career; and in 1884 and the following year first the investigation and then the actual trial of crime of this description had been taken out of the hands of these tribunals, and entrusted to special Commissions having the character and power of courts-martial. These Commissions were originally appointed for a few months only, but their powers were renewed by successive decrees, and for nearly five years they dealt with the great mass of criminal offences alike in Upper and Lower Egypt. They were not without an infusion of the judicial element, but their guiding spirit was administrative, and administrative of the Oriental type, for they were presided over by a Mudir. Moreover they were placed under the control, not of the Ministry of Justice, but of the Ministry of the Interior—of course a flagrant violation of the fundamental principle of separating the judicial from the executive power.

In October, 1887, M. Legrette, a Belgian, was appointed Procureur-General, and was authorized to institute an investigation of existing abuses. In 1888, the year of Nubar's dismissal, his inquiries bore fruit in a damning report, in which the irregularities, the injustice, and the cruelties of these tribunals were startlingly exposed. It was discovered that they had freely employed torture for obtaining evidence, that many persons had been imprisoned for years without trial, and that many others had been condemned to serve punishment on the flimsiest evidence. In one case nineteen people, all innocent, had been condemned on the evidence of a single man, who, as it subsequently turned out, had been coerced into falsely accusing himself and his associates.

Baring, of course, lost no time in pressing for the abolition of these tribunals—if tribunals they can be called; and, the new Prime Minister, Riaz

Pasha, who was at that time working fairly well with his British advisers, having yielded with some reluctance to the Consul-General's strenuous representations, in the early summer of 1889 these Commissions were suppressed.

Much more than this, however, was required to put the administration of justice in Egypt on a satisfactory footing : how much more it will need a fuller account of the Egyptian judicial system, or rather systems, to explain. For, to cite Sir Alfred Milner's admirable account of this subject, there are as many as four :—

(1) There is the old Koranic system, worked by the Mehkemehs or Courts of the Religious Law, which are now mainly confined to dealing with the personal status of Mahomedans.

(2) There is the system of the Mixed Courts, which deals with civil actions between foreigners of different nationalities, or between foreigners and natives, and in a small degree with the criminal offences of foreigners.

(3) There are the Consular Courts, which deal with the great body of foreign crime.

(4) There is the system of the new Native Courts, which deals with civil actions between natives, or with crimes committed by them.

It was practically with the Native Courts only that the English reformer was in a position to deal; for the Religious Courts are rightly regarded as institutions with which it is not advisable that Christians should meddle; the system of the Mixed Tribunals can only be modified with the unanimous consent of the fourteen Powers by which they were established; and the Consular Courts, unsatisfactory as in many respects they are, discharge a function of which they could not easily or indeed prudently be deprived, except by extending the jurisdiction of the Mixed Tribunals, or by so improving the quality of the "justice" meted out by the new Native Courts that Europeans could be fairly asked to submit themselves and their cases to them.

There remained then only the Native Courts, which had been left, as has been seen, to the control of Nubar Pasha, and with such results as have been recorded. Their signal failure to fulfil the purpose for which they were designed was only a new illustration of the very old truth that men are of more importance than machinery. *Quid sine moribus leges proficiunt*, asks the Latin poet, and the question which he then raises as to the efficacy of laws applies equally to the efficiency of law courts. On paper the native tribunals worked fairly well. Their codes and procedure were with some unimportant alterations borrowed from those of the Mixed Courts, which in their turn had been borrowed from the codes and the procedure of France. Excellently, however, as such a system might be suited to the case of a highly civilized country well equipped with all the necessary appliances and *personnel* of a complicated judicial mechanism, it was extremely ill adapted both to the requirements and to the capacities of Egypt, where the majority of the cases justiciable in the Native Courts are of a simple character, and where cheapness and expedition, unattainable under the too elaborate methods of French judicial administration, were objects of paramount importance. In a word, the system adopted by the Native Courts was at once too complex for the comprehension of the native community, and too costly for their pockets.

And it was too ambitious for the public purse. The numerical strength of the judicature was fixed absurdly high at a moment when the state of the finances was alarmingly low. It followed that the scale of the judicial salaries had to be adapted to the state of the finances, and even if the judges had been uniformly competent they would still have been exposed to the strongest temptation to become uniformly corrupt. But as a matter of fact their competency was far from uniform, as indeed may be readily imagined when we recall the fact that Egypt was called upon to man eight tribunals of First Instance with about a dozen judges each, and provide nearly twice that number for the Court of Appeal. It was ridiculous to suppose that the country could produce some six score of trained lawyers on demand, and, as might have been expected, the supply of functionaries thus qualified fell short of the demand by something like seventy-five per cent. Of the first occupants of the Native Bench only about one in four had had a regular legal training, and even of these a considerable number were lawyers in name rather than fact. Many of them had obtained their degrees from the law schools of some too easy-going university, and the smattering of jurisprudence which they brought with it ill compensated for the process of denationalization which they had undergone in acquiring it.

Moreover it is extremely doubtful whether, if there had been a sufficiency of judicial material to select from, it would have been drawn upon in fact. In the years 1883 and 1884 it was too soon to expect that appointment should be made by merit, especially in a branch of the public service which we had deliberately left to the un-controlled direction of native officials. Jobbery and nepotism are hard to suppress in practice, even in countries where they are disapproved of in theory : and in Oriental communities they are not even the objects of theoretical disapproval.

There the state of public morality in these
matters finds expression, as Sir Alfred Milner
aptly puts it, in the question : " Why on earth,
if a man is a decent person whom you like and
to whom you wish well, should you not appoint
him to any vacant post ?"

The idea of special qualification as a necessary
condition of the efficient discharge of special
duties is of comparatively recent growth even in
the West.   Neither the seed of it nor the soil for
it exists in the East.   Hence, when the Native
Courts were first constituted, "the judgeships"
were simply regarded as so many opportunities
for giving worthy people whom it was desired to
benefit a modest income.

As a first step towards the reform of this
intolerable abuse, the Consul-General proposed
to strengthen the Native Courts by increasing the
number of the European judges.   Here he found
himself confronted with more serious resistance
on the part of Riaz Pasha, but persevering in his
efforts with his usual calm tenacity he carried his
point, and in November, 1889, two additional
Englishmen were appointed to the Native Court
of Appeal, making in all three Englishmen and
three Belgians.   It soon, however, became evident
that a more radical reform was needed, and Baring
then urged the temporary appointment of an
eminent Indian judge to examine the whole

system of native jurisprudence, and to make proposals for its amendment. His recommendation was adopted, and in the spring of 1890 Mr. (now Sir John) Scott, a judge of the High Court of Bombay, came to Egypt to advise on the question, his appointment being in the first instance limited to one year.

At the end of 1890 Mr. Scott presented his report, in which he suggested a number of important changes in the constitution of the Courts, insisting especially on the necessity of a great improvement in their *personnel*. This proposal had the effect of stimulating Riaz Pasha's dissatisfaction to the fighting point. The Minister of Justice was inspired by him to draft a memorandum condemning Mr. Scott's recommendations from beginning to end. This step was obviously meant, and was promptly taken, as a declaration of war. Baring at once perceived that the whole question of reform or no reform in the native administration of justice was at issue, and, acting under instructions from home, he pressed more energetically than ever for the adoption of Mr. Scott's scheme, and for the appointment of its author to direct its application.

Upon this, history repeated itself. Riaz, like Nubar before him, turned at once to the Khedive and endeavoured to enlist him on the side of resistance. But Tewfik Pasha's attitude on this occasion was determined by the consideration expressed in the homely formula, "Once bit, twice shy." He had no mind to expose himself to a second rebuff from Downing Street, and as soon as he perceived that the consequence threatened he drew back. Mr. Scott's recommendations were accepted, and he himself appointed to a permanent post; and Riaz Pasha, like his predecessor, had to submit to a defeat which proved politically fatal. The relations between him and the Khedive became strained, and in May, 1891, on the plea of ill health, he resigned his office.

The reforms which he had resisted were now put in hand, and in the course of the few years that have since elapsed have virtually transformed the judicial system of Egypt. Had the matter been *res integra* the scheme of reorganization would probably have followed the lines of the Indian system, which has been proved by experience to be so well suited to the requirements of needy litigants, and the trial of what are in most instances simple causes. The Egyptian codes and procedure were, however, in existence; the native judicial body knew how to work with them, and with no other; the people were accustomed to them. It was wisely resolved, therefore, to proceed by way of improvement only, and not by way of demolition and reconstruction. Legal procedure had been slow, dear, and, as regards the redress of trifling injuries, inaccessible in a great measure to the majority of the people. To remedy these defects the number of judges which once formed the quorum in a multitude of cases, whether civil or criminal, has been reduced, and the system of summary justice extended ; for the five judges who were formerly necessary to construct a Court, whether of Appeal or First Instance, three have in almost all cases been now substituted. On the other hand, instead of there being only one judge of summary jurisdiction attached to each tribunal, there are now more than twenty employed throughout the country, and these are ambulatory instead of stationary. so that petty suits and offences can be dealt with on the spot. Their jurisdiction extends to all misdemeanours and to all civil actions not in- volving a sum of more than £100. An appeal lies from these single judges to a Three-judge Court at the respective tribunals of First Instance, where judgment on all misdemeanours and all the civil suits triable by a single judge is final. The general effect of these changes has been to expedite the action of the law, to economize the time of the judges and the money of the suitors, and to reserve the full strength of the highest Court for really important questions.

By extending the system of summary jurisdiction, however, and by reducing the number of judges sitting in each Court, an increased weight of responsibility is necessarily thrown on individual judges, and concurrently, therefore, with the reorganization of the Courts it became essential to improve the *personnel* of the judicial body. A considerable proportion of the old judges were pensioned off, and their places filled by men of upright character and of adequate legal training. A Commission of Superintendence was also established, consisting of three European members, who with the aid of three native inspectors examine the records of a certain number of cases decided by the Summary Court and Courts of First Instance. It does not usurp the functions of a Court of Appeal, and has no power to revise decisions. But to quote the most accurate description of it, it "calls the attention of individual judges to any flagrant errors which they may have committed, and at the same time it issues general circulars, containing explanations and instructions on important points of law and practice, on which from an examination of cases it appears that the judges in general have a special tendency to go wrong."

There is no denying that the very conception of a Commission appointed to "instruct" and keep in order a body of the judges is violently repugnant to the mind of the Western lawyer, and it is not surprising that the institution should have been severely criticized on its first creation. Nor is it quite successfully defended by its ablest apologist, who describes its method of supervision as "analogous to the inspecting powers possessed by the High Courts in India"; for the fact that in the latter case the inspectors are themselves judicial officers of a higher grade than the inspected, and are therefore only informally exercising the corrective authority which belongs to their regular jurisdiction, strikes at the very root of the alleged analogy. It would be better to seek the justification for the Commission not in principle, but in practice. It is stated to have proved a great success, not only in ensuring uniformity of action on the part of the Courts, but in promoting the zeal and efficiency of the judicial staff.

Curiously enough, however, it is not so much these Oriental tribunals as those latest products of Occidental (or Occidentalized-Eastern) statesmanship — the mixed tribunals — which have most recently attracted distrustful attention, and the working of which gives ground in one respect at least for somewhat grave anxiety. It is not, to do them justice, that they have in any degree disappointed expectations as to their judicial efficiency for the disposal of ordinary litigious business, involving no international jealousies.

The serious question which has arisen in regard to them is connected not with the legal but with the political aspect of their jurisdiction, and has indeed only illustrated the striking accuracy of the final criticism with which Sir Alfred Milner closes his account of them. The creation, he remarks, "of the mixed tribunals certainly tended to improve the administration of justice, but it evidently did not simplify the political constitution of Egypt. . . . They might nominally be the Courts of the Khedive, who appointed their foreign members, although on the proposal of the Powers. But they were in reality foreign Courts, deriving their authority from outside, and they have not hesitated to exercise that authority against the native Government whenever they thought it right to do so. . . . Judicially far better, they are at the same time politically far more formidable, than the authorities whom they have supplanted."

The collision between the Egyptian Government and the Caisse de la Dette has been noticed in an earlier page of this volume, as well as the method by which the quarrel was prevented from being pushed to extremities. It may be remembered that the Commissioners actually obtained judgment against the Government from the mixed tribunals through a Court of First Instance, and that the appeal against that decision, which would in all probability have been sustained in a higher Court, was only not proceeded with because in the meantime the Convention of London, concluded by the Powers in March, 1885, deprived the dispute between the Caisse and the Government of any practical importance. By a singular revolution of the wheel of fortune the successful plaintiff in that case has since become an unsuccessful defendant before the very same tribunals; and inasmuch as it has raised the question as to the extent of their competency and jurisdiction in an acute form, and in a connection with very grave issues of English and Egyptian policy, a brief reference should be made to it in this place.

When the recent advance upon Dongola had been determined on, the British Government, after taking the precaution of ascertaining that a majority of the Commissioners regarded the application as legitimate, and were prepared to assent to it, applied to the Caisse for an advance of £500,000 from the Reserve Fund, in order to meet the charges for the expedition. Four out of the six of the representatives of the Great Powers on this body gave their sanction, two only, the French and Russian Commissioners, withholding theirs. Nobody doubted then or now that the refusal of their assent was dictated

by political considerations, nor indeed would it
be easy to suggest any reason which would even
plausibly connect it with the interests of Egypt
herself. The Commission of the Caisse were
specially authorized to devote from time to time,
on the application of the Egyptian Government,
a portion of the Reserve Fund to meeting any
extraordinary expenditure which might be
required by that Government beyond the
ordinary expenses of the year. The majority of
the Commissioners held that the expedition to
Dongola was included among the purposes for
which such extraordinary expenditure might
properly be incurred; and assuredly if there is
any form of undertaking in which a Government
may be said to have a legitimate interest, one
might suppose it to be that of recovering a
lost and fertile province, together with the natural
wealth contained in its soil and the revenues
therefrom. One thing at any rate is clear, that
whether the expenditure in question was or was
not rightly included in this category, there was
not a human being in Cairo or elsewhere who
ever imagined that the decision of the majority
of the Caisse thereon was otherwise than final.
Many other questions had before this been decided
by a majority and action taken on the decision;
nor indeed was it less than preposterous to
suppose that when the Commission was estab-

lished by the decree of 1876 the Powers could have intended that it should be absolutely incapable of doing anything unless the whole of its members, representing in some instances the keen rivalries of European States, were absolutely unanimous.

Nevertheless, it was the operation of just one of those rivalries which prompted the attempt —unfortunately successful—to establish this intolerable situation by judicial decree. Certain Egyptian bondholders were moved to take proceedings against the Commissioners of the Caisse as for a breach of the Law of Liquidation by diverting the funds entrusted to them from the purposes to which they were confined, under the terms of that arrangement; and judgment went against the defendants in the Court of First Instance. An appeal was of course taken, but in the Appellate Court of the mixed tribunals the decision was confirmed. The preliminary contention of the Commission of course was, that a decision of the majority of their body was binding upon the remainder; but the Court acted apparently upon the view that the terms of the Law of Liquidation of 1880—differing in this respect, and differing, as was alleged, by the intention of the framers, from the decree of 1876 —vested separate rights of action in each Commissioner. That this assumed intention did not exist has been placed beyond doubt by the testimony of Lord Cromer himself, who himself took part in drawing up the Law of Liquidation, and who has stated that to his own knowledge the difference of the terms in which the power of the Commissioners are respectively described in the two documents was a mere accidental difference of drafting, and that it was not in the least designed by the authors of the law of 1880 to give to individual Commissioners any further or other powers than they possessed under the decree of 1876.

The point, however, is not of capital importance, since it is not clear from the decision of the Appellate Courts that its judges would not in any case have claimed to deal with the whole question on the merits, and to determine whether the advance of the money was or was not one made for a legitimate purpose, and within the competence of the Commissioners of the Debt to sanction. And of course if this is the extent of the tribunal's arrogation of jurisdiction, the unanimity or otherwise of the Commission, and the ability or inability of the majority to bind the minority, become immaterial points. It is enough that in the judgment as it stands the mixed tribunals have asserted a right not merely to decide questions of policy (for this it might indirectly become their duty to do in the regular discharge of their functions—as for instance, in their judgment in favour of the Caisse and against the Government with reference to the Northbrook financial *coup d'état*), but to decide them in a sense directly contrary to that of the body specially entrusted with jurisdiction over them by agreement of the Great Powers. The situation was thus described by Sir Michael Hicks-Beach in the House of Commons : " Here," he said, " was a Reserve Fund which at the time of the Dongola Expedition amounted to £2,750,000. A considerable part of it was not needed for any other purpose. It had been accumulated by the wise financial administration of the Egyptian Government acting under our advice. Its very existence was due to no other cause. The Egyptian Government decided that it was necessary that part of the fund should be applied to the cost of the Dongola Expedition. We who are responsible after all for the safety of Egypt —a responsibility which no other Power shares with us in any measure at all—we supported the view of the Egyptian Government ; but the whole thing is overturned and set aside by the verdict of the Mixed Court of Appeal."

The Court, by the way, was not very well " mixed," for it contained no representative either of Austria or of Great Britain—the last certainly by no means an unimportant ingredient in that particular judicial salad—and the decision, being given by a Bench equally divided in opinion, only operated in favour of the plaintiff by virtue of a rule, admittedly only of custom and not of law, whereby the opinion of the division which contains a majority of European judges is allowed to prevail. This very "prerogative," however, only brings into stronger relief the absurdity of a system which carefully provides for the representation of every one of the six Powers in the Commission appointed to determine questions of financial policy, and then permits its decisions to be overruled by a Court in which two of these Powers are without voice or vote.

It will at all events not surprise anybody that the Chancellor of the Exchequer should have added a strong expression of his opinion that when next year the time arrives at which the constitution and the powers of these Mixed Courts have to be reconsidered, "a very grave question ought to and must arise as to what shall be their powers and authority in the future, and whether they shall be allowed in this way to interfere in affairs which have been deliberately entrusted by the Great Powers to another tribunal altogether." Perhaps, however, the foregoing proposition that this announcement will not surprise anybody is a little too broadly stated. It should have been said that it would surprise nobody save those who, like Sir William Harcourt, were under the impression that a sort of halo of international sacrosanctity surrounded these same mixed tribunals. Such an impression, it is true, is more easily to be excused to the "man in the street" than to the member of a Government which actually did, and did more than once, what Sir Michael Hicks-Beach only suggested the advisability of doing. Yet that, unfortunately for the statesman, is in fact the difference between him and his fellow-critics of the Opposition. The exact state of the case, and the precise status of the Court, have been explained with a lucidity so helpful to the public, if so cruel to Sir William Harcourt, by the well-known correspondent of the *Times* who signs himself "A Twenty Years Resident in Egypt," that the following extract from one of his letters will probably dispel any lingering misconceptions on the subject :—

"The mixed tribunals were instituted by the Egyptian Government, not only without pressure from Europe, but in spite of the opposition of many Powers—notably France. They were instituted in order to do away with the existing Consular Courts. One of the first Powers to agree was Great Britain. The last great Power to come into the agreement was France, and she only joined when she found that it was going to be effected without her.

"It is important to bear in mind that it was not a concession extracted from Egypt by the Powers, but one extracted from the Powers by Egypt, and which Egypt had the technical right to relinquish by simple decree abolishing the Courts and returning to the Consular system.

"But every Power had the same right, for the French Government, opposed from the first to the tribunals, made an important proviso applicable to any other Power, that if the result of the experience was not satisfactory, she reserved the right of returning to the old system without waiting for the termination of the experimental period of five years.

"At the expiration of the first five years—1880 or 1881—the British Government desired a certain revision of the powers of the tribunals, and not obtaining it, only consented to renew for one year. This yearly renewal went on for two or three years, until the British Government, having obtained a part of what it asked, the five years arrangements began again."

So much for the absurd charge against the Chancellor of the Exchequer of the present Administration of having used "language of menace and defiance" in merely suggesting that Great Britain should exercise the right, expressly reserved to each one of the Powers, of examining the operation of the judicature to which she, like all the others, only provisionally assented ; and of making a renewal of that assent conditional on the removal of the grave political inconveniences and anomalies which have arisen from their interpretation of their judicial powers. Of these powers, and of those also of the Caisse de la Dette, the writer above quoted remarks with much pertinence, that "they were conferred when Egypt was financially and morally bankrupt." The arrangements then made " to control a bankrupt and corrupt despot are wholly inapplicable to the present situation in Egypt, and unless considerable modification is made, some means will have to be found for terminating the existence of the mixed tribunals established by Khedivial decree in 1875–76."

To anybody indeed but a political partisan or a legal pedant—or what is perhaps more common than either, a politician affecting the legal pedant in order to disguise the political partisan—the situation disclosed by this incident must appear plainly intolerable. On one side a Board of Commissioners, originally instituted only to protect the interests of the public creditor, but now virtually clothed with full power to control the whole financial policy of Egypt, yet with its omnipotence converted into impotence by the theory that each one of its members possesses that *liberum veto* which rendered the old Polish Diet the laughing-stock of the world: on the other side a tribunal which, if the Board were to recover its omnipotence by unanimity, could at pleasure reduce it again to impotence by an adverse decree. To pretend that that state of things is too sacred to be meddled with is simply ridiculous. Why, if it were to be discovered any day in this country that the judges of the High Court had judicially declared it to be within their jurisdiction to examine, say, the financial provisions embodied in a Budget Bill, and to pronounce them invalid, it may be safely said that, with all our reverence for the constitution, and jealous respect for the independence of the judiciary, we should not be long in legislating to curtail their powers. The Egyptian Mixed Tribunals are practically asserting the same sort of political authority as belongs under the American Constitution to the Supreme Court of the United States. And a Supreme Court of this description has to be deliberately created : no nation would allow it to come into existence by accident.

CHAPTER XIII.

The New Khedive

IN 1892 Sir Evelyn Baring was raised to the peerage under the title of Lord Cromer, and in the same year occurred the untimely death of Tewfik Pasha and the descent of the Khediviate to his son. Successions in Oriental countries are very often ticklish affairs. They are sometimes preceded by a murder and occasionally followed by an insurrection; while even in the case of States under Western tutelage they are not infrequently fraught with trouble and anxiety to the protecting Power. The succession of Prince Abbas Helmy had disturbing consequences of this description for the British Government. Tewfik's successor was a youth of eighteen, of unknown temperament and tendencies, and whose policy, therefore, it was impossible to forecast. That he had received a European education was a circumstance on which conjectures of a very diverse character might with equal plausibility be founded. It is possible, as our experience with the Indian Babu has too often proved, to occidentalize an Oriental without making anything better than an

inferior European. To acquire the enlightenment
of the West may mean no more than indoctrin-
ation with those Western ideas and theories which
are least susceptible of safe application to the
government of Eastern States. In the case of
the young Khedive, moreover, a European meant
a Continental education, and there is hardly any
Continental school to which one would by
preference send an Egyptian Prince on whom it
were desired to impress correct views as to the
relation of his native country to the British
Power. Whether the ideas he was actually found
to hold on this subject were imbibed by him
abroad or at home, before or after his accession
to the Khediviate, it is impossible to say; but
what is certain is that his behaviour during
the earliest days of his rule must have been
suggested, if it were the result of suggestion at
all, from a quarter unfriendly to ourselves and
to our authority in Egypt.

During the later months of 1892 there were
many indications of coming trouble, but it was
not till January of the following year that Abbas
declared war, so to speak, with the British
Government. On the 15th of that month he
suddenly startled the world by dismissing the
Prime Minister, Mustapha Fehmy, an adviser who
enjoyed the entire confidence of the Consul-
General and the Anglo-Egyptian officials as a

THE KHEDIVE.

From a Photograph by J. Heyman, of Cairo.

body, and by appointing Fakhri Pasha Prime
Minister in his place.   At that time, as had been
the case just ten years before, Mr. Gladstone was
at the Treasury ; but fortunately Lord Granville
was not at the Foreign Office.   His successor
was a Minister who had already shown a firm
grasp of affairs abroad and a high courage in
dealing with them, and he had entered this
particular Cabinet on terms which allowed him
exceptional freedom of hand.

With what admirable promptitude and decision
he met the crisis even the Blue Book—that grave
of all that is dramatic in diplomacy—cannot
wholly conceal.   The story indeed might almost
be left to tell itself in the series of telegrams
which flashed backwards and forwards between
the Foreign Office in London and the British
Agency in Cairo during these two or three
momentous January days.   For another reason,
too, the despatches deserve to be set out in full,
as showing incidentally how little this dispute was
sought by the British Government, and how
absurd therefore were the French insinuations that
we had fixed a *querelle d'Allemand* on the young
Khedive.   This is proved by a despatch from
Lord Cromer under date of December 19, 1892,
wherein, in view of the then serious illness of
Mustapha Pasha Fehmy and the possibility that
a successor to him might have to be appointed,

the Consul-General telegraphs : " I do not think it will become necessary for me to interfere directly, and unless the Khedive should wish to make any highly objectionable appointment, I propose standing aloof as much as possible." This attitude was formally approved by Lord Rosebery, and when Tigrane Pasha's appointment was proposed by the Khedive some days later, Lord Cromer, although the project met, he says, with a very unfavourable reception both from the English officials and the nation generally, contented himself with "discouraging the idea" on the ground that he considered it "advisable that the Prime Minister should under present circumstances be a Mahomedan." In this also the Foreign Secretary concurred; but with the recovery of Mustapha Fehmy the question of course dropped, only, however, to be renewed a fortnight later, when the state of Mustapha's health was put forward by the Khedive as a pretext for his evidently premeditated *coup*. The gravity of this move, and of the further action which it foreshadowed, was instantly discerned by the watchful eyes of our Agent at Cairo, who thus telegraphed without a moment's delay to Downing Street :—

" The last time I saw the Khedive it was fully understood that as Mustapha Pasha Fehmy was recovering there was no longer any question of naming another Prime Minister. This morning the Khedive's Private Secretary came to inform me that Mustapha Pasha Fehmy was dismissed and Fakhri Pasha named in his place. He was formerly Minister of Justice and was dismissed on my advice, as he was unfavourable to judicial reform. I have seen the Khedive. He bases the change on the argument that Mustapha Pasha Fehmy's state of health will not allow him to take up his work for some long while. There is no reason why he should be absent for more than six weeks. The intention to make the change is generally known, but the Khedive has promised me to stop the issue of any official notification till I could communicate with your Lordship. I beg to refer to Lord Granville's despatch of 4th January, 1884, on the subject of English advice being followed while the occupation lasts. The action of the Khedive must change the whole situation, both of the British Government and the English officials, and great trouble will ensue.

"The Khedive also wishes to change the Ministers of Finance and Justice. To these changes I would offer no objection. I wish to impress very strongly on Her Majesty's Government the importance of the present question."

The spirit of the new appointment, that of a Minister who had actually been dismissed by the Consul-General's advice, was unmistakable. It was and could only be meant as a deliberate affront to Lord Cromer, and, through him, to the British Government. The Foreign Secretary's telegraphic reply was prompt and decisive :—

"Her Majesty's Government expect to be consulted in such important matters as a change of Ministers. No change appears to be at present either necessary or peremptory. We cannot therefore sanction the proposed nomination of Fehmy Pasha."

On the day of the despatch of this telegram

another and still graver communication was received from Lord Cromer in these words :—

"I hear rumours from a fairly good source that if the Khedive is successful in the present undertaking the next step will be a wholesale dismissal of English officials. The latter, acting on my instructions, have declined to recognize new Minister pending receipt of instructions from London."

The Consul-General lost no time in acting on the Foreign Secretary's despatch. He called on Abbas Pasha the next morning, and thus reports the result of his interview :—

"I have seen the Khedive, and given him a copy of your Lordship's telegram dated yesterday. In doing so I said that in the event of his agreeing to reinstate Mustapha Pasha Fehmy as Prime Minister no objection would be offered to the proposed changes as regards the Departments of Finance and Justice. In the contrary event I must reserve the liberty of action of Her Majesty's Government as regards all these Ministers. I said I did not think it would be just of me to press him for an immediate answer, and that unless he sent for me at an earlier date I would call to-morrow morning to hear his answer. I added that it was not yet too late to yield, and that I earnestly hoped he would do so, as otherwise affairs might become more serious and complicated. The Khedive said nothing from which I could gather probable nature of his reply."

To this Lord Rosebery instantly made answer :—

"Your Lordship should inform the Khedive, in case of his refusing to take your advice, that His Highness must be prepared to take the grave consequences of his act, and that you must at once refer to Her Majesty's Government for instructions."

As usual at the acutest stage of an Egyptian crisis France intervened, and the Foreign Secretary soon found himself in the favourite attitude of the British sailor in the palmy days of nautical drama—the central figure in a "combat of three." He had to keep a tight hold of the young Khedive with one hand, while he parried the thrusts of M. Waddington with the other. Thus he writes to Lord Dufferin :—

"The French Ambassador inquired to-day about the recent proposed change of Ministry in Egypt and its causes.

"As to the facts, I told him that I could give him no more information than was in the papers, except that we had presented our formal protest against the appointment of the new Prime Minister.

"M. Waddington intimated that our course of action appeared to indicate that we claimed the right to nominate the Prime Minister ourselves. I said that that was not the way in which I should put the matter, but we did claim the right to give authoritative advice in conformity with the terms of Lord Granville's despatch of the 4th January, 1884, as to the choice of Ministers. Indeed, so long as the British flag was there and the British forces were in occupation it would not be possible for us to allow the whole Administration, beginning at the top, to be reversed at the mere whim of the Khedive. The situation was undoubtedly grave, and I trusted that the Khedive would be brought to a more reasonable frame of mind without further measures.

"The Ambassador then said he had received a despatch stating that in conversation the Khedive had stated that when there was a question of nominating a successor to Mustapha Pasha Fehmy, then at the point of death, Lord Cromer had refused the sanction of Her Majesty's Government to the appointment of any Christian Prime Minister. I expressed my belief that Lord Cromer had used no such general expression.

"The French Government, M. Waddington went on to say, believed that the Khedive had been moved to this serious action by irritation at hearing that Lord Cromer had assured Mustapha Pasha Fehmy of his support, even against the Khedive, his master.

"I rejoined that I was not aware of this report, which was probably due to mere exaggeration by some members of the Khedive's Court."

The rumoured incidents at the interview which preceded the surrender of the Khedive will be referred to hereafter. In the official account of it Lord Cromer telegraphs that " His Highness expressed his regret at occurrence of recent incident, and pointed out that it would humiliate him and make him lose all his authority in the country if he were obliged to reinstate Mustapha Pasha Fehmy." He suggested the compromise of his being allowed to nominate Riaz Pasha in his place — a proposal which was accepted by Lord Cromer, whose assent to it was duly ratified by the British Government.

But it would be unjust to the brilliant Statesman who then presided at the Foreign Office, and who dealt so vigorously with this anxious crisis, to close the narrative without reporting the last and neatest passage of arms between him and M. Waddington. Thus he describes it to our representative in Paris :—

"At a further interview with the French Ambassador to-day His Excellency stated that he was instructed by his

Government to lay a formal protest against the action taken by Lord Cromer with regard to the nomination of Fakhri Pasha as Prime Minister in Egypt. What the French Government chiefly objected to was the high-handed nature of the proceeding. It amounted to this, that the Khedive was not to appoint any Minister, except at the goodwill and pleasure of the British Government. Such an event was unprecedented in the history of the British occupation. It went, in the opinion of the French Government, far beyond the terms of Lord Granville's despatch, and would, His Excellency feared, be taken throughout Europe, as in France, to be a long step in the direction of actual annexation.

"As regards the nature of the proceeding, I said in my reply to M. Waddington that I was aware that there had been some high-handedness; but that it had been on the part of the Khedive, who without notice, warning, or consultation had selected as his Prime Minister a person notoriously unfitted for the position. To admit such a pretension would be to deprive the British occupation of any reason for existence, as it would open the door to the very maladministration to prevent which this country had in concert with France intervened in Egypt. For as a matter of fact, if His Highness had *carte blanche* to appoint whom he pleased to any post in the Administration, beginning at the top, there would be no safeguard whatever against the return of the worst abuses which existed under the *régime* of the ex-Khedive Ismail.

"His Excellency had said that the proceeding was unprecedented, and indeed it was so for one obvious reason. It had never happened in the reign of the Khedive Tewfik, for though that Prince had often changed his Ministers, he had always been wise enough to take the British representative into his counsel. And when His Excellency spoke of the high-handed nature of Lord Cromer's proceeding, I was at a loss to understand his meaning. The Khedive had named an unacceptable Minister, and Lord Cromer on the grounds I had mentioned had entered a protest. At any rate, when His Excellency called to mind the express purpose for which he had sought the present interview, he could hardly contend that a protest was in itself a high-handed proceeding."

T

One does not know whether most to admire the urbanity of form which distinguishes this verbally effective retort, or the genial audacity which characterizes its essentially inconsequent matter. We are not told what or whether any reply was made to it by M. Waddington, but it would not at all surprise us to learn that His Excellency was for the moment too taken aback to question the soundness of the analogy, and that it was still "holding the field" when the interview came to an end. Perhaps it was closed before the thought occurred to him that there are "protests" and "protests," and that the cases compared by Lord Rosebery would have somewhat better satisfied the true conditions of a parallel if the French Army had been in occupation of London, and M. Waddington had been like Lord Cromer, in a position to support his protest by an irresistible body of arguments, held in reserve at not much greater distance than the barracks in Birdcage Walk. It is easy to say that this retort was obvious, but it was one of those obvious retorts which to a man whose breath has just been taken away by so daring a sophism may only suggest itself in the form of a *bon-mot d'escalier*. It is quite possible, therefore, that M. Waddington might have already descended the stairs at the Foreign Office before it struck him that the protest he had just delivered was not exactly

" on all fours " with that which Lord Cromer had lodged at the Abdin Palace.

It is to be noted, however, that, before being staggered by this unexpected comparison, the French Ambassador had retained sufficient presence of mind to declare that the action of the British Government " went far beyond the terms of Lord Granville's despatch "; and so in truth it did. It is all very well, and no doubt legitimate as diplomatic " fence," to contend that our method of treating the sudden emergency which had arisen was constructively prescribed in the famous document referred to, and that to anyone acting in the spirit of that admirably firm deliverance of a deplorably weak Statesman the course was clear. But it must be remembered that merely to act in its spirit in the circumstances which now presented themselves involved a very momentous extension of its letter. " It should," Lord Granville had written, " be made clear to the Egyptian Ministers and Governors of provinces that the responsibility which for the time rests on England obliges Her Majesty's Government to insist on the policy which they recommend, and that it will be necessary that those Ministers and Governors who do not follow this course should cease to hold their offices." But what was here in question was not the disposition of officials, but the acts of their

Sovereign; what the British Government were confronted with was not the individual recalcitrancy of Ministers who were unfriendly to the British policy, but the deliberate design of the Khedive to appoint and sustain in office such Ministers as would assist him to bring that policy to nought. To act, therefore, in the spirit of Lord Granville's declaration it was necessary for his successor to take the very decisive step of inserting the words "and the Khedive himself" after the words "Egyptian Ministers and Governors," and of so amplifying the final words of the declaration as to make it not only impose on contumacious Ministers the penalty of dismissal from office, but threaten an impracticable Khedive with deposition from the throne.

This was an undoubtedly logical corollary from the declared policy of the British Government; but it is not every Government that has the courage of its logic. Thanks, however, to its representative Minister at home, and its representative agent abroad, the Government then in power fortunately had. Lord Rosebery telegraphed his instructions to Lord Cromer, with full confidence in the strength of the man who was to carry them out; and Lord Cromer executed them with equal assurance of the firmness of the man from whom they had been

THE ABDIN PALACE.

From a Photograph by J. P. Sebah, of Cairo.

received.   The result was a sharp but short struggle, followed by a complete victory.   What passed between the British Consul-General and the young Khedive at that fateful interview on January 17 belongs of course to the secret history of diplomacy, and Blue Books cannot be expected to divulge it.   But it is tolerably well known that on the side of the British Consul-General very plain language had to be used.   It was currently reported in Cairo that at a critical point in one of their colloquies Lord Cromer had to invite His Highness to look from a window of the Abdin Palace on a British regiment paraded for some military purpose or other on the square without, and thus tacitly to remind him of the irresistible power which lay behind the measured and courteous remonstrances of his adviser.   If so blunt an appeal to the visible symbols of coercion became really necessary, we cannot doubt that it was painful to the Consul-General to employ it against an inexperienced youth, possibly less to be blamed for his self-will than to be pitied for the misfortune of having fallen under the influence of unscrupulous and intriguing councillors.   But as little can we doubt, or could Lord Cromer have doubted, that the sternest was also the kindest treatment of the misguided Khedive, and that however his feelings may for the moment have been wounded, he would live to thank the inflexible monitor who had saved him from rushing upon his ruin.

Abbas Pasha gave way, and on the 18th of January the crisis was at an end. The appointment of Fakhri was cancelled, and though, to break the Khedive's fall, the reinstatement of Mustapha Fehmy was not insisted upon, Abbas was obliged to accept Riaz Pasha as Prime Minister, with the consent of Great Britain. The Ministers of Finance and Justice, however, Boutros and Mazlum Pashas, though their loyalty to the existing *régime* was certainly not conspicuous, were allowed to retain their offices. More mischief, however, had already been done than could be thus easily remedied. The revolt of the Khedive had thoroughly unsettled the native mind, and the friction between the English officials and their Egyptian subordinates, which had been reduced to a minimum, once more became acute. Riaz Pasha, though appointed with the concurrence of the British Government, showed no disposition to further the ends of British policy. It may be that his defeat by Lord Cromer two years before still rankled in his mind, and that the demise of the Khediviate had inspired him with hopes of avenging it. Tewfik, he knew by bitter experience, was not to be relied on for steady support in a conflict with the Consul-General; Abbas, apparently of stronger and more masterful dispositon, might prove stancher in his backing. Whatever may have been the cause of the Prime Minister's attitude, there was at least no doubt of its nature. It was one of stubborn opposition to British influence, and it was imitated, as in such cases always happens, throughout every rank of the Administration.

Nor was this anti-British movement confined to the official world. " The spectacle of the Khedive at open variance with the British," writes Sir Alfred Milner in his graphic account of the crisis, " naturally gave fresh encouragement to all those elements of Egyptian society which are permanently hostile to us, and incited them to unprecedented activity. . . There are the fanatics, to whom even intercourse with foreigners is more or less repugnant, and foreign predominance intolerable. There are the old-fashioned Pashas and their following, who from self-interest or mere conservatism long for the return of autocratic native government. There are a certain number of young men, ambitious, clever, sympathizing with modern ideas, who believe themselves capable of governing the country on progressive principles without external aid. Finally, there are the turbulent elements of the population—partly Egyptian, partly low-class foreigners and Levantines—who are always in favour of change, and who find the orderly and honest administration of to-day less congenial than the system which preceded it. None of these parties is very formidable by itself, and their positive aims are quite inconsistent with one another. But in the negative policy of Anglophobia they were all able to unite, and encouraged from above they made an influential coalition. The greater portion of the Press, whether native or European, is inspired by one or other of these factions; and though the Press is still an inconsiderable power in Egypt, its vehement tirades, however childish and mendacious, were not without effect in creating the appearance of a genuine national movement. Moreover, the bulk of the people, who at heart are far from dissatisfied with the *status quo*, find it prudent to give a demonstrative though hollow support to the policy of their rulers. It did not occur to them to doubt that the Khedive and his Ministers, before placing themselves in open opposition to the English, had made sure that they were strong enough to carry such a policy to a successful issue, and this being so they naturally desired to be on the safe side."

It is in fact this calculation, always more or less operative in the native mind, which tends—and so long as the future of Egypt remains uncertain must perpetually tend—to embarrass us in that country. If it were known to-morrow that we intended to hold Egypt as we hold India—that is to say, as so much territory, of which nothing but superior force will ever dispossess us—the situation would still be difficult. We should still have our opponents to deal with among the native politicians and the official class, and the forces of bigotry, corruption, and self-seeking which we have now to combat would, though perhaps in diminished intensity, still exist. But outside this hostile camp, as one may call it, we should be surrounded by a ring of benevolent, instead of as now indifferent, if not positively malevolent neutrals. In other words, we should receive the passive support of all those persons—everywhere a large, and in Eastern countries an over-whelming body—who desire to be on the winning side. As it is, we do not get the passive support, and we cannot expect to have it. It is not that we are unpopular with the great mass of the people, or at any rate to such an extent as to make them wish to get rid of us. Free to choose, without fear of the consequences, they would undoubtedly prefer the present state of things to the arbitrary system that preceded our advent. But to borrow once more from the terse and lucid account of the situation given by the brilliant writer above quoted, "with the Khedive and the native magnates conspicuously against

us, they shrewdly reason thus : ' If we do not
take sides against the English we shall be
prejudiced while they remain, and punished when
they go. If we do take sides against them
we shall curry favour with our native rulers in
the present, and we are perfectly safe whatever
may be the result in the future; for should
the English remain they will not hurt us, and
should they go we shall be able to make
capital out of the fact that we belonged to the
patriotic opposition while they were here.' "

Such were the standing difficulties of our
position in Egypt, which at once aggravated, and
were aggravated by, the immediate consequences
of Abbas Pasha's outbreak. For a whole year
their combined force continued in operation, and
with the result that what one may call "the
coefficient of friction," on the wheels of the
Anglo-Egyptian administrative machine, rose to
a higher point than it had reached at any time
within the last seven or eight years. Almost
every Englishman engaged in the work of
administration found the dead-weight he had to
lift appreciably heavier. His native subordinates
yielded him a less cheerful obedience ; his native
colleagues, of equal or superior rank, gave him
no help. Outside the official circle men who had
formerly been friendly now showed a disposition
to hold aloof—in some cases frankly explaining

that they were afraid to appear on good terms with the English. It was even said that the manners of the common people towards Englishmen became visibly discourteous and menacing; and it is the fact that the signs of popular feeling were regarded, if not with actual apprehension, at any rate with uneasiness, by experienced observers not wont to take alarmist views on any matter.

In short it was an anxious year for all Englishmen in official positions, and of course most anxious of all for him on whom the chief responsibility rested—the British Consul-General. How long this state of tension might have lasted if the Khedive had been an older and less impetuous man, and a better player of the dangerous game upon which he had entered, it is impossible to say. Fortunately for us, or rather perhaps for him—since it is rather he than we who would have suffered from a prolongation of the crisis— his impulsive temper brought matters to a head, and forced on a second conflict with the British authorities. He might have continued with impunity to thwart and embarrass the civil administration of the country, but he was imprudent enough to lay a hostile hand upon the one wheel of the machine with which we cannot allow anybody, from the Khedive himself down to the smallest of discontented native officials, to intermeddle. His attack, however, upon the military system, as remodelled by English officers, was not fully developed until the beginning of the following year, and in the meantime the situation was rendered more irritating, though not perhaps to any material extent complicated, by the action of the Egyptian Legislative Council, which assembled as usual at the beginning of December, and at once set to work to show its hostility to English ideas. It began by attacking two of its members for having as a matter of courtesy called upon Lord Cromer in Cairo, and on that point brought upon itself a sharp rebuff, alike from the British representative and from the Egyptian Government. It then proceeded to attack the Budget, especially the estimates of the War Department, and the expenses of the army of occupation. It proposed to abolish the Prisons Departments, the Municipality of Alexandria, and the Department for repressing the slave trade. It recommended a large reduction of the grant for Public Works, and of the salaries of European officials. It appointed a Committee to inquire into the alleged unsatisfactory administration of the Domains, demanded a reduction of the secret service money, denounced the extravagance of the Government, deplored the "rapidly increasing poverty and distress of the Egyptian people," and in short behaved itself generally as an Oriental legislative body, called into existence by Western experimentalists, would be likely to comport itself towards the authors of its being.

As it turned out the Council proved to have gone a little too fast and too far, even for its own friends, and to have offended not only the English Administrators, but the Egyptian Government also. They were snubbed by Riaz Pasha, and their allegations as to the financial condition of the country were met by Sir Elwin Palmer with a clear and conclusive contradiction. Eventually the Government rejected nearly all the Council's proposals. There can be little doubt, however, that native opinion in Cairo, so far as it expressed itself, was delighted with the action of the Council, and this is a fact which may well have weighed more with the Khedive and his Government than the behaviour of the legislative body itself.

In the autumn of 1893 Abbas took his first step on the path of danger by appointing Maher Pasha Under Secretary of State for War. In the nomination itself there might not at another moment have been anything particularly objectionable. But at this particular juncture of affairs it was understood, and it proved, to be an appointment made with intent to create trouble, and to further the Khedive's hostile designs against

British policy. Its true character, as a blow aimed at the authority and influence of the Sirdar, the English Commander-in-Chief of the Egyptian Army, Major-General Sir Herbert Kitchener, became speedily apparent; and unwilling as Lord Cromer is, and always has been, to meddle with the everyday business of Egyptian Administration, or to intervene between the English and native servants of the Khedive, his summons to such intervention had now become clear and imperative. The existing Egyptian Army had been created by British officers, and for ten years the supreme authority of the Sirdar in all purely military questions had remained undisputed. If the reorganization of the defences of Egypt were, as beyond question it was, the most conspicuously successful of our administrative achievements in that country, it was so by reason of its having been also the one undertaking in which we had the most absolutely free hand. In the interests of Egypt, and indeed of Europe in general, it was essential to maintain that freedom at all costs, and to oppose the promptest and sternest resistance to any attempt to impair it. Fully alive to this, Lord Cromer delivered instant check to the Khedive. Supported as before and with the same vigour by the Foreign Office, he quietly but firmly insisted on a modification of Abbas's policy, and with some trouble a compromise was

THE SECOND CATARACT (AT LOW WATER).

From a Photograph by J. P. Sebah, of Cairo.

arranged, which left the Sirdar's authority nominally unimpaired.

But the truce was of short duration. In January of 1894 the Khedive set out from Cairo for a "progress" to the frontier at Wady Halfa. To his subjects the occasion was a highly interesting one, for this was not only his first tour of his dominions since his accession to his dominions, but, as was understood, his first introduction to the scenery and monuments of the Nile. The Father of Waters was *en fête* for a thousand miles of its length. At Keneh, at Luxor, at Assouan, elaborate receptions were prepared for him, and turbaned crowds of fellaheen flocked from all the neighbouring villages to the landing-places to pay their homage. But even here and to his Mahommedan subjects he showed signs from time to time of his arbitrary and impracticable temper, and he lost no opportunity of publicly slighting the British officers who accompanied or received him. It would almost seem as if he had been deliberately working himself up to the calculated outburst of petulant rudeness which was shortly to follow. On his arrival at Wady Halfa, where he was of course received with all due deference by the military authorities, the usual review and inspection of the troops was held in his honour; and at its close, in place of the few words of formal commendation which are looked for on such occasions, the Khedive complained publicly and pointedly to the Sirdar of the military inefficiency of the force under his command.

The significance of so carefully studied an insult was of course impossible to mistake. General Kitchener understood it as a blow aimed directly at him and his authority, and he at once tendered his resignation. The Khedive, however, his object being sufficiently attained by the humiliation of the highest British military authority, requested him to withdraw it. In the circumstances, no doubt, and in the immediate interests of discipline, the Sirdar had no choice but to comply, but it was of course impossible that the matter could be allowed to end here. It was essential that something should at once be done to re-establish the undermined authority of the British commander of the Egyptian forces, and it was rightly judged that to this end it was necessary that the slight offered to General Kitchener should be atoned for as formally and publicly as it was inflicted. Acting accordingly under instructions from Lord Rosebery, the British Consul-General waited on the Khedive, and then and there demanded that he should issue a general order expressing his approval of the discipline and efficiency of the Army, and his satisfaction with the officers whose authority he

GENERAL KITCHENER.

From a Photograph by J. Heyman, of Cairo.

had so deliberately attempted to overthrow. The position in which Abbas Pasha thus found himself was if possible even more painful than that into which his imprudence had betrayed him just a year before. But as had happened previously on two separate occasions to his father, and as always happens with Oriental Sovereigns who rely upon Oriental Ministers to back them in a conflict with a great Western Power, the Khedive looked around him in vain for supporters. The Ministry of Riaz Pasha, by whom he had been up to this point supported in his campaign against his British tutors, now shrank back in dismay at the rashness of his latest act, and urged him to submit. The French Minister, and the other foreign elements usually most hostile to Great Britain, were alarmed at the possible consequences of a collapse of discipline in the Army. It is even possible that the Khedive himself was somewhat disconcerted at the evidence of the universal uneasiness which his recent conduct had inspired. Anyhow, he retreated with the best grace he could muster, and issued the order which had virtually been dictated to him. It was published in the first instance only in French; but with this the British Government was not satisfied. They held it, and no doubt rightly held it, necessary to force the unhappy young Sovereign to drink the cup of humiliation to the very dregs, and the general order had to be published in Arabic also. Nor was even this all. Lord Cromer was further instructed to demand the removal of Maher Pasha from his post at the War Office. Here again the Khedive was at first inclined to make a stand. He then endeavoured to temporize with the demand, and sought to delay the dismissal of the Under Secretary until another suitable post could be found for him. Once more, however, the requirements of the British Government were inflexibly insisted on, and within a few days Maher Pasha was sent elsewhere and replaced in his post by Zohrab Pasha, a Minister whose loyalty to British policy could be relied on.

With this last and in some respects sharpest encounter the struggle ended. Its consequences for the half-hearted advisers who had instigated Abbas, only to abandon him, were exactly what historic precedent might have taught him to expect. History indeed repeated itself with curious exactitude in the case of Riaz Pasha, who, just as he had fallen into disfavour three years before through his having embroiled Tewfik in a contest with the British representative, in which the Khedive and his Minister got the worst of it, so now was he about to lose·power again through precisely the same error committed as counsellor of Abbas. The confidence of his present, like that of his former master, was entirely destroyed. Mutual recriminations on the failure of their joint attempt at revolt may not improbably have ensued, and what was practically a two months' ministerial crisis was at last brought to an end by Riaz's resignation, and the recall of Nubar Pasha to office after six years of retirement.

It was to all intents and purposes a signal of surrender, for though Nubar Pasha has had passages of arms with Great Britain and her representative, and though he chafes occasionally under the restraints which British policy imposes upon him, he is far too able a statesman not to perceive that the future of the country depends on its working cordially with the one Power which can save it from what he has himself called the "curse of internationalization." There are still, as there have ever been, but two possibilities before Egypt. Her native rulers, the Khedive and his Ministers, may frankly accept the assistance of Great Britain in that still far from completed work of administrative reform which can alone make Egypt capable of ultimate autonomy; or they may revert to their recent policy of hostility and obstruction—a policy which will render the accomplishment of our undertaking impossible on its present lines, and must eventually lead to the formal and permanent establishment of British dominion over the country. The one result in which it could not possibly issue would be the escape of Egypt from foreign control. To substitute European for English tutelage with all its consequences, some of them doubtful, others proved by past experience to be disastrous, is the utmost that Egypt under existing conditions could hope to achieve.

Happily there is good reason to believe that Abbas Pasha—thanks to the firm and tactful diplomacy of Lord Cromer, aided by the teaching of events—has at last had his eyes opened to the real facts of the situation. More than three years have now passed since the Khedive made his last and most desperate attempt to free himself from British control, and they have been years full of instruction for any not unteachable mind. In 1895 he paid an official or semi-official visit to his suzerain at Constantinople, and he returned from it in a most wholesome condition of disenchantment. His reception by the Sultan and his *entourage* was disappointing ; and his departure was allowed to take place with a lack of ceremony which gave him not unnatural offence. He came back to Cairo convinced that no substantial aid was to be expected from Constantinople, and he has in the meantime learnt to estimate the support of European intriguers in his own capital at its true value. He has discovered that these false friends of his, though they are willing enough to egg him on in a course of obstruction to British policy, have neither the will nor, if they had it, the power to render him any efficient assistance in the difficulties which he thereby brings upon himself. In a word, he has now convinced himself not only that the English are his most helpful friends and his most powerful enemies, but that wherever else he turns, either at Cairo or elsewhere, he will find no so-called friends who are not enemies in disguise. And for the last year and a half the effects of the discovery have been visible not only in the attitude of the Khedive himself, but in that of his native subjects. The so-called National party in Egypt consists largely of that time-serving element among the Arabic and Levantine population who habitually take their cue from their ruler, and the temperature of whose patriotism rises and falls with the variations of the thermometer at the Abdin Palace. It is therefore a most hopeful sign of the political weather that patriotic ardour at Cairo subsided many months ago into a cold but contented acquiescence in British rule.

CHAPTER XIV.

The Advance to Dongola

THE history of Lord Cromer's official career has now been brought nearly down to the present day. It only remains to add a brief account of the important military movement which has again directed the attention of the British public to the country wherein after a brief period of service, not indeed more able or faithful, but rendered more conspicuous by the dramatic events associated with it, he had settled steadily down to twelve years of comparatively unnoticed though invaluable work. It must be a satisfaction to him, as assuredly it has been to all who have formed a correct conception of his views on Egyptian policy, that the forward movement into the Soudan has taken place during his Consul-Generalship at Cairo, and promises to be crowned with the recovery of the Soudan before its close.

It will not have been forgotten how desperate were the attempts of the " Little Englander " party to make out, when the advance from

Wady Halfa was first announced, that the step was taken, not only without consultation with Lord Cromer, but in opposition to his well-known and decided belief in its inexpediency. How far it may have been found possible to take counsel with him at the moment one cannot say. Urgent reasons of State may have compelled the Government to take immediate action; in so far indeed as they were actuated by that desire to assist Italy which they put forward in their Parliamentary explanation of their policy, there was undoubtedly no time to be lost. It may be, then, that the order to advance took not only the "politicals" in Egypt, but the soldiers by surprise. Still there is a wide difference between being unprepared for, and being opposed to, an expedition to the Soudan; and even if it be the fact that the former word correctly describes Lord Cromer's attitude towards the movement, there is not the slightest warrant for applying to it the latter. The Radical members of Parliament who "heckled" the Government so pertinaciously on the point during the early session of 1896 were unable to point to a single scintilla of evidence to justify their interrogations, and in fact no such spark of testimony exists.

The Consul-General simply suffered, in fact, from a revival of the impression to which he owed so much unmerited misjudgment of the position taken up by him thirteen years before. The Radicals believed, or more probably pretended to believe, that the diplomatic adviser who—in common, be it remembered, with every single military authority who was consulted on the question—had recommended the evacuation of the Soudan in 1883, must necessarily be opposed to an expedition for its reconquest in 1896. As well might it be pretended that the triumphant march in which Wellington halted not till he had swept the French invaders of the Peninsula across the Pyrenees, was unwillingly commenced by him in 1811 because he had retired behind the lines of Torres Vedras in 1810. The retreat in the one case as the other was a matter of military necessity, and in one case as in the other it was executed by men who cherished at the time the confident hope of retracing their steps and recovering the country from which they had retired. That Sir Evelyn Baring was to be numbered among them in 1883 it would doubtless be too much to affirm. He surveyed the situation in those days with the eye of the politician rather than with that of the soldier; and the political future was then too dark for forecast of any remote future. For all that was visible at that time to the most prescient of observers, the English tenure of Egypt might any day have been determined ; and of course if it had come abruptly to an end, with its work unfinished, the Native Government—which had been too weak to hold the Soudan—would manifestly, and *à fortiori*, have been unable to recover it. But so soon as it became certain that England had no mind to leave Egypt till her work was completed—and still more when the military portion of that work was so far advanced as to place the country in possession of a well-drilled and disciplined army—the situation was entirely altered. Recovery of the Soudan became at once an attainable object of Egyptian policy, and the only question that remained was whether it was a desirable one. To affirm that Lord Cromer, though obliged to recognize its possibility, disputed its expediency, would be to impute to him such a lack of political perception as no man of his powers and experience could, without gross absurdity, be charged with. As a matter of fact, and as is well known to all who have been admitted to his confidence on the subject, the British Consul-General has long been as firmly convinced as anyone of the absolute necessity of the Soudan, not merely to the due development of Egyptian prosperity, but to the mere safety of the country and the stability of the Khedive's rule within his own borders ; and that whether he was or was not prepared for the advance of the Egyptian Army at that particular juncture, the general policy of the enterprise had his hearty approval, and was promoted by him not only as a matter of official duty, but with all the energy of personal good will.

The insinuations—for there were no materials for anything more than insinuations—of Lord Cromer's hostility to the movement were the more absurd because if he had been opposed to it that fact could hardly have failed to become known at a much earlier date. For it is not as though the forward policy had but recently come to the front. For at least two years before, the question of the recovery of the Soudan had been a subject of discussion in diplomatic and military circles; and the changes in the "international" situation in Central Africa, which have tended to make that question an urgent one, had been under observation for a longer period still. It was matter of common remark among those who had followed the progress of affairs in that region, that at least one European Power was pursuing a policy of extension and conquest in the Dark Continent which seriously menaced our position in Egypt, and which, if persisted in, would at no distant date enable that Power to obtain the command of those head-waters of the Nile on which the prosperity, not to say the very life, of Egypt depends. And that those advances would have sooner or later to be met by a counter movement on the Egyptian side was never doubted by any competent authority. That it was precipitated by other causes—by the growing restlessness of the Dervishes, and by apprehensions of the agitating effect likely to be produced upon them by the defeat of the Italian arms at the beginning of the year 1896—is true enough; but these influences could have done little more than hasten the despatch of an expedition which could not in any case have been long delayed.

Still it was thought by the British Government, and perhaps wisely enough, that the desire to help a great and friendly Power in a position of extraordinary difficulty might well determine the moment for striking the blow. Driven back in the direction of Massowah by their defeat, the remains of the Italian army found it impossible to lend a helping hand to their sorely pressed comrades in Kassala. There were threatening signs of movement among the Dervishes in the direction of the beleaguered stronghold, and one of the avowed objects of the British advance was to effect a diversion in its favour. Accordingly on March 21 Sir Herbert Kitchener, Sirdar of the Egyptian Army, accompanied by Major Wingate, the chief of the Intelligence Department, and Slatin Pasha—the romantic story of whose long captivity among, and ultimate escape from, the Dervishes is well known—left for Assouan and Wady Halfa with the First Battalion of the North Staffordshire Regiment, while simultaneously an advance column of the Egyptian and Soudanese troops pushed forward from the last-named place to Akasheh, which they captured without opposition, occupied, and proceeded at once to fortify.

Here it was necessary to make an enforced halt of two months' duration until the rise of the Nile permitted the land-advance to be assisted by river operations. In the meantime the railway from Wady Halfa was being pushed southward with all possible despatch. On the 6th of June the forward march was resumed, and the expeditionary force at last got to close quarters with the enemy at Firkeh. The behaviour of the Egyptian soldiery—which had been the subject of many misgivings—did the greatest credit to their English training. Even their Soudanese comrades, whose pluck and staunchness had often already been tried and tested, were not braver or steadier in the field. The Dervishes occupied a formidable position, and defended it with their usual desperate valour, but after hard fighting were routed with great loss. It was a brilliant success, and demonstrated once for all the ability

A GROUP OF NUBIANS.

From a Photograph by J. P. Sebah, of Cairo.

of the fellah, when properly drilled and led, to hold his own against the wild warriors of the desert. Every detail of the engagement confirms this most gratifying conclusion. The Dervishes at one point of the position were repeatedly called upon to surrender, but refused, and died sword in hand. Eighty of them were killed in one hut, and thirty of their Emirs, including Hammuda, their commander, were killed. This obstinacy of defence means equally hard fighting on the side of the attacking force, while its steady behaviour when the positions were reversed is sufficiently attested by the fact that a charge of the Dervish cavalry was repulsed at the point of the bayonet by the Egyptian line. The moral effect of the victory was instantaneous and immense; its military result followed promptly in the evacuation of Suarda, which had long been the headquarters of the Dervishes, and the abandonment of a large quantity of supplies.

From Suarda the march was pursued without resistance to Kosheh, which became the next halting-place of the expedition and the point of departure for the final advance to Dongola. It was at this stage of the enterprise, however, that its real difficulties were to begin. The Dervish was an enemy much less to be dreaded than disease. Cholera broke out among the troops in the midsummer heats, and during the

months of July and August the camp suffered
somewhat severely. As, however, is the case
with every visitation of the kind at the present
day, its ravages were undoubtedly much exaggerated. It was ascertained on good authority
by one of the most active of the newspaper
correspondents engaged in a review of the
campaign after its close, that the mortality from
the cholera among the troops was somewhere
between 15 and 20 per thousand, which, though
of course regrettable, cannot be considered as at
all approaching calamitous proportions. Apart,
too, from cholera the health of the troops was
singularly good, the sick-rate from all other causes
being no more than 11 per cent. Among other
notable over-statements of that time were the
accounts of the alleged inordinate losses among
the transport animals through overwork. As a
matter of fact, to quote the same trustworthy
authority, out of 3000 camels, the whole number
with the Expedition, only 300 succumbed or
had to be turned adrift throughout the whole
campaign. More than that number were lost in
a single day during the campaign of 1884, in
which, too, the total proportion of loss amounted
to no less than 70 per cent. As little, too, did
the cavalry suffer in the Dongola Expedition,
not more than 76 out of a thousand horses
having perished either in action or from other

causes. And lastly, a word must be said of the famous Absarat desert march, over which there were as many portentous shakings of the head at the time as though for rashness and reckless indifference to human life it had been a sort of second Balaklava. It is true that its length —thirty-six miles—was considerable; but except for a few miles the marching was fairly easy, and in the last campaign watering-places had been established. The extravagant language in which the operation was described was not justified by its intrinsic severity or difficulty, but was in reality provoked by certain disastrous accompaniments of it for which no human foresight could have provided. On their march the troops were overtaken by a violent storm of wind, sand, and rain, and in the dust and confusion of the scene men strayed wholesale from the route. In the result probably about 300 of the Soudanese blacks turned about and eventually came back, weak and exhausted, into camp at Kosheh, having lost some eight or ten of their number. This disaster, therefore, considering the extraordinary rarity in the African desert of such visitations as the terrible tempest which directly caused it, ought in justice to be reckoned as among those mischances of a campaign for which commanders are not responsible.

Nevertheless it may be said, and indeed has been said, that although military experts cannot foresee Soudanese storms, they know the seasons of the year in which such storms are likely to occur, and should avoid selecting such seasons for difficult operations. Here, again, the average readings of the thermometer for the months of July and August in the tropics are not (it might be said) inaccessible statistics, nor the mortality from sunstroke and the risk of cholera outbreaks among incalculable contingencies. "Apparently," it was remarked the other day by a critic of one of the narratives of the campaign, "every reasonable purpose would have been served by sending the Expedition in September instead of March." If for "every reasonable purpose" we read every purpose within the extremely limited knowledge of the "man in the street," the proposition might pass; but if we are to talk of what is reasonable, it surely stands to reason and to common sense that if with all the obvious inducements to despatch an expedition in September instead of in March a Government in fact despatches it in March instead of September, that Government must have had very strong motives for making such a choice.

Surely, too, it was plain from the first on the patent facts of the case that though the advance itself into the Soudan were dictated by purely administrative and military reasons, the selection of the moment for making it might have been almost exclusively determined by considerations of *la haute politique.* It is too readily forgotten that the interests of Egypt on the Upper Nile are in a far more precarious condition to-day than they were on the morrow of the evacuation of the Soudan, and that movements of Great Powers in Central Africa, influenced, as they well might be, by the turns of European politics, may at any moment expose them to a far graver menace than that of the fanaticism or rapacity of Dervishes. At any moment, therefore, rapidity of precautionary action may be imposed upon an English Government by information to which Governments alone have access, and which it is from the nature of the case impossible for them to divulge.

Apart, moreover, from obscure considerations of this kind, it is going much too far to assume that the purely military work of the Expedition would have been no more difficult in September of 1896 than it proved to be in March of the same year. If the crushing defeat of one European army to the east of the Nile had not been followed as speedily as it was by the advance of another Power up the river valley, it is impossible to say what effect the elation of unchallenged victory might not have produced in the minds of the desert tribes, and what it might not have done to concentrate their forces and to attract new recruits to their banners. What we do know, and it should be surely enough to satisfy us, is that the prompt despatch of the Egyptian troops from the frontier at Wady Halfa produced an instantaneously disconcerting effect on the Dervishes, and that before they had time to recover from it we had routed and rolled them back many scores of miles to the south. But to resume the story of the march.

It was on the 19th of September that the final blow of the year's campaign was struck. Nothing could have been more decisive or less Homeric than the battle at which it was delivered, which has been well described as "a cross between an artillery duel and a naval engagement." After a toilsome desert march throughout the previous day, the force bivouacked at about a mile to the north of the rock of Abu Fatmeh, and some six miles from the Dervish fortified post of Kerma, where it was supposed that the enemy, led by Wad el Bishara, the Governor of the Dongola Province, who had come north with reinforcements, intended to make a determined stand. At four in the morning of Saturday the 19th the troops set out again, and by daybreak arrived at Kerma, only to find the fort deserted. From a report afterwards brought in by a spy they learned that at midnight, or very early that morning, Wad el Bishara and his men had withdrawn across the Nile to Hafir, on the west bank, where, it was again alleged, they were resolved to fight to the last man.

Bitterly disappointed at this retreat of the foe whom they had hoped to encounter, the army continued without halting to advance in battle array for another mile and a half, until nearly opposite Hafir, where, as soon as day had broadened, the enemy's position was plainly discernible. It had been selected with no little judgment, commanding the very point on the river at which the Sirdar had purposed transporting his troops to the opposite shore. Wad el Bishara's defences, too, were strong enough to offer a considerable resistance to light field guns, such as constituted the only artillery which could be brought to bear upon them from the opposite bank. Fire was, however, opened upon them about seven o'clock, though with comparatively little effect, at a range of about 2000 yards, and without eliciting any reply.

The fight did not begin in earnest until the arrival of the three gunboats, which shortly afterwards came steaming up the river, and when within a thousand yards of the Dervish forts opened fire upon them. Even this failed for a time to provoke any return, but at last the enemy opened fire with cannon and small arms from the works along the bank, while swarms of Dervish riflemen armed with Remingtons poured down to the water's edge and raked the advancing gunboats with a galling fusillade. So hot was the fire of artillery and small arms combined that the boats slackened speed, stopped, and then retreated down stream for some 1500 yards, though in the meantime still keeping up a brisk bombardment at longer range. After a short interval the steamers were again swung round into line, and once more advancing up stream made vigorous play with their machine guns on the forts; and thus for two hours the artillery duel went on, the superiority in number and power of weapons being all on the Egyptian side, but the Dervishes showing their old pluck and tenacity in sticking to their guns. Again and again, as one gun after another was temporarily disabled, it was supposed that the enemy's batteries had been silenced; but again and again, whenever the firing ceased from the steamers, a gun would be run out and a shot discharged at them. At last, at about 10.45 a.m., the three gunboats were sent forward, and running the gauntlet of the Mahdist lines under a fierce fire, which, moreover, they returned with such good will as temporarily to silence the shore works, the little flotilla steamed up the river past Hafir under orders to proceed to Dongola.

Though the land forces had taken little or no part in this engagement, it practically opened the way for them to the goal. It had, in fact, broken the neck of the Dervish resistance; and when three or four days later the Sirdar's army advanced upon Dongola, the gunboats at the same time steaming side by side with them up the Nile, they encountered no serious opposition. At five o'clock in the morning the first movement was made, and just an hour afterwards the enemy's encampment was reached. Wad el Bishara, though severely wounded at Hafir, was reported to be still full of fight, and to be "encouraging" his troops in Oriental fashion by threatening all those who showed signs of wavering with instant death. As a matter of fact, however, his nerve was shattered. An artillery engagement between the forts and steamers delayed the advance of the Egyptian force for a brief space, but before ever they got to blows with the Dervishes the Dervish leader and his principal lieutenant had fled. Against such a discouragement it would be difficult even for the best disciplined European troops to bear up; to an Eastern army it is inevitably and promptly fatal. The Dervishes were completely disorganised, and the Egyptians gained an almost bloodless victory. The cavalry by land and the gunboats by water pursued the flying foe, but armed resistance was for all practical purposes over, and hundreds surrendered themselves passively to the victors. That night the army of the Sirdar encamped within the mud walls of Dongola, and on the very same evening Lord Cromer arrived in Egypt on his return from a stay of some weeks in England.

It was an inspiriting welcome to his official home, and a most gratifying episode to have interpolated itself in a long and often monotonous history of hard administrative work. Representing, too, as it did, but the first stage in our enterprise of reconquest, this little campaign is nevertheless one on which the country has good cause to congratulate itself, and which may well inspire us with just pride in the organization, civil and military, by which it was carried out. The Expedition of 1896 was, like most adventures into the formidable wastes of the Soudan, beset with difficulties requiring a large measure of capacity and wise forethought at headquarters, and of courage, resource, and endurance in the field to ensure its success. But Lord Cromer and the Sirdar had so thoughtfully provided for all contingencies at all capable of prevision, and Sir Herbert Kitchener showed such promptitude in

NUBIAN VILLAGE (ABOVE KOROSKO).

From a Photograph by J. P. Sebah, of Cairo.

grappling with and overcoming all unforeseen obstacles, that the campaign "went" from start to finish almost without a hitch. Even reckoning in the hindrances entailed by an unprecedented succession of violent sand and rain storms, the advance was, on the whole, so admirably managed that the losses and hardships incidental to it have been trivial as compared with those of similar warlike operations, either in the Soudan or elsewhere.

A few facts and figures may help perhaps to impress this truth upon the minds of those to whom it has not yet been fully brought home. Wady Halfa, the frontier and advanced post of operations, is distant, roughly speaking, 1000 miles from Cairo, and all communication had to be carried on by alternate railway and river travel. An army numbering with non-combatants about 20,000 men, together with their transport animals and materials of war, a camel transport corps of 2000 men, many of whom knew nothing of that peculiar animal, had to be trained, armed, set to work, and kept at it; and so rapidly and thoroughly was this work accomplished that these raw amateurs, as they were at starting, became one of the most efficient arms of the force, making long and toilsome marches, sometimes of forty miles a day, without the slightest abatement of their good spirits or good humour. When further it is stated that the amount of food and forage required by the expeditionary force amounted to some fifty tons a day, all which had to be sent not only over this distance of 1000 miles, but latterly five hundred miles further, some idea may be formed of the labour entailed in forwarding such quantities of material, and keeping a month's stock ahead in case of accidents. It meant the employment of steamers as well as sailing craft by hundreds on the various reaches of the river, and in addition camel transport round the cataracts, and from the railroad to the army in the field.

Individual ability and energy play of course an important part in an achievement of this kind; but its success must always be due in an even larger measure to loyal and harmonious co-operation among all the various parties and departments engaged in the work of organization. And the best if not the only security for this is to be found in unity of aim and counsel among the civil and military authorities. To the native administration of the Egyptian War Office, under the guidance of the Sirdar, the chief share of credit must no doubt be ascribed; but without the constant cordial support of their coadjutor at the Agency, and without the animating influence of that zeal and public spirit which Lord Cromer and the school of English administrators trained under his eye have infused into the Egyptian officials, the military operations which began in March 1896, and ended six months later in the capture of Dongola and the restoration to Egypt of a rich and fertile province, would assuredly not have run so smooth and unchequered a course.

CHAPTER XV.

Personal Characteristics

AS this imperfect memoir draws near its close, its irremediable but, as I venture to think, excusable inadequacy impresses itself more and more upon the writer. The difficulties with which he had to contend were from the first patent, and were indeed dwelt upon with perfect frankness by the distinguished subject of the biography in the course of a conversation with his biographer. If it be an almost impossible task to give a full and faithful account of the political career of a leading English statesman during his lifetime, or perhaps until a good many years have passed since his death, it may well be contended that in the case of an English diplomatist this impossibility becomes complete. If much remains unknown to the biographer in the former instance, in the latter hardly anything is revealed to him. In the one case our Parliamentary system exacts a certain amount of self-disclosure from our public men ; in the other the traditions of our diplomatic service enjoin upon them the

utmost amount of self-effacement. The statesman is sometimes compelled to step forward
into the light; the diplomatic agent lives perpetually in the shadow.

It may be said—though it would of course be
only an utterance of *sanctissima simplicitas*—that
the true record of the diplomatic agent's career
is to be found in the correspondence which has
passed between him and his official superiors
for the time being in Downing Street; but there
is no Ambassador, Envoy, or Consul-General,
of however melancholy a temperament, who
could entertain this proposition without a smile.
" Do not read history to me," said Sir Robert
Walpole on his death-bed, " for that I know must
be false." It would need less than the long
experience of that Minister, and none of the
profound solemnity of that moment, to make a
diplomatist willing to say the same of the Blue
Book. As an official narrative of the facts which
Governments are supposed to lay before the
representatives of the nation—or in other words,
as such a careful selection of communications
from their agents abroad as may best help their
Parliamentary case at home—the Blue Book is
all that can be desired. But as a record of the
part really played by such agents in the determination of the policy which their employers
have to defend in Parliament it is of most

doubtful and variable value. If the agent happens to be an enthusiast for the policy of his employers, and that policy happens to be one which is popular and successful, one, in fact, which they are proud of and eager to avow, why then, indeed, the agent, though he may not get full credit for his share in it, may count upon his action and opinions in the matter being placed beyond the reach of public misconception. Should he, on the other hand, be the instrument of a policy of which he either actually disapproves, or at any rate is not ardently enamoured, and if at the same time that policy is neither successful nor popular, nor a source of pride to its authors, he need not expect that Blue Books will give any adequate account of his opinions, or even of his action. Rather he may think himself fortunate, or at any rate he may congratulate himself on his discretion and exactitude in expressing himself, if it does not create or help to perpetuate a totally false impression concerning them.

That Lord Cromer has at least escaped this fate reflects great credit on his abilities as a despatch writer ; and the fact that even the Blue Books of 1884 leave his official reputation unimpaired is one reason why they have been so freely drawn upon for extracts in the pages of this volume. We may depend upon it that if the Gladstone Government could have laid even a portion of their responsibility for the many blunders committed by them between September, 1883, and January, 1885, upon the shoulders of their Egyptian advisers they would have been all eagerness to do so. As a matter of fact they took shelter behind the Consul-General and his military colleagues whenever that retreat was open to them. For every backward step they took, for every interval of delay, for every mood of hesitancy, for every qualm of misgiving, they were only too glad to be able to refer to the correspondence of their Blue Books for a Parliamentary explanation. If they could have shown that Sir Evelyn Baring's advice proved prejudicial to their Soudanese policy at any stage of it; if they could have shown that whether from motives of personal jealousy, as has been absurdly suggested in a recent biography, or from any other cause, Sir Evelyn Baring had opposed the mission of Gordon until it was too late for it to be successful, or that he had delayed the susception of measures for Gordon's relief, or that, in short, he had in any way, by act or default, contributed to the tragic result of that mission, all possible care would have been taken that this point in the defence of the Government should be duly brought out in the "papers," and properly impressed upon the mind of Parliament. That Ministers could find nothing in Baring's despatches out of which to make this sort of Parliamentary capital has, I think, been fully shown already. The published correspondence entirely exonerates the Consul-General from any further or other responsibility in the whole matter of the retirement from the Soudan than such as belongs to every diplomatic servant of the country abroad who accepts a policy not of his own choice, but dictated to him by his official superiors, and does, as he is bound to do, his loyal best to carry it to a successful issue.

More than that, however—and it is little enough—the Blue Books cannot be expected to show. Their negative evidence is as valuable to Lord Cromer as any negative evidence can be; but of positive evidence as to his services in the capacity of adviser and agent, they contain as little as such documents usually do. In the private advices which Ministries at home receive from Her Majesty's representatives abroad; in the warnings that are addressed to them, to be noted or neglected, as the case may be; in the reports of the steps taken by such agents on the spot, and of their own responsibility, in anticipation of some danger to the interests of the country—it is in these that the true record of a diplomatist's official career is to be found, and these seldom or never see the light. The tacit understanding with the diplomatic servant is that if his observations turn out accurate, and his recommendations wise, the credit is to go to the home Minister whom he has advised; and that if the reverse should be the case he should be willing to act as that eminent person's Parliamentary scapegoat, and accept a position in the desert of unpopularity without a murmur. It seems a singularly one-sided arrangement, but our diplomatic service has always dutifully accepted it—on, of course, the implied consideration that their faithful and silent service will be duly recognized by the Crown— and it is acted upon with remarkable dignity and self-control. The diplomatist, however unappreciated be his services, or however misconceived his opinions, will rarely consent to lend his assistance to any public vindication of the one or explanation of the other at the hands of anybody, be he biographer, essayist, journalist, or what not. And Lord Cromer is perhaps of all men the least disposed to swerve by one hair's breadth from this salutary rule.

To these general considerations of the difficulty which interposed itself to the construction of any complete biography there are others of a special character to be added. Anglo-Egyptian politics possess an exceptionally delicate and complex character of their own, and their governing events are still recent.   Hence one is confronted with a twofold obligation to reticence in the fact that many of the actors in the drama wherein Lord Cromer played so prominent a part are still alive, and that of the many burning questions which it has been his lot to deal with some are not yet cold.   " Even in these rapid days," writes a personal friend and first-hand observer of the Consul-General's entire career in Egypt during the last thirteen years, " the occurrences of 1883–1886 cannot be labelled ' Ancient History ' ; and though for convenience sake we may divide the history of the British Occupation into distinct acts and scenes, and speak of certain transactions as finished, we have no guarantee that the event of to-morrow will be intelligible save by observing its close connection with the speeches made or the obligations undertaken a dozen years ago.   The scenes of the drama have hitherto had a close connection with each other, and in spite of many transformations the characters have preserved a consistency which forbids us to treat them as personages whose past is unknown to us.   Thus there are many despatches and documents which would present the history of the last thirteen years in an entirely new light, but which it is as impossible to publish now as it would be to disclose prematurely the incidents on which the

playwright relies to justify his *dénoûment.*" For
the purposes, in fact, of any complete survey of
the official life of the distinguished subject of
this memoir we shall have to wait—as we do in
the case of public men more highly placed still—
for the disclosure of those private records which
are usually withheld from the world until not
only he who preserved them, but most of his
contemporaries also are in their graves.

In such a case, and in default of adequate
materials for setting forth the work of the
diplomatist, a biographer must be content with
such a portrait as he is able to draw of the man.
His personality is in itself an attractive one,
and is rendered additionally so by the peculiarities
of his career. An officer of artillery, who began
life by making a serious study of the scientific
part of his profession, who first brought himself
into notice by his ability as a financier displayed in what is perhaps the most important
financial position in the British Empire outside
the United Kingdom, and who has in the later
stages of his official life developed the highest
capacities and won unbounded confidence as a
diplomatist, he can at any rate boast a unique
history. It is rare for a soldier to distinguish
himself as an economist and administrator of
great revenues; and it is perhaps rarer still
for any man to break through the somewhat

narrowing influences of the financier's employment, and rise to such conceptions of national
and international policy as have directed Lord
Cromer's diplomatic course in Egypt.   Rarest of
all is it to find any servant of the Crown who has
passed from its military to its civil service, and
then from one branch of the latter service to
another, and who while attaining to an eminent
position in both civil capacities has in each case
added to his personal reputation for ability, and
has in neither provoked challenge of his deserts.
Such an experience, especially when we consider
the jealousy, under a strictly regulated system
like our own, of all transfers from one department
of the service to another, would in itself stamp
him who has undergone it as the possessor of no
ordinary gift of adaptability, and of a truly many-
sided genius.

The last of Lord Cromer's promotions was
no doubt the most remarkable, and might have
been expected to provoke the greatest amount of
criticism.   It is not that the faculties which it
called for differed to any very great extent from
those which he had displayed in his previous
employment: on the contrary, it was well known
that the Anglo-Egyptian problem was largely a
financial one, and that whoever was selected to
deal with it must be a financier first and foremost.
What made Baring's appointment to the Egyptian

Consul-Generalship a peculiar one, and might have made it a subject of jealous comment, was not so much that it was conferred upon a man of his proved aptitudes, as that the Government did not seek for someone of the same qualification within the ranks of the diplomatic service. And this was the more likely to be grudged because the Agency at Cairo had, since Tel-el-Kebir, become a post which any diplomatist ambitious of distinction might well have been glad to fill. Its duties were in the highest degree interesting, and having regard to the entirely new situation created by the English occupation of Egypt, the able and tactful discharge of these duties already promised to become a matter of international importance. In short, the post to which Sir Evelyn Baring was appointed in 1883 was one which must have been coveted by many a man who had been " through the mill." It had been previously held by Sir Edward Malet, and before him by Mr. (afterwards Lord) Vivian, both in the usual line of promotion; and indeed it appears to have in only one other case in recent times been bestowed upon anyone not in the regular diplomatic service. It is thus among the strongest of testimonies to Baring's reputation, not merely for financial, but for general adminis- trative ability, that no audible voice of criticism was raised against his appointment either by the press on its own account, or acting as a medium of remonstrance emanating privately from the official world.

Nevertheless, it is probable that his financial skill and reputation filled the most prominent place in the estimate at first formed of him by his colleagues at Cairo. At an official dinner given to him on entering upon his duties as Consul-General, Sir Auckland Colvin, who had succeeded him as Controller of the Finances, referred pointedly to this reputation of his in proposing the toast of his health, and with humorous solemnity warned the heads of departments to be careful as to what they submitted "to the spectacled eyes of the most remorseless of financiers." Even Sir Auckland Colvin probably did not foresee the notable expansion which, under the influence of a transformed situation and new responsibilities, was to be effected in the remorseless financier's ideas of Anglo-Egyptian policy. But even with widened conceptions and designs the instincts and habits of the remorseless financier remained unchanged. On this point I may cite the testimony of one who has enjoyed the intimacy and, from a peculiar point of vantage, studied the career of the Consul-General during the last fifteen years, and who thus writes to me of him :—

"In time it was discovered that he was much more [than a mere financier]; but still his first object everywhere and always is to set things on a firm financial basis. Loosely-kept accounts, vague statements as to the extent of a debit balance, his soul abhors. He is as anxious that the nation should pay its debts as that the individual should pay his, because he knows that there is nothing so fatal to public or to private morality as laxity about pounds, shillings, and pence. The reign of the Khedive Ismail was an object-lesson on the evils of extravagance that might have converted Dickens's Micawber or Charles Lamb's Mr. Bigod to thriftiness, and the man whose task it was to repair the ruin caused by this prodigal misrule, even if he had not been a Baring, would naturally have learned to place sound finance before everything else. Not only in figures, but in all matters small and great, Lord Cromer values accuracy. Half the misfortunes in life, he is fond of saying, are due to inaccurate statements."

And here is what the same appreciative observer says of Lord Cromer's methods of procedure in his new and wider sphere of duties :—

"The work in Egypt grew upon the English representative, but it was work under imposed conditions. The necessity of fiscal reform was admitted on all sides, but beyond this Lord Cromer was not given a perfectly free hand. He was to work on the lines of Lord Dufferin's celebrated despatch, and this document prescribed certain conditions which were attractive on paper but difficult to establish in practice. Lord Dufferin could not boldly place Englishmen at the head of the various departments, but leaving the native Pashas in their high offices he provided each of them with an English Under-Secretary, who was to guide and influence him in his administrative duties. Had each of these subordinates been endowed with the tact or sympathetic dexterity, as well as with the unexampled experience of Lord Dufferin himself, the result might have been successful, but when the Under-Secretary was deficient in those gifts friction immediately resulted.

"However, Lord Cromer had to carry out the programme as best he could with the materials that he found provided for him. One by one he took in hand the various departments, and laboured to substitute order for chaos, honesty for corruption, and industry for inertness. The hardest task was, and is still, to develop in native officials a sense of responsibility and self-reliance. Timid and suspicious, nurtured in a hot atmosphere of gossip and intrigue, fond of subterranean ways and tortuous paths to promotion, the Egyptian did not take kindly to the English *régime*, because he did not and could not believe in it. He cannot understand even now that hard work, and not backstairs influence, is the passport to promotion.

"The British Representative and his band of subordinate workers had the hard task of impressing this lesson on the natives, and their work has been rendered doubly hard by the persistent hostility of the French. The explanation of this hostility, and of the phases through which it has passed, belongs to the history of the British Occupation, and I need not go into it. My only object is to show how Lord Cromer's special gifts have enabled him to proceed with his reforms, when to this irritating opposition were added the dangers of pestilence and war.

"His first rule is to take one thing at a time. His mind is like a large bureau with many pigeon-holes, each labelled with a docket specifying its contents. He has that rare gift, an accurate sense of proportion; and he decided when he took charge of Egyptian interests what were the relative sizes of the questions to be dealt with. Then he studied each thoroughly, first satisfying himself what work had to be done, and then selecting men qualified to do it.

"Here of course occasional mistakes have been inevitable. It was impossible to find always the right men in Egypt, and the workers imported from India, though superior to the Englishmen on the spot, failed sometimes to realize the anomalous part they had to play, and either effaced themselves too much and became Egyptianized, or effaced themselves too little and were hated as domineering Englishmen. But to all his countrymen associated with him in Egypt Lord Cromer has been absolutely loyal. He has upheld them through evil report and good report. He has encouraged the shy, checked the over-confident, backed up those who wanted support, and left those who had stuff in them judiciously alone.

"His philosophy leads him to take kindly views of men. He likes to think generously of those about him, and he often says that as he grows older he thinks better of the rank and file of humanity than he did when young. All those who have worked under him feel that he trusts them, and that he requires at their hands equal candour. He loses no opportunity of praising his subordinates and of recommending them for promotion; but he requires from them staunch and thorough loyalty in return. His attitude towards his men is not unlike that of Dr. Arnold, of Rugby, when he said that 'he *must* have confidence in the Sixth.'

"Lord Cromer's resemblance to the great Headmaster is specially shown in his relations with the junior members of his staff. The Agency at Cairo is an excellent diplomatic school. The Chief treats his subordinates with perfect frankness, and the result is that he is served with unswerving devotion. He requires thoroughness and hard work. His conversation—rich in quotations, historical references, and shrewd criticisms of men and things—is full of instruction and stimulating suggestion. Dull indeed must that Secretary be who does not learn something from the daily talk Lord Cromer pours out over the luncheon table. In his relations with his 'boys,' and above all in his happy domestic life, the warmth of heart that underlies the brusque manner is apparent. For one of the young men who was associated with him in the most trying time in his Egyptian career he cherished, as he has himself told us, a fatherly affection; and those who saw his sorrow at the untimely death of Gerald Portal realized that, like all the other sides of Lord Cromer's character, his affections are strong. There is nothing weak or superficial in the man.

"Sir Alfred Milner pointed out, when sketching the difficulties of the Egyptian problem, that it required above all other things *patience;* and indeed without this, tact, energy, financial adroitness, and financial ability would have availed little. Lord Cromer knows better than most men how to wait without losing time, when it would be inopportune to push one of his chief projects, for which he never loses a moment, but turns aside and puts in some smaller work which is auxiliary to the main object. And the name of these tasks is legion. The British Agent and Consul-General is the universal referee, and is applied to by petitioners of every nation, and 'in all causes ecclesiastical and civil.'

"In a single morning he may be requested to give his verdict on a proposed economy on the Budget, on the dismissal of a postman, on a plan for augmenting the Army, on a quarrel between two rival Jewish sects, on the deportation of a drunken Irishman, on a question of precedence of the wives of two Egyptian officials, and on the best method of preserving the remains of a Ptolemaic temple. These and a score of other matters pass in review before 'the spectacled eyes,' and are investigated and adjudicated on with a care and thoroughness alike untiring and inexhaustible. And during six months of the year to these multifarious duties are added social engagements — luncheon parties, dinner parties, and receptions to 'all and sundry' who may be furnished with letters of introduction to the Agency— not to mention interviews with journalists and members of Parliament who wish to prove the Occupation a failure, and projectors whose *nostrums* have only to be tried and paid for to convert it into a triumphant success.

"All these claimants in turn receive appropriate treatment. They are not sent away with frothy assurances of support which mean nothing, enforced by emphatic shakes of the hand which mean less. They are not snubbed or handed over to an Under-Secretary ; each has his claims listened to, and he may be sure that if Lord Cromer has promised to write a letter on the matter that letter will be written before the day closes, and in his next interview he will find that his proposal has been thoroughly sifted, and subjected to a glance as penetrating as a search-light.

"My sketch has shown Lord Cromer as an indefatigable worker. He is also an omnivorous reader, but with a high critical standard. He likes no inferior work. This is largely owing to the fact that he lays a sound foundation. Like Coleridge, he regards the Bible as the 'Statesman's Manual.' Few divines know the Book of Job and the prophecies of Isaiah better ; but though again with Coleridge he would say that 'Sublimity is Hebrew by birth,' he begins every day with a page of Greek or Latin authors. He loves his Homer. The 12th Book of the *Iliad* is his favourite, Cicero and Juvenal he enjoys. His favourite study is history, and his favourite period the French Revolution. Indian questions of course interest him keenly.

"His knowledge of the English poets is remarkable. Dryden's masculine verse attracts him, but his voluminous note-books contain extracts from writers of every century. He loves a good novel, and enjoys healthy stories, like those of the new romantic school of novelists ; but he never fails to express his loathing of the nauseous fiction of the day, and has been known to put chance-found volumes of it into the first fire he could find alight.

"Among his favourite passages from the Latin poets may be cited the noble lines of Claudian on the maternal and beneficent function of Imperial Rome :—

> " ' Hæc est in gremium victos quæ sola recepit
> Humanumque genus communi nomine fovit
> Matris non dominæ ritu, civesque creavit
> Quos domuit, nexuque pio longinqua revinxit.
> Hujus pacificis debemus moribus omnes
> Quod veluti patris regionibus utitur hospes
> Quod sedem mutare licet ; quod cernere Thulem
> Lusus, et horrendos quondam penetrare recessus
> Quod bibimus passim Rhodanum potamus Orontem
> Quod cuncti gens una sumus.'

"Will any Egyptian poet ever celebrate the beneficent work of England in the nineteenth century as Claudian celebrated the work of Rome in the fifth? It seems as if we should be too sanguine to expect such a eulogy, though it would be in many respects just. At all events, such a panegyric would be incomplete without a tribute to the man who has been 'the voice of England in Egypt,' and who has directed her efforts for good with such distinguished vigour, wisdom, and perseverance—EVELYN BARING, LORD CROMER."

Side by side with this unofficial testimony to the great qualities of the Consul-General let me place the no less admiring estimate formed of him by one of the ablest and most distinguished of the young Englishmen who served under him—in fact if not in form—during the darkest and most difficult years of the British Occupation, and recorded in what has become the standard work on this remarkable chapter in our history. Sir Alfred Milner writes (*England in Egypt*, p. 437) as follows :—

"In the art of government the Englishman seems to be as handy and adaptable as he is clumsy and angular in society. There are other nations with equal and perhaps greater gifts for the creation of an ideally perfect administration, if they have a *tabula rasa* wherein to construct it. But I doubt whether any of them could have made anything at all of a system so imperfect, so incongruous, and so irritating as that which we found in Egypt, and which we have not been permitted radically to alter. The logical Frenchman would have been maddened by its absurdities. The authoritative temper of the German would have revolted at its restrictions. They would have insisted on governing in their own way, or they would have despaired of governing at all. It needed that incarnation of compromise, the average Briton, to accept the system with all its faults and set to work. quietly plodding away to do the best he could under untoward circumstances.

"The qualities of the race have triumphed. But our success might have been less complete; perhaps that success might never have been attained at all had it not been for one remarkable piece of good fortune. The stars were indeed gracious when at the beginning of our greatest troubles it occurred to the British Government to entrust the conduct of its policy to the hands of Sir Evelyn Baring. It would be difficult to overestimate what the work of England in Egypt owes to the sagacity, fortitude, and patience of the British Minister. His mental and moral equipment—very remarkable in any case—was peculiarly suited to the very peculiar circumstances in which he found himself placed. Perhaps the most striking feature about him has been a singular combination of strength and forbearance; and he needed both these qualities in an exceptional degree. On one side of him were the English officials, zealous about their work, fretting at the obstruction which met them every time, and constantly appealing to him for assistance to overcome it. On the other side were the native authorities, new to our methods, hating to be driven, and keen to resent the appearance of English diplomatic pressure. The former were often induced to grumble at him for interfering too little, the latter were no less prone to complain of his interfering too much.

"What a task was his to steer an even keel between meddlesomeness and inactivity! Yet how seldom has he failed to hit the right mean. Slowly but surely he has carried all his main points. And he has carried them without needlessly overriding native authority or pushing his own personality into the foreground. He has realized that the essence of our policy is to help the Egyptians to work out as far as possible their own salvation. And not only has he realized this himself, but he has taught others to realize it. By a wise reserve he has led his countrymen in Egypt to rely upon patience, upon persuasion, upon personal influence rather than upon rougher methods to guide their native colleagues in the path of improved administration. Yet on the rare occasions when his intervention was absolutely necessary he has intervened with an emphasis which has broken down all resistance. Criticize him as you will—and he has made mistakes like other statesmen—the record of his nine years of arduous labour is one of which all Englishmen may well feel proud. The contrast between Egypt to-day and Egypt as he found it, the enhanced reputation of England in matters Egyptian, are the measure of the signal services he has rendered alike to his own country and to the country where he has laid the foundations of a lasting fame."

This tribute from one who knew Lord Cromer so well as did the author of *England in Egypt* could be swelled, if need were, by many confluent streams of eulogy from members of what may be called the Anglo-Egyptian Civil Service. Those who have come into closest contact, official and personal, with Lord Cromer, bear testimony with one voice not only to the confidence and the admiration, but to the feelings of regard and affection with which he inspires his subordinates. That "brusque manner," to which reference has been made in one of the foregoing extracts, belongs so essentially to the mere external aspects of demeanour, that no one who has ever got beyond the first few phrases of a ceremonious introduction to the British Consul-General would be even conscious of its existence. It is the thinnest of crusts on the surface of a genuine

and genial nature, and the warmth engendered
by a five minutes' conversation suffices to thaw
it.   There could be no greater mistake than to
imagine that it is due to any defect of sympathy
in the man.   The truest measure of the magni-
tude of such an error is to be found in the whole-
hearted devotion which animates the co-operating
efforts of his staff—a sentiment which only sympathy can create and sustain.   It is no small part
of the debt for which a Minister in Lord Cromer's
position becomes the creditor of his country, that
he has been enabled to enlist support of this description from those who work with him.   Ministers
who fail, even only from faults of temperament or
manner, to secure it lose half their usefulness;
and apart altogether from the Consul-General's
diplomatic gifts, apart from his skill in dealing
with the difficulties which were created for him
by native ill-will, native inertia, native intrigue,
it is certain that his capacity for managing his
own countrymen of the official class, and for
evoking from each of them the best that he
had to give, contributed immeasurably to the
splendid success of our administrative undertaking in Egypt.

And whatever be the ultimate issue of that
undertaking, its record, let us be sure, will retain
a lasting place in history, as its memories will
abide in the traditions of the Egyptian people.

If England, concentrating her strength for self-defence, were forced to-morrow to retire from Egypt—even as Rome, our prototype in history, withdrew her legions from our own shores when her enemies gathered on her frontier—the last two decades of the nineteenth century would still be remembered in the Nile Valley as a period when for the first time for countless generations law and order and security reigned under the ægis of a Power which has spread these blessings over half the world ; when the stream of justice flowed pure from its fount, and the rich man could no more deflect its course than he could divert the waters of the Nile from the plot of the poorest cultivator ; when the hand of the oppressor was stayed over the people, and the extortions of the tax-gatherer were made to cease, and the lash was wrested from the task-master, and the peasant everywhere ate of the fruit of his labour, no man making him afraid. The recollection of these things will not soon pass away in Egypt; the experience is too sadly strange, too pathetically novel for that. It will be engraven on the hearts of the people as upon a stela as enduring as the sepulchres of their kings. And wherever the tale of this great and beneficent work is told, the name of the English administrator who guided its whole course from commencement to completion, whose unconquerable patience overcame one by one all the obstacles that impeded it, whose sagacity foresaw and whose firmness averted all the dangers that threatened it, will claim a place at the head of every chapter of the noble narrative, and be recalled with honour on every page.